W9-CKP-865

Praise for *X Marks the Scot*

"For a complex story brimming over with pride and passion, betrayal, trust, and most of all the power to make a bad boy a hero, pick up this read."

—*RT Book Reviews*

"This is one author who just keeps on getting better... One of the most exciting Highland romances I have read. Definitely worthy of five stars!"

—*Night Owl Reviews*, Top Pick

Praise for *Temptation in a Kilt*

"An exciting Highland adventure with sensual and compelling romance."

—*Amanda Forester, acclaimed author of*
True Highland Spirit

"Well written, full of intrigue, and a sensual, believable romance, this book captivates the reader immediately."

—*RT Book Reviews*

"Roberts's debut features appealing characters and an interesting background of ancient clan feuds and spurned lovers."

—*Publishers Weekly*

"Everything a Scottish romance should be. Beautifully written, this story will captivate you from the very first page, bringing the highlands to life right before your eyes."

—*Romance Junkies*

To Wed a Wicked Highlander

VICTORIA ROBERTS

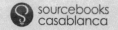

sourcebooks
casablanca

Published by Sourcebooks Casablanca, an imprint of Sourcebooks,
Inc.
P.O. Box 4410, Naperville, Illinois 60567-4410
(630) 961-3900
Fax: (630) 961-2168
www.sourcebooks.com

Printed and bound in Canada.
WC 10 9 8 7 6 5 4 3 2 1

To Rita Spak, beloved mother and biggest fan of her daughter's romance novels. Even though you are watching from above, I can only imagine what you must be thinking. There is not a day that goes by that I don't think of you. I miss your smile, your laughter, your hugs…I miss you, Mom. And I hope you're proud.

There is more treasure in books than in all the pirates' loot on Treasure Island and at the bottom of the Spanish Main...and best of all, you can enjoy these riches every day of your life.
—Walt Disney

Prologue

"Ye're just a lass. Ye cannae jump," said her brother with a smirk. "We ne'er should have let ye come with us in the first place."

Colin never knew when to keep his opinions to himself, and this was clearly one of those times. He continued to taunt her when she wanted nothing more than to strangle him with her bare hands. Family or not, he was an idiot. And worse yet, he scolded her in front of her cousins. Not that this matter was any of their concern.

John stood in his braies and then leapt from the giant rock above. When her cousin plunged into the pond, water droplets sprayed the top of Sybella's head. The heat was unbearable. All she wanted to do was swim, while Colin clearly was trying to make something out of nothing.

Angus laughed and turned to Colin. "If Sybella insists on jumping, let the wee lass jump."

Wee lass, my arse, she thought. She was just shy of her

sixteenth birthday, and there was no reason she couldn't do anything her brother or her annoying cousins could do. Why should they get to have all the fun?

Colin shook his head and ran his hand through his wet hair. "Ye donna come down exactly right and ye will break your neck. Ye know Father would give me a thrashing if I didnae watch over ye. And I told ye, ye shouldnae do something because someone else does it. Ye're only a lass. Ye could be hurt."

Sybella threw back her head and placed her hands on her hips. "*Only a lass?* Because ye have th-th-that…*thing* hanging between your legs doesnae make ye a man, Colin MacKenzie."

Her cousins chuckled while Colin's voice rang with command—or so he thought. "Ella, I am nae going to tell ye again. Enough of this foolishness."

Her brother was in for an awakening. Her father was not a man to back down from a fight, and after all, she had her father's blood, did she not?

Sybella whipped off her boots and hastily tossed them aside. She hefted her skirts over her head, sporting her brother's old trews and tunic underneath. She threw her dress to the ground, and Colin stood before her with his hands placed on his hips.

"I give ye fair warning, Sister. Donna even think upon it. Ye can swim, but ye arenae going up there."

"'Tis so unfair, Colin. Ye, Angus, and John did it." There was defiance in her tone as well as a subtle challenge.

Colin rolled his eyes. "I have had enough. Angus and John," he called over his shoulder, gesturing for them to depart.

Her eyes lit up in surprise. "Ye cannae yet leave. I didnae even swim."

"Then mayhap next time ye will think twice before ye follow us." Colin glowered at her and then turned away.

Her brother might be four years her senior, but the dolt was not her father. She learned a long time ago that she did not have to take orders from him. She glanced over at her cousins and brother as they paid her no heed.

Perfect.

Sybella dashed along the outer boulders of the waterfall and climbed undetected. As she nearly reached the top, her foot slipped and her heart leapt in her throat. The waterfall was a lot higher than she'd realized.

"Sybella, ye stay put! I am coming! Donna move!" ordered Colin.

And that was the problem with her brother—always barking orders and telling her what to do. She found perverse pleasure in openly defying him. She stood at the edge, cool water lapping against her feet. A warm breeze blew her hair. She tossed her head and eyed Colin with cold triumph. She could do this and once and for all prove she was his equal. She paused, her eyes widening, and she shook her head, puzzled. What did they think they were doing? She continued to watch the fools in awe.

Colin ascended to her left and Angus to her right, while John stood with his mouth agape. She wouldn't give the men an opportunity to catch her and would only accept one way down—unescorted.

Sybella used all her strength to jump clear of the rocky ledge. She was headed dead center into the shimmering pool. It would be a perfect landing, and despite Colin's worries, he would be impressed.

She hit the water with a loud splash that was immediately silenced as she descended into the pond's cooling depths. Her tunic lifted and wrapped around her head and arms as she tried to pull it down. It was so tight and heavy. She tugged on it again, but it refused to budge. The cloth swathed her hands and arms, tying them so close together that she could not maneuver to the surface. Fear knotted inside her as she made several attempts to calm her racing heart. She had almost given up hope when something exploded beside her and tiny bubbles rushed to the surface.

Colin.

Her brother grabbed her waist and kicked up from the bottom of the pool. When his strong arms pushed her to the surface, Sybella involuntarily gulped for air and received a rush of water into her lungs. As soon as her head had cleared the water, John ran into the pond and scooped her into his arms.

She needed air.

John lowered her to the ground and Colin bent her over, pounding her back. "God's teeth, Sybella, breathe," said Colin.

As she gasped for breath, a mouthful of water escaped her and she coughed uncontrollably. She placed her hand over her chest, tears streaming down her cheeks. "I would have done it had my tunic nae tangled," she said, not noticing the tremor in her voice.

John, Angus, and Colin shook their heads. "After

ye intentionally disobey me and almost drown, those are the words which escape your lips," spat Colin, a shadow of anger spreading across his features. "'Tis a great wonder ye are a MacKenzie, ye daft lass. And that is *my* tunic ye wear. We will get the horses. Pull yourself together and get dressed. Meet us at the top of the ridge and donna go for another swim, Ella. I warn ye for the last time."

Sybella tried to look meek, but as her brother retreated, she couldn't help eyeing the waterfall again. If only she'd been able to strip down like the boys, she wouldn't have become tangled in Colin's tunic. As she heard footsteps behind her, she was ready to give Colin a tongue thrashing for watching her like a hawk. How typical of him not to trust her. She was so disgusted that she didn't even bother to turn around.

"I didnae go back into the water, Colin," said Sybella with impatience.

"Ye MacKenzies are naught but trouble. The last my father needs is a dead one on MacDonell lands."

Whipping her head around, Sybella came face to face with...the most handsome man she had ever seen. He wore a loose-fitting tunic and the MacDonell plaid of blue, green, black, and red. His light brown hair brushed the outlines of his broad shoulders, and wisps of dark hair curled against the V of his open shirt. She guessed he was around the same age as Colin.

Sybella pulled herself to her feet and brushed down her skirts. "We meant ye nay harm."

The man entered the glade and placed his hands upon his lean hips. "I saw ye take the leap. Ye landed right in the center. Cannae ye swim?"

"I can swim. My tunic was caught under the water and I couldnae untangle it." She shifted from foot to foot. If the MacDonell man raised an alarm that MacKenzies were on his lands, there would most definitely be a thrashing—even for Colin. Although she did not currently hold her brother in a favorable light, she would not intentionally get him in trouble. "Please accept my apologies and donna call a warning. We will nae do it again. Ye have my word."

"Stealing our cattle wasnae enough for ye MacKenzies? Now ye have to encroach on our lands?" he asked with a heavy dose of sarcasm. When Sybella played with her skirts in front of her, he gave her a slight nod. "*Dè an t-ainm a tha ort?*" *What is your name?*

"Ella." She cleared her throat. "Lady Sybella MacKenzie."

"The MacKenzie's daughter?"

"Aye. And ye are…?" she asked, lifting a brow.

"Alexander, son of Laird Dòmhnall MacDonell of Glengarry."

Sybella picked up her drying cloth and smiled. "Again, please accept my apologies." She spun on her heel and was halted by the tone in his voice.

"And where do ye think ye are going?"

She turned around slowly. "My brother waits—"

"All I have to do is shout, and my father's men will come."

Taking another step closer to the MacDonell's son, Sybella felt the color drain from her cheeks. "Please donna." If she started a battle with her father's enemy over a swim…She cringed at the mental image.

Trouble would not escape her this time. "Tell me. What can I do?"

The man's eyes sparkled and he rubbed his chin, a devilish grin playing on his lips. "A kiss."

"What?" she gasped.

"Ye heard me. A kiss. One kiss from your lips and ye are free to take your leave." He waited, challenging her to go through with it.

"Surely ye jest." She flashed him a look of disdain. "*Do thoil fhèin.*" *Suit yourself.*

When he raised his hand and encircled his mouth to shout a warning, Sybella blurted out, "*Fine.*"

Her lips were pressed shut so no other sound would burst out. If she cursed the reprehensible brute, he might go back on his word. She jumped when he quickly closed the gap between them and impaled her with his steady gaze. Her breath caught in her lungs and she merely stared, tongue-tied. She felt like a complete dolt.

Her reaction seemed to amuse him, and his mouth curved wryly. Lowering his head, he whispered, "May ye always remember a MacDonell was the first to taste your lips, Lady Sybella MacKenzie of Kintail."

His lips pressed against hers. Similar to her experience of jumping off the cliff, his kiss sent her stomach into a wild swirl.

"Sybella!" called Colin from a distance.

If her brother came back down to get her, there would be bloodshed. She pulled away slightly and took a sharp intake of breath. "*Feumaidh mi falbh.*" *I must go.*

He wiped his lips with the back of his hand like she

had the bloody plague. "Ne'er forget…your enemy was the first to taste ye." When the beastly man had the audacity to smirk, he broke the last thread of self-control she had managed to hold on to. MacDonell or not, she would not let herself be put down by this brute. She met his accusing eyes without flinching.

"I donna like ye, Alexander MacDonell."

"Aye, but ye will ne'er forget me," he said, then turned his back and disappeared into the trees.

One

Glengarry, Scotland 1606

Dear Alexander,

If you are reading this, I have joined your beloved mother. Do not be saddened, my son. First and foremost, you are a MacDonell. Never doubt the decisions you make.

Now that you are laird, the entire clan is in your hands. It is up to you to keep our MacDonells safe and provide for them during the harsh Highland winters. I strove to raise you as a strong and kind chief, and my wish for you would be that you become a better man than I was.

One of your first responsibilities is to seek a wife and beget an heir so as to carry on the MacDonell line. When all else fails, I know my beloved sister will torture you until you do.

As we discussed, John will replace Donald as the captain of your guard.

Lastly, at all costs, keep the stone safe within the walls of the Rock of the Raven.

I have never been disappointed in you, Alexander, and I have no doubt you will fulfill the duty that has been entrusted to you.

Laird Dòmhnall MacDonell of Glengarry

Alex sat in the chair behind his father's desk, now his own desk, shaking his head. "Father mentions to keep the stone safe within the walls of the Rock of the Raven. What stone?"

Donald's eyes narrowed. "I donna know."

"Why would he write me and then nae explain his words? This doesnae make sense."

"Your father sealed the letter and gave it to me over a year ago. Mayhap he meant to speak with ye and then became ill. But he ne'er mentioned anything to me about a stone. If ye donna know of what he writes, then this stone is probably already safe."

"I will speak with Aunt Iseabail. Father may have spoken to her." Alex pulled a pouch from a drawer and placed it on the desk in front of Donald. "I thank ye for the years of service and your continued loyalty to my father."

"It was my honor to serve him. I wish I could do the same for ye, but I am afraid these aging bones are weary. John will serve ye well. If ye ever want or need for anything, ye need only ask. Your father was a dear friend to me and ye are as a son." Donald rose and picked up the pouch. "Ye will make a fine laird, Alex."

Alex watched Donald walk out the door, and then once again, he glanced at the opened letter. He couldn't help but wonder if there was anything else his father had neglected to mention.

The remainder of the afternoon passed as a blur. All he was mindful of was the fact that last eve he had stood over his father's lifeless body and now he returned to stand over his father's grave. Time could not be turned back. He had to accept the fact that his sire was truly dead.

Alex glanced at his aunt as tears welled up in her eyes. Neither one of them spoke. The knowledge that he was now Laird Alexander MacDonell of Glengarry knotted and turned inside him, for he was a man who faced a harsh reality.

It was time to take his father's place.

Alex's hand seemed somewhat large as he rested it on his aunt's frail shoulder. "Take all the time ye need, Aunt Iseabail. I will stay as long as ye wish."

She patted his hand in response. "He was a good man, my brother."

"Aye."

There was a heavy silence.

She nodded toward his father's grave and murmured, "*Dia leat.*" *God be with you.*

Touching her elbow lightly, Alex guided her back toward home. "I have been meaning to ask something of ye. Before he died, Father wrote a letter that spoke of keeping some kind of stone safe within the walls of the Rock of the Raven. Do ye know of it?"

He sensed a slight hesitation, and then Aunt Iseabail's gaze lowered in confusion. He had been afraid that might happen. She had her good days and bad. Perhaps he would try again when she wasn't so burdened by grief.

"I must confess my mind sometimes fails me," said Aunt Iseabail with regret.

"'Tis all right. Why donna ye take some time to think upon it?"

After seeing to his aunt and barely muddling through the day, Alex sought the solace of his father's study. He closed the heavy wooden door and secured the latch, pausing a moment to welcome the blessed silence. He grabbed a tankard from the shelf and opened the bottom desk drawer. Pulling out MacGregor's ale, compliments of his cousin, he poured himself a healthy dram.

Without thought, he walked around the edge of the desk and then caught himself. What the hell was he doing? Backing up, he pulled out his sire's chair and sat down. He kicked back a long, burning mouthful and welcomed the numbness the fiery liquid brought. With a shiver of vivid recollection, he was flooded by memories of his father and realized he hadn't nearly had enough to drink. He would keep the bottle of ale on the desk. Hell, maybe he'd even down the whole damn thing.

Alex continued to stare at the walls that encased him until he heard a soft tapping at the door. He rubbed his hands over his eyes. Perhaps if he ignored the sound, it would go away. When another rap repeated even louder, Alex grunted. He pushed himself to his feet, walked over, and reluctantly lifted the latch. He swung open the door, and what he saw was certainly not what he had expected.

"Doireann." He was too tired to notice the woman's slim waist that flared into rounded hips or her hair, which was a rich auburn. He'd taken the lass so many times he knew every curve by memory.

"Alex." She raised her hand to touch his arm in a gesture of sympathy. "I thought you might need comfort. And since my father's service to your sire has come to an end, we will be taking our leave on the morrow to join my mother's kin. Unless, of course, there is a reason ye would want me to remain…"

When he did not immediately respond, she closed the distance between them. She smoothed his hair with her hand and offered something else with her eyes. "We have been together for years, Alexander. I know ye as well as I know myself. I think ye should find an opportunity to speak with my father and discuss our future. If ye so desire."

Alex sighed heavily. "Doireann, ye know I'm fond of ye, but we've discussed this before. We cannae have a future together, and ye always knew that. I am laird now."

A playful smile curved her lips. "I thought as much, but ye cannae blame a lass for trying." She fingered the edge of her gown above the swell of her ripe bosom. "But still, I offer ye comfort. For old times, if naught else. Do ye want me one last time?"

He studied her thoughtfully for a moment, and then his eyes sent her a private message. He traced his finger across her lip and then his hand slid down. There was no time for words. All of the pent-up energy he had been feeling for days rose in one heated moment. He needed a welcome distraction and she was more than willing. Before sanity crept back in, he tossed her skirts and lifted her to the wall.

If Doireann was shocked by his urgency, she did not say so.

Right now, Alex was not the laird of Glengarry. He was only a man with a single purpose. He looked her over seductively and tugged down her dress over her shoulder. When he exposed her breast, he lowered his head and his lips touched her nipple. She let out mewling sounds, and one of his hands slid down her taut stomach to the swell of her hips, between her legs.

Leave it to the skillful Doireann—she was ready for him.

He lifted his kilt and his body imprisoned hers. She was so wet and welcomed him into her body. With thrust after blessed thrust, he yielded to the burning sweetness. She pulled him closer, riding him harder, deeper, burying her hands in his thick hair.

Her soft curves molded into the contours of his lean body. She was panting, her chest heaving. He took her like an animal, and the degree to which she responded stunned him. She rose to meet him in a moment of uncontrolled passion.

When she moaned aloud, she roused him to the peak of desire. She gasped in sweet agony, and with one last heavy thrust, he spilled his seed.

"Alex, ye are going to kill me," she said, panting.

He grunted in response. That may not have been one of his most prolonged performances, but it had sated his needs nonetheless. He gently lowered her to the ground and supported her until her legs stopped wobbling. She brushed down her skirts and adjusted her bodice, casting him a wry smile.

"Are ye dead?" he asked, the huskiness lingering in his tone.

She stepped around him, and her eyes grew openly amused. "I donna think so. I suppose there is naught much else to say except I will sorely miss that and *ye*, Laird Alexander MacDonell of Glengarry."

A sad smile played on his lips. The carefree moment ended as he suddenly felt burdened by a heavy weight on his shoulders. "Be well, Doireann."

She walked to the door and turned around. "Ye and John be sure to stay out of trouble…and harm's way, Alex."

He nodded as she took her leave and then he smirked, realizing the irony. Doireann had walked out of his life and closed the door just like the last chapter of a book. Just as well. All that mattered now was the future. He was laird. He had responsibility, and Alex was bound and determined to make his father proud.

Two

Kintail, Scotland

LADY SYBELLA MACKENZIE HUFFED. "I DONNA KNOW why 'tis so important I learn to do this. Why is it expected that women must learn to sew and stitch? 'Tis truly ridiculous and has nay value whatsoever. I feel as though I'm losing my mind."

"Nay wonder, Sybella. Ye arenae concentrating. Look at your stitching. What a mess." A smile played on her cousin-by-marriage's lips as Mary tucked her nut-brown hair behind her ear. She was petite and fragile, everything Angus would favor in a woman. "When ye wed, do ye want your husband to have tattered clothing? He would look like a fool."

Sybella giggled. "It doesnae matter if his clothes are tattered. Men always look like fools."

"Angus takes pride in his appearance," Mary added.

"And my cousin takes ye for granted. Why do ye want to sit here bored to tears when we could be out in the open air?"

Mary promptly ignored her, resuming her latest

project, while Sybella glanced around the ladies' solar. She shook her head at the womanly touches. Dainty pictures of the fairer sex wearing delicate gowns hung on the walls. There were flowers and all of the feminine furnishings someone would expect to be placed in a room where the ladies were presumed to congregate.

How very original. Who made those rules? She would love to hang the bow that had landed her four rabbits in one single hunt. She wondered what the ladies would say about that. The women of propriety would surely shudder, including Mary. At least the bow might turn conversation to something other than the usual acceptable, boring subjects.

Sybella sprang to her feet, dropping the embroidery to the floor. "'Tis a beautiful day and ye are clearly wasting it. I dare ye to stop what ye are doing and come out and enjoy the sun." When Mary hesitated, Sybella knew she was going to relent.

Sybella headed toward the door and turned her head over her shoulder. "Grab your cloak and I will meet ye in the bailey."

"Ye know? One of these days ye're going to meet your match. I wish to be there when ye do."

"There has ne'er been such a man." Even as she spoke the words, Sybella couldn't help remembering a stolen kiss in a sun-kissed glade and the sound of a waterfall rushing in the distance. She quickly shook her head to clear the thought. She wouldn't give the beastly MacDonell man the satisfaction.

Sybella ambled through the bailey to wait for Mary.

"Cousin."

Sybella turned to face Mary's husband, Angus. "Your father wants to speak with ye in his study."

"Now?" she asked, disappointed.

Angus ran his hand through his brown locks. "Aye."

"All right. Will you tell Mary for me?"

Sybella hoped whatever her father wanted wouldn't take long. It was too beautiful to remain inside one minute longer than necessary.

As she approached the study, she could hear raised voices coming from inside. The argument sounded heated, but she couldn't quite make out the words.

The voices silenced.

"Enter, Sybella," called her father from the other side of the door.

How he could have heard her was beyond her comprehension. She pushed open the door to see her father seated behind his large wooden desk with Colin nearby. A shiver went up her back at the dour look on her brother's face. This did not bode well.

"Come in, Daughter. I wish to speak with ye." Her father gestured for her to sit.

There was no denying a command from her father. He was a man used to having his orders obeyed—instantly. His graying hair, broad shoulders, and sharp features gave him an innate air of authority.

She glanced at Colin, who cast her a bleak, tight-lipped smile. His eyes were dark and unfathomable. What was this about? If her father was going to chastise her about catching more rabbits than Colin and, therefore, making her brother look like a daft fool…It wasn't the first time and it certainly wouldn't be the last. Straightening her spine, she waited for her father's censure. What would it take to prove to him that she could be just as reliable as her brother? When would he understand that her talents were wasted on sewing and other women's work?

Her father leaned back in his chair and folded his hands over his stomach. "I donna expect ye to understand the ways of politics, Sybella, but ye know enough to realize marriages are often arranged to better our clan."

She heard herself swallow, not sure she liked where this conversation was headed.

"Since your dear mother has passed and ye nay longer care for her, nae to mention with our conquest of Lewis, the MacLeod clan—"

She stirred uneasily in the chair. "Surely ye arenae going to offer my hand to the MacLeod, Father," Sybella blurted out, unable to disguise a trace of panic in her voice.

Her father sat forward and rubbed his thumb over her fingers. "Daughter, what kind of father would I be if I offered your hand to that savage?" he asked in an offended tone.

She didn't see the muscle ticking angrily in Colin's jaw.

"I wouldnae think of it," said her father. "Howbeit there is another clan with which we wish to keep the peace."

Perhaps it was her own uneasiness, but her misgivings increased by the moment. She regarded her father with searching gravity, and something in the back of her mind cautioned her not to ask. She had an underlying feeling in the pit of her stomach that his next words would forever seal her fate.

"The MacDonell of Glengarry has recently passed, and we need to make an alliance. I am offering your hand to his son, the new laird of Glengarry. And I am fairly certain he will accept my offer."

Her mouth dropped. "Ye cannae offer my hand to him!" Fury almost choked her. "He is naught but an arrogant, brooding, conniving excuse for a man, and he is our enemy! All of the treasures in the world wouldnae make me wed—"

Her father's voice hardened. "This isnae open for debate. My decision is final, and there is nay more to discuss. Ye will do as ye're told. Besides, ye have ne'er even met the man."

Sybella growled in frustration, but she couldn't very well admit to her father what had occurred those years ago. The MacDonell rogue still made her blood boil when she thought about him. Not that she did—well, maybe sometimes but not a whole lot.

She fingered a blond curl behind her ear. "Our clans have been warring for years. Why would the MacDonell even want a MacKenzie for a wife? Or is it that nay one will take his bloody arse?" she asked.

Her father rose and sat down on the edge of the desk. He gazed down at her and smiled, speaking in a tone filled with awe and respect. "Daughter, I am verra proud of ye. There has been enough heartache all around us with the passing of your poor mother. We need to attempt to make peace with the MacDonell. Think about making your mother proud, Sybella. I need ye to gain your husband's trust and be a dutiful wife. For now, that is all I ask of ye."

"I donna understand, Father. The MacDonell has been our enemy for years. Why now?"

"Now is the perfect time." He tapped his finger on the desk. "But there is another matter which ye need to know." When she looked puzzled, he continued. "Ye arenae to speak of this to anyone. Do ye understand?" She nodded as he continued. "For a verra long time our clan has been blessed with good fortune because we have been gifted with a seer. There are less than a handful of men who know of this, and I want to keep it that way."

"*A seer?*" She sat back, momentarily rebuffed.

Colin's voice was calming. "I have seen it with my own eyes, Ella. Our conquest of Lewis was the last he foretold."

"Who is this seer and why have I ne'er heard of him if he is a MacKenzie?" she asked doubtfully.

"For your own safety, 'tis better ye donna know. Dòmhnall MacDonell was quiet and circumspect in burning our church to ash when his real purpose was to steal our clan's seeing stone. And there is another purpose for your vows...I need ye to find the stone and return it to your clan where it belongs."

Sybella pulled back. "I donna understand. Are ye and Colin in your cups?"

Her father's eyes darkened. "Still your tongue and listen. Once ye find the stone, I will take care of the MacDonell. I would ne'er make my daughter suffer under the same roof as a bloody MacDonell," he spat.

Colin shifted uneasily next to her.

"But what if the man will nae agree to such a union?"

Her father chuckled. "Leave the politics to me, Daughter. Ye just find me that stone."

She sat back and rubbed her hand over her brow. She needed time to absorb this. How could she marry the man who had haunted her dreams for years and then be expected to betray him?

Three

FOR SEVERAL WEEKS, SYBELLA HAD OCCUPIED HERSELF
with meaningless tasks. But no matter what she tried,
her mind kept returning to its tortured thinking. What
would the future hold when she became the wife of
her father's enemy? To her regret, she could no longer
hold off the inevitable. By this time tomorrow, she
would know.

As she, her father, Colin, and members of their
clan rode toward Glengarry, the clomping hoofbeats
that surrounded her drowned out her silent screams
of desperation. She wasn't daft enough to believe her
father would never arrange a marriage for her, but she
found it hard to accept that the MacDonell would be
her husband. Day after day, night after night, the same
pompous man by her side. Her only hope was to find
the stone quickly and bring this nightmare to an end.

"How are ye holding up, Ella?" asked her brother,
riding up beside her.

Her eyes widened and she finally gave in to the
tension that had been building all day. "How in the
hell do ye *think* I am holding up, Colin?"

He lowered his voice. "I know ye arenae pleased with wedding the MacDonell, but ye do realize it could've been much worse."

"And who could possibly be worse than the MacDonell?" she asked, raising her brow.

"The MacLeod of Lewis."

She smiled smoothly, betraying nothing of her annoyance. "Father would have ne'er arranged for me to wed the MacLeod. Besides, ye were there when he said as much."

Colin's mouth pulled into a sour grin. "I only want for ye to be safe, Sister. Give yourself some time to settle in with the MacDonell. Donna be reckless and start your search for the stone if your husband has yet to trust ye." He paused. "And if ye ever want for anything, ye need only call upon me and I will be at your side." She raised her eyes to find him watching her. "I mean every word."

As if her dormant wits had renewed themselves, she straightened herself with dignity. "I am a MacKenzie. I will do what is required of me. Donna worry. I will make ye and Father proud."

"I am always proud of ye. Ne'er forget that." Colin gave her a brief nod and then trotted up next to her father.

One of the many things she would miss about home was her brother. Colin never wanted more from her than she was able to give and basically never expected her to be something she wasn't. She would sorely miss times like these when he talked to her and spent time with her, when he'd taken her on jaunts in the woods. She'd treasure those memories forever. She wasn't exactly thrilled to give up any of that. And now she found herself momentarily saddened. This was her family. She couldn't help but wonder if she would be welcomed into another or kept isolated simply because her last name was MacKenzie. No matter, she would make the best of it. She always did.

Something flashed at the corner of her eye.

A handful of MacDonell guards thundered toward them, the MacDonell tartan whipping in the wind. For a moment, she breathed in shallow, quick gasps. The men looked formidable riding their gigantic steeds, their hands placed strategically on the hilts of their swords. Could it be any more apparent that the MacDonell men did not trust the MacKenzies?

Colin moved protectively to her side. "'Tis only the MacDonell guard. We are now on the MacDonell's lands. The men will escort us to Glengarry."

She nodded because words simply failed her.

Sybella continued to study her surroundings—the lochs, trees, anything that would help her escape from her purpose. It didn't matter. She couldn't see the bonny sights anyway through her haze of swirling emotions. She suddenly felt ill-equipped to undertake such a task.

As if Colin read her mind, lines of concentration deepened along his brow and under his eyes. He'd flanked her the entire way, and she had to admit, his mere presence made her feel secure. Perhaps he only did it to make certain she would not flee, but she was comforted nonetheless.

Overlooking beautiful Loch Omhaich, Glengarry was an imposing gray stone structure boasting a gigantic L-shaped tower house with a round tower. The castle was somewhat elegant and formidable. Although the beastly MacDonell would need a place large enough to house his big-headedness, his home was not as Sybella had imagined it.

As her father entered the bustling bailey, he was immediately greeted by a wall of MacDonell men. Their untrusting eyes continued to survey him as he dismounted.

"Your new home is quite lovely," said Mary, her eyes glowing with delight.

Angus lowered his voice. "Here comes your betrothed. Let him assist ye from your mount."

And there he was.

His kilt rode low on his lean hips, and Sybella would recognize that arrogant swagger anywhere. He had a strong chiseled jaw, blue eyes, and light chestnut hair that was long enough to brush the outlines of his broad shoulders. The muscles under his white tunic quickened her pulse, and his stance emphasized the force of his thighs and the slimness of his hips. Praise the saints. He was definitely not the same boy she had met at the waterfall.

When the MacDonell spotted her, his smile broadened and he walked to her side. He held up his hand to assist her. "Lady Sybella MacKenzie, welcome to Glengarry." He had the nerve to wink at her when he caught her eye, and then his gaze roamed over her figure as if he undressed her with his eyes.

Sybella couldn't help herself. She refused to let the man get the best of her—again. She returned a frank and admiring look at him, studying his body unhurriedly, feature by feature. As if he enjoyed her subtle challenge, featherlike laugh lines crinkled around his eyes.

"Sybella!" Mary's tone was coolly disapproving.

Ignoring the MacDonell's hand, Sybella shifted her leg and slid from her mount. She would make it perfectly clear that she didn't need the dastardly man or his help.

A soft gasp escaped Mary, and Angus interjected. "Please excuse my cousin's lack of—"

The MacDonell chuckled in response. "There is nay need for apologies." When an older woman with silvery hair walked up behind him and nudged his back, he turned and wrapped his arm around the woman. "Lady Sybella MacKenzie, pray allow me to introduce Lady Iseab—"

The older woman reached out and fingered Sybella's curls. "Praise the saints. Ye are a bonny lass. I always wished to have honey-colored tresses myself." The woman brought her hand to her own hair. "Now I am only graced with death-gray. And please donna listen to my nephew. Ye may call me Aunt Iseabail."

It was hard to believe that the arrogant MacDonell could have an aunt who was kind and free spoken. Sybella sensed a kindred spirit, and there was something warm and enchanting about this woman. She smiled and gave the MacDonell's aunt a small curtsy. "'Tis a pleasure to make your acquaintance, Aunt Iseabail." Leaning in close, Sybella added, "I think your silvery tresses are verra becoming on ye."

The woman's smile brightened. "Come inside, my dear. All of ye."

❦

To say there was tension among the people in the room would understate the situation. Granted, it was hard to erase all the years of turmoil and hardship the MacKenzies had caused, but Alex's clan needed to at least try to make amends. He hoped his impending marriage would open that door and only prayed it wouldn't close before he had the chance to complete the task.

Pulling himself to his feet, Alex lifted his tankard. Silence enveloped the room and all eyes were upon him. He chose his words carefully. "Let us nae speak of the past, but look toward the future with hope and promise." An unwelcome tension stretched even tighter among the clans and blank stares continued to gaze back at him. They did not look convinced—at all. Not a smile was to be had, unless he counted Aunt Iseabail. He needed to do something fast.

When he glanced down at his betrothed, she sat in the chair, her thin fingers tensed in her lap. Her emerald gown clung to the luscious curves of her body, and for a moment, Alex had to be honest. MacKenzie or not, the lass had grown into a beautiful woman. He had a hard time keeping his eyes from her. She was still the same wild beauty he had met at the waterfall so many years ago. Back then she was just a young lass, straight as a stick. But now, she had filled out in all the right places and was feminine—very feminine.

He extended his hand and pulled her to her feet. "And let me introduce my future bride, Lady Sybella MacKenzie." He lifted Sybella's hand, and when he brushed a soft kiss on her ivory fingers, the MacKenzie men cheered. It was only a matter of time before Alex's kin followed.

"Now let us all enjoy this bountiful feast and welcome the union of our clans. 'Tis indeed a celebration," said Alex, his voice laced with pride. He and his future bride sat back down at the table. Damn. The woman had no idea how captivating she was when she smiled.

The tables were covered with meat, cheeses, and breads, and Aunt Iseabail's flowery touches were placed in bundles on each of the tables. He had to admit that he was rather pleased. Glengarry looked welcoming for the new lady of the castle. He only hoped Sybella felt the same.

"Nicely done, MacDonell," said the MacKenzie, giving him a brief nod.

Alex returned the same gesture and then leaned in close to his betrothed. "Are ye pleased?"

Her tankard froze at her lips, and a puzzled look crossed her features. "What?" She hesitated and then quickly added, "Pardon, my laird?"

When Alex repeated the question and she still held the same look of confusion, he smiled. "Our clans, they are conversing." She nodded slightly and then took another sip from her tankard. "Since ye are to be my wife on the morrow, ye may call me by my given name, Alexander. My friends call me Alex."

"Verra well. If ye insist. The food is verra good, *Alexander*," she said with quiet emphasis.

So that was the game his future wife wanted to play. He couldn't help but turn up his smile a notch. "Aye.

Cook prepared a fine meal. The meat is actually from your father."

"Mmm...I wondered how much cattle I was worth," Sybella retorted with cold sarcasm.

He raised his brow. "Pardon?"

She shook her head and rubbed her temples. "*Tha mo cheann goirt.*" *I have a headache.*

"Would ye like to retire to your chamber?"

Sybella squared her shoulders, her creamy breasts rising over her formfitting gown. "Please accept my apologies. I am nae yet ready to take my leave."

As he was about to return to his own meal, he noticed a woman waving to his betrothed. In fact, he believed the woman had been introduced as Mary. When his eyes met Mary's, she quickly looked to the ground at the same time he felt Sybella stiffen at his side. Not thinking it was his imagination, he continued to look in the woman's direction several additional times. She was definitely giving his betrothed some type of signal.

"Do ye think it will rain on the morrow? I would-nae want mud to dirty the gown I had made for the occasion," said Sybella in an odd tone.

His eyes widened in surprise. "I donna think it will rain. I am sure your dress will be fine. Are ye all right?" He couldn't help but notice the forced words that seemed to escape her lips. It was also hard to miss the fact that she had adjusted her posture and sat ramrod straight as if bound in the tightest corset imaginable. In truth, his betrothed looked uncomfortable and pained.

"Of course," said Sybella, returning to her meal.

Alex made another quick and involuntary appraisal

of her features. The lass had certainly grown in more bountiful places since the last time he had kissed her innocent lips. It seemed not that long ago when he had discovered the young girl at the waterfall. Although only a boy himself, the memory of her unsullied touch stayed with him long after their encounter. He often wondered what had become of her.

The corner of his lips lifted into a smile when he realized he would fulfill the nagging fantasy that plagued him as a lad. He discreetly reached down and adjusted the front of his kilt, finding a great sense of satisfaction in the fact that on the morrow, his fantasy would no longer be a dream.

❧

Mary was annoying. The infuriating woman's unrelenting gestures for initiating polite conversation or for sitting up straight were making Sybella daft. And the amusing part was that her foolish cousin had no idea how close she was to being pummeled into oblivion. Sybella tried desperately to disguise her annoyance in front of others but didn't think she was fooling Alexander.

The man continued to survey her, and her pulse skittered alarmingly. She cleared her throat, pretending to be unaffected by his gaze. Her heart began to hammer in her chest, and she wondered what the hell was wrong with her. Her cousin rattled her. Of course, that most definitely was not because of the man sitting beside her, devilishly handsome. His strong features held a certain sensuality she could not deny; however, she could ignore it—more or less.

Alexander leaned back, sizing her up, and that was the point when Sybella realized her behavior was absolutely ridiculous. The position of her back was causing it to ache. Why should she care what notion the man held of her feminine qualities? She never pretended—for anyone.

She sat back casually in the chair, relaxing to the best of her ability and soaking up the air of the celebration. Once the men lightened their moods, the sounds of laughter spread throughout the great hall. The reason for their merriment could have been the result of the flowing ale, but it was a somewhat enjoyable occasion nonetheless.

The MacDonells truly did everything they could to make the MacKenzies feel at home. And Sybella's kin must have felt it too because as the evening progressed, some of them sat at the table with Alexander's family. By the jovial expressions among the clans, they were all at least feigning to mend the past. Although the idea was somewhat unbelievable, Alexander even treated her with dignity and respect. Granted, they barely spoke, but she gave him the credit he deserved. Perhaps this wouldn't be as terrible as she had initially thought.

Her father should be proud. Moreover, the man appeared downright pleased as he mingled with the MacDonell men, Colin by his side. She was glad to see that her father's spirits weren't dampened by her impending union. Even though her only purpose was to steal back the stone, she knew it must be difficult for her father to not only lose his wife but now his daughter as well.

The hour grew late and her back was sore between her shoulder blades. The women would probably seek their beds shortly, and the men would more than likely drink themselves under the table. As long as everyone remained in their cups, no one should really bother her. Undoubtedly, they wouldn't even notice she was missing. She briefly wondered if she'd be able to search for the stone now, and then she remembered Colin's words to earn the MacDonell's trust first. Damn. She knew that finding the stone this eve and not having to speak her vows in the morn would be too much to hope for. At any rate, it was time to make her escape.

"Alexander," Sybella said softly. When her betrothed glanced toward her, she cast her gaze downward. "I think it best to seek my chamber now."

He rose to his feet and pulled out her chair. "Let me have someone escort ye."

She shook her head. "That isnae necessary. My trunk was brought up and I know where 'tis found. I thank ye for this fine celebration." When she started to walk away, he called to her.

"Lady MacKenzie…" When she turned around and raised her brow, Alexander lazily appraised her. "I will see ye on the morrow. Sleep well," he said, his voice low and consciously alluring.

As their eyes met, Sybella felt a shock run through her. It was too easy to get lost in the way the man looked at her. She felt a curious swooping pull at her innards. Unsettled, she moistened her dry lips and turned on her heel.

⤞✦⤝

Colin approached his father, pushing him toward an unoccupied wall. He slapped his father's shoulder. "All of the men are knee deep in their cups. It appears the MacDonells have welcomed Sybella into their home. Her charm is fairly catching. How could they nae?"

"They arenae but a bunch of daft fools," spat his father. He glanced around the great hall and then lowered his voice. "I assume ye will take this opportunity then."

A heavy silence fell.

"To do what? The MacDonell seems verra pleased," said Colin in a reassuring tone.

His father's coolness was evidence that he was not amused. "*Find my bloody stone.*"

Four

"I HONESTLY DONNA KNOW WHY YOUR FATHER AND Colin donna throttle ye." Mary sat down on a chair in Sybella's bedchamber. "Whether ye like it or nae, the MacDonell is to be your husband. Ye need to act as a lady, Sybella. Ye barely spoke to your betrothed this eve, and your posture was just dreadful at the table. Didnae ye see me? I tried to tell ye. If ye keep up with that type of behavior, the MacDonell may have ye eating in the stable with the other animals."

Sybella recognized that Mary meant well in her own way, but her cousin-by-marriage didn't know the true purpose behind this marriage. If she did, Sybella knew Mary wouldn't understand. The woman loved and doted upon Angus, and she was foolish enough to think that women should be allowed to marry for love as well as convenience. But for Sybella, it was too late. As Sybella, Colin, and her father had discussed, they would tell no one, including Mary and Angus.

Although Sybella's loyalties lay with her father, she couldn't help but feel somewhat deprived. She would never know the feeling of what Angus and

Mary shared. She would never know love, because her marriage was nothing more than a ruse.

While Mary continued to ramble, Sybella fell back on the bed and studied the stone walls of her prison—well, her permanent residence for the rest of her days. The bed in which she lay had tall, carved corner posts, and its heavy wooden frame took up the majority of one wall. A beautiful golden coverlet displayed fine needlework, something she would surely never master, and was draped over the feather mattress, which was surprisingly comfortable. On the far side of the room, a painted portrait of someone she had assumed to be Alexander's mother hung above a fairly large stone fireplace. And her cousin-by-marriage currently occupied the small sitting area, refusing to cease her incessant chatter.

"Angus and I tried to tell ye—"

Sybella pressed both hands over her eyes as if they burned with weariness. She was tired, drained from another lecture.

"God's teeth! Will ye *cease*?" asked Sybella, spacing the words evenly. "If the MacDonell decides to call off the wedding, it will nae be because of my lack of comportment."

As if her arse was afire, Mary flew to her feet. "I only look after ye, and your first impression was far from a good one. Do ye want your betrothed to see his bride as some uncivilized, unmannered woman? Ye didnae let him assist ye from your mount, and then ye stared verra boldly at him. Ye barely spoke to the man at sup, and must I remind ye again of how dreadful your posture was at the table? Ye sit as a man, Ella.

If I may be so bold, ye have made enough errors in judgment that ye should be taking my instruction willingly. Now if ye will excuse me, Angus awaits. Mayhap we will be able to speak again on the morrow when ye arenae so sensitive."

Sensitive?

"Mary, I love ye dearly, but take your leave before I strangle ye with my bare hands," Sybella warned.

Stunned by Sybella's bluntness, Mary snapped her mouth shut. She turned on her heel and strode out the door. Even though it pained Sybella to admit as much, Mary did have a valid point. She had barely conversed with *Alexander* this eve. She needed to remind herself to make it a personal goal not to call him Alex. God forbid she surrendered that easily and gave the rogue the satisfaction of knowing she'd lowered her defenses.

Taking a deep breath, she drew the conclusion that this was probably not the best way to start a marriage. She hadn't tried to speak or make pleasantries with the man because frankly, she didn't give a damn about him. But granted, the last thing she wanted to do was disappoint her father. It was important she please him, make him proud. Laird Kenneth MacKenzie was truly a great man and deserved a daughter who was not an embarrassment to the clan.

Sybella rose from the bed and straightened her gown. What she needed was some fresh air, a new perspective. Perhaps a brisk walk on the parapet would help to clear the haze. She was proceeding out the door when a scraping noise sounded from the opposite end of the hall.

"Is anyone there?" asked Sybella. When no one answered, she closed the door and continued with her purpose.

When she reached the door to the parapet, she saw a disheveled man who had his arm draped over a voluptuous woman with fiery red tresses. Sybella presumed the drunken man was a MacDonell from his bawdy laughter—well, that and the fact that he was wearing a MacDonell plaid. The man pulled the woman roughly, almost violently, to him against the stone wall.

Sybella's temper flared.

She was about to defend the helpless woman when she froze midstep. The woman responded—by burying her lips against the MacDonell man's throat and sliding her leg up around his waist. Suddenly, she didn't appear as helpless as Sybella had initially thought. When the woman proceeded to slip her hands underneath the MacDonell man's kilt and his expression tightened with strain, Sybella's eyes rounded with comprehension.

The woman did not need saving.

It wasn't as if Sybella hadn't spied on Colin enough to know how the act was done, but she couldn't disguise her body's reaction to the sight displayed so openly before her eyes. The man and woman pawed at each other out in the open, not in a bedchamber. At least her brother had enough sense not to be so visible. He would've taken his leman to a bed or at least sought a hidden hayloft. But no matter how disturbed she was by witnessing their carefree touches, Sybella could not find the strength to pull away.

The man repositioned himself, and when he let out a guttural moan, Sybella could not help the loud gasp that escaped her lungs. The man's head turned slightly toward her, and then he gently pushed the woman away from him.

"M'lady." He attempted to give her a low bow as his companion steadied him. The woman tried to straighten her clothing while the man spoke, his words barely comprehensible. "We were heading to the p-p-parapet. Unless of course, ye w-w-wanted..."

Sybella was glad of the semidarkness that hid the flush on her cheeks. "Nay, I was returning to my chamber. Thank ye." The last thing she wanted was to be in the middle of a lovers' tryst, let alone spying on one. What the hell was the matter with her? Why hadn't she fled when she had the chance?

She walked hastily through the halls, thoroughly embarrassed by the scene she had witnessed. She should've stayed in her chamber and sought her bed. That's what she wanted to do in the first place. Now she was paying a humiliating price for her stupidity.

She had almost reached the safe confines of her bedchamber when she spotted someone ducking into one of the rooms at the end of the hall. In fact, that certain someone looked vaguely familiar.

Moving quietly down the hall, Sybella approached the room. But as soon as she bent over to see if a light was illuminated from underneath the door, the chamber went dark. She hesitated, questioning what she thought she saw. Perhaps it was only her imagination, but she could have sworn...

She lifted her hand and gently knocked on the door.

When no one answered, her curiosity was most definitely aroused. This may not have been one of her brightest ideas. Who knew what she could be walking into? The thought barely crossed her mind when someone reached out and pulled her abruptly into the room.

She gasped.

"What the bloody hell are ye doing here, Ella?"

≪∽≫

Alexander reveled in the aftermath of the celebration. A few MacDonell men were passed out with their heads down on the tables, not to be outdone by the MacKenzie men who were splayed upon the great hall floor. He never thought he'd see the day when MacKenzie men slumbered on the MacDonell crest inlaid in the stone floor. In any event, Alex sat in the laird's chair, his father's chair, pleased at conclusion of the day's events.

"I see your betrothed has retired for the eve." John pulled out a chair and sat down. "Did ye fire her ire, or did she run back to Kintail with her tail between her legs?"

Alex chuckled in response and poured John a tankard of ale. "I donna know. In either instance, at least we have the cattle."

"I hope to hell ye know what ye're doing."

Imposing an iron control, Alex spoke confidently. "We already had this discussion. 'Tis a lot of cattle for our clan to be fed and the MacKenzie has taken so much from us already. Think of it as them paying us back for all the things they've taken."

John lowered his voice. "I didnae mean the cattle. Ye've shackled yourself with a wife—and a *MacKenzie* one at that."

Alex favored many things about John, but sometimes his friend's truthfulness was more of a pain in the arse. "And that MacKenzie lass brings two hundred fifty cattle with her as her dowry—two hundred fifty *MacKenzie* cattle."

A grin overtook John's features and he held up his hands in mock defense. "Ye donna need to convince me. The men seemed to enjoy themselves." He nodded to the drunken men.

"Aye. For a time I thought our clans would actually be warring in the middle of the great hall." He ran his hand through his hair in a tired gesture. "I was somewhat concerned, but at least everyone is still in one piece—well, more or less."

"Ye gave a fine speech, Alex." John took another swig of ale and lowered his voice. "The men are still on guard."

"Good. Make certain they arenae in their cups, and they will be rewarded when the MacKenzies take their leave. I want a watchful eye kept on them at all times. The MacKenzie retired with a lass a short time ago. Where is his son?"

"I have Ian following him. Nay worries, Alex. Enjoy your celebration because on the morrow, ye will be a married man. 'Tis too bad Doireann took her leave with Donald. Ye could have had at least one more night of freedom before ye spoke your vows."

"I doubt I will be getting much rest with my new bride if Aunt Iseabail has her way. The woman has been constantly hounding me about an heir. Praise the saints I should forget such a task."

"That is one duty I know ye will nae mind performing." John gave him a friendly punch in the arm. "At least the MacKenzie lass isnae so sore on the eyes. I cannae help but wonder if ye would have accepted the offer so willingly had she been a troll."

Alex shrugged. "'Tis late. I suppose I should gather Aunt Iseabail, but she doesnae look as though she is ready to part company."

John gulped the remainder of his ale and placed his tankard down on the table. "And I should be checking on the men to make sure they stay at their posts." He rose from the chair and slapped Alex on the back. "Ye better seek your bed, my laird. Ye will want to give your bonny new bride all of the attention she deserves on the morrow."

Alex smiled. "Aye, as soon as I am able to rouse Aunt Iseabail from the table and the company." He watched John walk away, and then he shook his head, thinking about his aunt. She'd drunk most of the men under the table and still was able to hold a conversation. The MacDonells were indeed strong stock.

Alex approached the table, and the older MacKenzie man looked thoroughly engaged in the conversation—well, either that or completely taken by Alex's aunt. The man sat forward, hanging on the edge of her every word.

"So my dear departed husband stripped them of their clothing, took their mounts, and made them all walk back as bare as the day they were born," said Aunt Iseabail. "They ne'er encroached on our lands again." She was friendly, smiling and bantering in a relaxed manner. As though she sensed someone beside her, she turned. "Alexander, I was sharing stories with William."

"Aye, your aunt has some amazing tales," said William, his eyes never leaving hers.

Alex knelt down beside her. "Aunt Iseabail, 'tis late. Why donna ye let me escort ye to your chamber?"

To his surprise, she pushed him away. "Nephew, William and I are having a delightful time. Right, William?"

"We only stay here to talk. I will make certain your aunt seeks her chamber." William met Alex's eyes without flinching. "Alone."

When Alex raised his brow at his aunt, she smirked, shooing him away. "Please, Nephew. 'Tis been a long time since I required a chaperone." And with that, Aunt Iseabail promptly ignored him and continued her conversation with William. "Now what was I speaking of?"

Alex knew when he wasn't wanted. Recognizing that sleep would not come, he wasn't ready to seek his bed and walked out into the bailey. Against the far wall, John spoke in raised tones with Ian. When John threw his hands up in the air, Alex knew something was amiss.

He approached his men and John's words were hostile. Ian received a verbal thrashing and looked none too pleased.

"What the hell is going on?" asked Alex. "I can hear ye from across the bailey."

At the sound of his voice, Ian turned. "My laird,

the MacKenzie has sought his chamber, but I cannae find the MacKenzie's son."

❧

"Colin, what do ye think ye are doing?" Sybella scolded him, pulling her arm out of her brother's grasp.

Colin lit the candle and she glanced around. Several pieces of unfinished embroidery were laid upon the table, and a handful of dresses were thrown carelessly on the bed. The room was smaller than hers but just as enchanting. The dark wooden frame of the bed and the ornate furnishings complemented one another. And with bunches of floral stems that were placed upon the mantel, Sybella knew in an instant whose chamber this was.

"What are ye doing in here?" she asked, her voice unintentionally going up a notch.

"I was searching for you," Colin responded with returning impatience.

"Searching for me? Why would ye be searching for me in Aunt Iseabail's chamber? I will have the truth, Brother."

His stare drilled into her and he cleared his throat. "I didnae know it was her room."

"Ye didnae know," she repeated.

"Aye, ye heard me. What other reason would I have to be in her chamber, Ella?"

She walked around him. "Let me tell ye what I think."

"Ye always do," Colin murmured under his breath.

"Surely ye arenae so bold as to search for the stone before I am wed. Ye told me as much. That being said,

I think ye cannae help but sneak around Glengarry and wonder how Kintail compares," she simply stated.

He held up his hands. "Aye, ye found me out. Can we please take our leave now before we are discovered?"

She gave a brief nod. "That would probably be best. If we were to be discovered and Father found out ye—"

"Exactly. Let us seek your chamber. I would like to know what kind of poverty my sister is living in," he said in a jesting tone. He opened the door and gestured her through as he blew out the candle.

They walked down the hall and entered Sybella's bedchamber. She had just closed the door when Colin smirked. "There is nay way this is your chamber, Sister."

"What do ye mean? Of course this is my chamber."

He spoke in his casual, jesting way. "'Tis far too clean to be your room, Ella."

She tossed a pillow at him and he caught it with one hand. He placed the pillow back on the bed and sat down beside her. His eyes had a burning, faraway look in them.

"What is it, Colin?"

"Are ye going to be all right here with the MacDonell? I would expect the truth."

His smile was almost apologetic, and she punched him playfully in the arm. "Is that what is troubling ye? In truth, I am nae thrilled to be the MacDonell's wife, but as I told ye before, I will do what is expected of me. Like all things in life, I am sure I will grow accustomed."

"Do ye mean that?"

"I wouldnae speak the words if they werenae the truth." She couldn't figure out if Colin's concern was that of an older brother or if there was some other meaning to his words or lack thereof. He was always direct with her and never made a play upon his words—yet, she had an underlying feeling something was off. "Are ye certain that is all that troubles ye?"

He hesitated, studying her for a moment. "I am only concerned for your welfare. Father made this alliance for the sole purpose of finding the stone. 'Tis dangerous, Ella. I want ye to be careful and donna be so quick to search for the stone. It will probably take the MacDonell a little while to lower his guard around ye. Give him time to know ye, and I am sure he will be besotted." He smiled warmly. "Most importantly, earn his trust. Make him realize that his wife stands by his side. I know it may be difficult for ye, but be a dutiful wife and please try to hold your tongue."

"This is the second time ye and Father have made such a reminder. Why do I get the feeling ye donna trust me to take this responsibility seriously? I am a MacKenzie. I know what is to be gained from recovering the stone." When his eyes flashed with the same familiar display of impatience, she added, "But I understand what ye mean. I will make certain I have the MacDonell's trust before I start to search for the stone so he isnae suspicious of me."

Colin kissed her on the cheek and then rose. "I will see ye in a few hours for your wedding, Sister. Try to get some rest." He was about to open the door when she spoke.

"And Colin?"

He turned around and raised his brow. "Aye?"

"Seek your own chamber and stop your wanderings lest we both find ourselves upon the gallows."

He rolled his eyes and closed the door behind him.

&cts;

"Where the hell is he?" asked Alex for the hundredth time.

"Donna worry. We will find him," said John reassuringly.

"And ye searched the chambers?"

"Aye."

"The bailey, stables, parapet." Alex knew there was no need to continue because Colin MacKenzie had simply walked into the great hall. Turning to John, Alex snarled, "Make sure Ian keeps a firm watch on the MacKenzie's son now. I will see ye on the morrow or in a few short hours."

Alex reached the hall to his chamber. When he heard laughter, he glanced up as Aunt Iseabail and William walked from the other end of the hall, arm in arm. Alex made a mad dash inside his bedchamber and closed the door. When William's voice carried through the hall, Alex couldn't help himself and he paused inside the door.

"Lady Iseabail, I must thank ye for a most enjoyable evening. I havenae had the pleasure of such delightful company for quite some time."

"I thoroughly enjoyed your company as well, William. Ye have many entertaining stories. I am especially fond of your tales as a young lad. They were verra charming."

"'Tis been my pleasure. I shall see ye on the morrow for the wedding."

"Aye, the wedding. We have waited so long for Dòmhnall to wed, and frankly, I ne'er thought it would happen. My husband and I are verra proud of him."

William paused and Alex cringed. But he had to give William credit when the MacKenzie man simply made a polite farewell and left his aunt to her own devices. Poor Aunt Iseabail. Alex wished he could cease his aunt's memory lapses, but at least she was otherwise healthy and happy.

He finally crawled into bed only to find himself staring at the ceiling. When he grew tired of that, he gazed at the wall. He lay in the drowsy warmth of his bed, thinking. He wasn't sure how long he had remained in the same position when an image popped into his mind.

Five years ago, Alexander first laid eyes on the fair-colored lass with her golden tresses and dusty rose cheeks. She was going to jump from the top of the waterfall. Alex admired a lass who showed some bollocks. Of course, that was before he realized the wily female was a dreaded MacKenzie. At the time, he could not say what had surprised him more. The fact that the damn MacKenzies stepped foot on his father's land or his own brazen mockery of kissing his enemy's daughter.

The lass had barely spoken with him this eve, but he knew he hadn't really gone out of his way to initiate conversation with her, either. He probably should have made more of an effort, been more attentive.

Sybella said she had a headache. Perhaps he should show her some kindness and ask if she needed anything—well, if she was still awake.

Alex threw the covers from the bed and stood. Hastily, he donned his kilt. He walked toward the adjoining door, completely aware that the headstrong MacKenzie lass probably had it barred. He was momentarily taken aback when he tried the latch and found it unlocked. He knocked softly and then slowly pushed open the door.

One bedside candle remained lit, illuminating Sybella's long golden tresses. He stood close to the edge of the bed and simply watched her. Her nightrail had slipped down over her shoulder and displayed the milky color of her skin. Her hair tumbled carelessly down her back, and her seductive young body and wholesome good looks tightened his groin.

Her smooth skin glowed with pale undertones, and her cheeks were of rose and pearl. She looked more delicate and ethereal than ever. The prolonged anticipation of touching her was almost unbearable.

He stepped forward and extended his fingers over the contours of her shapely figure. He was close enough that he could almost caress her. When reality sunk in, Alex hastily pulled back his hand, knowing the mere touch of her body would be his undoing. With one last look, he lazily appraised her.

She was beautiful. And in a few hours she would be his.

He walked back through the adjoining door and gently closed it behind him—completely unaware that Sybella's eyes were open.

Five

Sybella's eyes burned from sleeplessness. Her mind kept turning to last eve—or should she say a few short hours ago—when her betrothed had snuck into her chamber through the adjoining door. Alexander had some bollocks; she would give him that. Did he presume their wedding night would start earlier than expected? She had feigned sleep to deter any advances and had breathed a sigh of relief when he eventually left. Only the gods knew what went on in that man's head.

She pulled out her wedding dress and tossed it on the bed. At least her tiredness would keep her sanity at bay. She splashed some water from the bowl onto her face, but it was not as cold and bracing as she'd hoped it would be. She needed something to snap out of this tired stupor. When there was a knock at her door, she picked up a cloth and dried her eyes.

"Sybella, 'tis Mary."

Praise the saints.

Mary swung open the door, and Sybella didn't think fast enough to close it again. Mary stood with her hands on her hips, assessing Sybella from head to toe. "Look at ye. Ye arenae even dressed. Your hair is a mess, and your eyes look as though ye were in a brawl."

"And good morn to ye as well, Mary," said Sybella with a bright smile.

Mary closed the door and spoke in a rush of words. "Come now. Ye must make haste." She approached the bed and then brushed the top of the feather mattress with her hand as if she were wiping crumbs from the table. "I am nae saying anything about last eve because I know ye were distraught, but there is something we need to discuss before ye speak your vows."

Sybella cringed. "And what might that be?"

"There is nay delicate way to speak upon such matters so I will be blunt."

"I would expect naught less," Sybella said dryly.

"There are certain duties a man expects from his bride on the eve of his wedding."

When stains of scarlet appeared on Mary's cheeks, Sybella gave her a polite smile. "Please spare us both. Ye donna need to discuss such subjects with me."

"Since your dear mother is nay longer with us and I am the only woman of close relation, 'tis my duty, Sybella. How will ye know what to expect if nay one tells ye?"

A suffocating sensation tightened Sybella's throat. From the look upon Mary's face, she was not going to give up on her commentary any time soon. With a sense of dread, Sybella knew the battle of wills was lost before it had even begun. It didn't help that Mary was right. Sybella didn't know what to expect on the eve of her wedding, and frankly, she was more than a little curious and nervous.

While Mary talked in very specific terms, Sybella studied the furnishings. She gazed at her gown. She stretched her neck and almost forgot to give the occasional nod. With that, the detailed instruction on coupling was finished, and they got back to the task at hand.

Sybella was lifting the gown over her head when Mary asked, "Are ye all right?"

After pulling down the dress, Sybella straightened her bodice. "Of course."

"Ye can talk to me. I know this must nae be easy for ye." When Sybella gave her a wry smile, Mary studied her intently. "Come sit down and let me fix your hair."

Sybella sat on the bed while Mary brushed her hair. For some reason, Sybella's palms had started to sweat. Closing her eyes, she took a deep breath. "I donna know what is the matter with me, but my stomach is verra unsettled. I think I feel ill."

"'Tis perfectly normal for all new brides. Once ye see your betrothed at the altar, ye will find your nervousness disappears. Trust me. The man will only have eyes for ye. There. Ye are all done. Ye look beautiful, Sybella, and I'm sure your mother would be verra proud."

For the first time since she could remember, Sybella hoped that was true.

❧

Alex stood in front of the altar in the stone chapel, waiting patiently for his betrothed. Bloodshot eyes stared back at him, and some of the men leaned up against the wall. Everyone was indeed a sorry sight. His clan sat to the right and Sybella's kin to the left. Aunt Iseabail was the only MacDonell who sat next to a MacKenzie. She sat in the pew next to William, beaming approval. Alex hadn't seen that spark in her eyes since last eve, when she was in her cups and doting on the MacKenzie man. Alex briefly contemplated whether or not his betrothed had fled when a vision of beauty stepped foot through the entrance.

The MacKenzie plaid was proudly draped over Sybella's shoulder, and her sky-colored gown displayed a slim waist that flared into rounded hips. The sun illuminated her long golden tresses, making them look like strands of lustrous silk. She was simply…enchanting.

Escorted by her father, she walked slowly and moved with an easy grace. She nodded at a few people along the way and approached Alex at the altar.

He couldn't help but smile. "My lady." His voice was shakier than he would have liked.

She curtseyed in response. "My laird."

The priest asked something of Sybella's father and the MacKenzie may have answered, but to be truthful, Alex only half listened. Sybella was simply beautiful, and he could barely take his eyes from her. Everything that happened next would remain a haze around the edge of his mind.

He believed he had spoken his vows when he heard his stammering voice, which was nothing but a buzz in his ear. But when Sybella spoke, there was a gentle softness to her words. Her tone was comforting, calming. Or maybe it only sounded that way because he'd barely slept.

"Ye are now man and wife," said the priest.

When everyone clapped and shouted in response to the priest's words, Aunt Iseabail's voice could be heard above all others. "Give her a wee kiss and make it a good one, Alexander!"

He looked directly at Sybella, and they exchanged a subtle expression of amusement. "I cannae disappoint my aunt."

Sybella gave him a gentle smile. "Of course ye cannae."

Her eyes froze on his lips and he lowered his head. Standing on tiptoe, his wife pressed her lips to his, his hands locking against her back. She was soft and warm, and suddenly he was very conscious of where his wife's flesh pressed up against his.

When their kin whooped and hollered, Alex pulled back slightly and gazed into her eyes. Ignoring everyone, he spoke only to her. "Welcome to Glengarry, Lady Sybella MacDonell."

Aunt Iseabail rushed to the altar and handed Sybella a tartan sash. "This belonged to Alexander's wife. Ye should have it."

"It was my mother's," he said.

Sybella accepted the sash with gentle kindness. "Thank ye, Aunt Iseabail. 'Tis quite lovely and I shall wear it proudly." She removed the MacKenzie plaid and draped the MacDonell sash over her dress, fastening the garment with the MacKenzie badge.

"I also have a gift for you," said Alex. He handed her a bejeweled dagger. "I thought of ye and had it made."

"Thank ye, Alexander."

Although she was reluctant to admit it, the man looked positively dashing in the MacDonell kilt and plaid. God help her, but his blatant good looks were hard to ignore. When he touched his lips to hers, Sybella felt as though she'd been struck by a bolt of lightning. In truth, she was shocked at her own eager response to his touch.

"Are ye ready for another feast?" Alexander's hand came over hers possessively and he smiled.

"I am, but I am nae sure I can say the same for our kin." She glanced around the chapel at the tired faces. "It seems they are still recovering from last eve."

"There is that," said Alexander.

A hand clamped down on Sybella's shoulder and she jumped.

"Let me be the first to congratulate ye, Sister. *Gu meal sibh ur naidheachd.*" *Congratulations to both of you.*

"Thank ye, Colin," she said with a warm smile.

Sybella stepped around Colin, and her father tugged her close. His lips whispered lightly into her ear as he rubbed her back. "Best wishes, my daughter."

"Thank ye, Father."

Her father gave a brief nod to Alexander. "Congratulations on your union to my daughter, Laird MacDonell. I am sure ye will find Sybella to be a faithful and obedient wife."

Sybella stiffened as Alexander clasped her father's arm.

"Let us hope so, for 'tis too late to go back on our agreement now," said Alexander, a trace of laughter in his voice.

Her new husband glanced at her for any sign of

objection and so did her father. Sybella bit her lower lip before her mood veered sharply to anger. She didn't think it wise to have heated words with both men on the day of her wedding. When she looked up at Alexander, he gave her a broad wink as if he knew how she felt.

"Is everything all right, *Wife*?"

"Of course...*Alexander*." She paused as soon as the word "husband" attempted to escape her lips.

"'Tis so wonderful to have ye here." When Sybella turned, Aunt Iseabail brought her hands to Sybella's cheeks. "I hope ye and my nephew will be verra happy for many years to come."

"Thank ye, Aunt Iseabail."

The kind woman lowered Sybella's head and kissed her on the forehead. "'Tis a pity the wedding is over. My husband and I wish we could have spent some time with ye, but we must return home on the morrow."

Sybella's heart sank and she wasn't sure what to say. She rubbed her hand over the aging woman's frail shoulder, giving her a compassionate smile. Sybella was relieved that Alexander was by her side, but she watched as his features grew more concerned the more Aunt Iseabail spoke.

"Dòmhnall, ye have yourself a bonny new bride, and I am looking forward to plenty of bairns under this roof. More than one, I tell ye—and they donna need to be all lads. I donna think my poor heart can handle it." She raised her hand over her chest and laughed.

His gaze was filled with sympathy. "I am Alexander."

Aunt Iseabail waved him off. "Of course ye are. Ye remind me so much of your father."

"Will ye be sitting with William for the meal?" Alexander asked, his tone holding a degree of warmth and concern.

Sybella saw William and gestured him forward. "William, Aunt Iseabail will sit with ye for the meal."

"It would be my pleasure to enjoy such company again." William held out his arm to Aunt Iseabail, his smile courteous. "What other tales do ye have for me, Lady Iseabail?" Alexander's delightful aunt rewarded William with a large smile of her own.

Alexander escorted Sybella to the great hall, accepting felicitations along the way. Once again, she took her place beside him on the dais and watched men and women flow into the hall for the celebration. She couldn't help but glance at him and notice the worried expression on his face. She sensed his disquiet, and frankly, the feeling of hopelessness was all too familiar. Watching the health of loved ones fade was by no means an easy feat.

"Does Aunt Iseabail lose her thoughts often?" asked Sybella in a soft tone.

Alexander had opened his mouth to reply when her father raised his tankard and spoke in an impressive voice. "May you travel in the truth on straight paths—be moderate and civil and never abandon reason; may your race be numerous throughout the land. And may you see your great-grandchildren following in your footsteps."

Cheers were shouted out in response to the marital blessing.

Alexander took a drink from his tankard and then looked directly at Sybella. When he realized she was still waiting for an answer to her question, he sighed. "More often than I would like. Ever since my father passed, her mind has worsened."

Sybella looked around at the celebratory crowd and began to speak as memories flooded her. "I cared for my ailing mother and barely left her side. This was the same woman who raised me and loved me from the time I was a bairn. When her days were good, they were verra good. When they were bad…"

When he raised his brow, she added, "I think 'tis harder on us to watch their health fail. Aunt Iseabail may call ye by your father's name and forget the reason for the celebration, but ye still have her. Other than her mind, she seems hale. I know it pains us greatly to see our loved ones nae as they once were, but in truth, 'tis truly a blessing they are still with us. Donna mourn for the past, Alexander. We should be grateful for the time we have left with them—now, in the present."

Angus and Mary approached the table and Sybella was irked by the intrusion. "Congratulations again, Cousin," said Angus, giving Sybella a slight bow. "Mary and I are verra joyful for you both." Mary stood silently by Angus's side—ever the dutiful wife.

"Thank ye."

Angus stretched his arm around Mary's waist. "We shall be taking our leave on the morrow and thank ye for the hospitality, Laird MacDonell. Colin and I are looking forward to getting back to some hunting."

Sybella tried to stay the pang of regret that washed over her when she remembered all of the things she would miss with her brother. It was almost as if Angus had intentionally rubbed salt on an open wound, a subtle reminder that she was no longer a part of the MacKenzies.

Alexander leaned forward in his chair. "Are ye both skilled with a bow?"

"I am more accomplished than Colin," said Angus. "It doesnae take too much to best my cousin at anything."

When Angus gave Mary a conspiratorial poke in the ribs with his elbow, Sybella's instinctive response was to reach over the table and throttle her witless cousin. Granted, Colin was not adept with a bow, but Angus had no right to tell that to a MacDonell. Although it was difficult, she willfully restrained her tongue, lest there be bloodshed on the day of her wedding—caused by her own hand.

As a peaceful alternative, Sybella shifted in the seat toward Alexander, clearly dismissing her vexing cousins. "My laird, pray excuse me for a moment." She rose from her chair and walked to her brother's table without a backward glance.

❧

"Ye must forgive my cousin. She doesnae yet know her place," said Angus. The MacKenzie man spoke as if he and Alex were longtime friends.

Alex sat back casually in the chair and tapped on the rim of his tankard. "And what place might that be?"

Angus and Mary exchanged a glance full of secret meaning, and then Angus bent his head slightly forward. "If I may speak freely…"

Alex raised his brow and waved his hand. "By all means. I would expect naught less."

"'Tis nay great secret that my cousin needs lessons in matters of comportment. Ye see…Sybella cared for my aunt for two years, locked up within the stone walls of the castle. 'Tisnae my cousin's fault, mind ye, but the only companionship to be had was that of her ailing mother and the woman's soiled linens."

Angus scrunched up his features in disgust. "That is part of the reason why my cousin is such a spirited lass. In my humble opinion, her father and brother give her far too much leave. But I am sure in time Sybella will come to understand your rules. She only needs a firm hand." Angus gave Alex a conspiratorial wink.

Alex sat very still, his eyes narrow. "Let me tell ye what I think. The lass watched her mother die, and there was naught my wife could have done but offer her mother comfort—whether by changing her linens or holding her hand. And with ye as my wife's cousin, nay wonder she stayed within the walls of her mother's chamber. I donna share your views, and ye will keep them to yourself under my roof. The woman ye speak of is my *wife*. Do ye understand?"

Angus was puzzled by Alex's stern attitude, but Alex didn't care. How typical that they would judge Sybella's behavior when they had absolutely no idea what circumstances molded the lass. Having had a similar situation with his father, Alex was sympathetic toward her plight.

Clearly dismissing Sybella's annoying kin, he stood. He had no patience for daft people. He approached Sybella, who still remained at her brother's table, and she stiffened when Alex touched her waist. "Pray excuse me while I steal my bride for a moment," he said to Colin. The lass looked startled by the intrusion.

Colin smiled and gave Alex a brief nod. "We will speak later, Sybella."

"Come. I have something to show ye."

"Should I be worried?" she asked, raising her brow.

Alex didn't answer as they walked silently through the bustling halls of Glengarry. When they reached the parapet door, he swung it open and gestured her through. "After ye."

He followed her swaying hips up the stone staircase and only needed a few seconds to realize that his attempts not to be an arse were not working. When she stepped out onto the parapet, she came to a dead stop. For a moment, the lass forgot to move and let him through the door. He reached out and touched her waist as a gentle reminder.

Sybella moved hastily to the side. "My apologies. 'Tis beautiful."

The day had turned cloudy, and the sun's rays peeked sporadically through the clouds in the blue-gray sky. Mossy-green grass surrounded the loch, and the water glimmered with the reflective light of amber hues. This was the view that Alex treasured and often sought.

"I thought ye might be in need of a respite from the celebration."

"Ye thought that right. 'Tis truly breathtaking."

"Aye, the view is verra bonny as well."

Sybella rolled her eyes and smirked. "How long did it take ye to think up that one? I bet ye say that to all the lasses."

"Only a few."

When she ignored him, Alex thought to try again. He reached out, swinging her around to face him. "I know this must nae be easy for ye, Sybella. Our clans have been battling for so long that everyone has come to expect it. I am comforted by the thought that the warring will cease with our marriage. There has been too much bloodshed. I am probably the last man ye would want for a husband, but I will be a good one nonetheless. I will protect and care for ye as long as ye stand by my side. In return, my only request is that ye are truthful and stay true to your vows. I donna want a marriage filled with lies and distrust. And I offer ye the same courtesy."

A strange look flashed in her eyes, and she gently tugged away from him. She spoke as she stared out at the loch. "Then ye will nae mind me saying that your kiss wasnae appreciated."

"My kiss?" Alex hesitated, puzzled. Then as if he were knocked on the head, he realized she was talking about that first kiss by the waterfall, and he chuckled in response.

"Ye know damn..." Clearing her throat, she added, "darn well what I am speaking of, Alexander MacDonell. How dare ye threaten to call a warning if I didnae kiss ye?"

"Now, lass, if ye remember correctly, I did give ye a choice."

Her eyes narrowed. "Some choice," she said dryly. "Kiss ye or ye'd call your father's men. What kind of choice was that?"

"When ye and your brother decided to encroach

on our lands, ye gave me verra little choice. And besides, it doesnae matter. Ye are now my wife, Lady MacDonell."

His expression stilled and grew serious.

Licking her lips nervously, Sybella turned her head promptly away from him and remained still.

Alex moved even closer until he left her no room at all.

❧

Sybella swallowed hard and squared her shoulders. Alexander's fingers took her arm with gentle authority, and he turned her to face him. Briefly closing her eyes, she felt his hand brush the hair back from her neck. His hand remained on her shoulder for a moment too long.

She noticed he was watching her intently, his nearness overwhelming. At the base of her throat, a pulse beat and swelled as though her heart had risen from its usual place.

He lowered his head, and his kiss was surprisingly gentle. The touch of his lips was a delicious sensation. He planted a tantalizing kiss in the hollow of her neck, and she felt her knees weaken.

His lips recaptured hers, more demanding this time. He forced open her mouth with his thrusting tongue and she savored every moment. Her thoughts spun, her emotions whirled and skidded, and her body arched toward him instinctively.

She was shocked at the impact of his gentle grip. Her response to him was so powerful that for a long moment, she felt as if she were floating.

He slowly pulled back, and something unexplainable passed between them. She had to admit that she was strangely flattered by his interest.

"Wife, 'tis still too early to seek our marriage bed. We must return to the celebration." His voice was low and alluring.

An unwelcome blush crept onto Sybella's cheeks as she tried to swallow the lump that lingered in her throat. She was humiliatingly conscious of her husband's scrutiny. She was perfectly aware that she needed to gain his trust, but surely Alexander must think his new wife some type of harlot for kissing him so wantonly in broad daylight.

She was an idiot.

Six

SYBELLA DONNED HER NIGHTRAIL AND SAT IN THE chair in her bedchamber. Should she be sitting? Maybe she should be standing. She rose and started to pace. Perhaps she should be still. She folded her hands together and then crossed her arms over her chest. What was she supposed to be doing? She felt like a daft fool. When Alexander did not walk through the adjoining door, she sat down on the bed. She sure wasn't going to appear as though she was waiting for the man to grace her with his presence.

When her husband finally walked through the door, he was dressed in his tunic and kilt. His warm eyes were full of something she could not quite identify, and although what he expected was not clear, there was something captivating in his look. Since Alexander still wore his clothes, maybe he had decided not to consummate the marriage this eve. If that was true, Sybella felt completely underdressed for the occasion.

He placed a tankard down on the bedside table. "Wife."

"Alexander."

His gaze lowered, as did his voice. "Ye have yet to call me husband or Alex."

"We barely know one another," she said quietly.

"Now that simply isnae true. We have known each other since the day at the waterfall." His tone was laced with subtle amusement.

Her mouth dropped open. "The *waterfall*? We hardly spoke."

He gave her a roguish grin and Sybella cast her eyes downward. All too quickly, she had run out of diversions. How much longer could she postpone the inevitable? She tried to force her confused emotions into order and couldn't stand the unwelcome tension. Praise the saints. There was no sense worrying about what could not be changed. One way or another, after tonight, she would no longer be an innocent woman.

She took a deep breath and consciously masked her inner turmoil with deceptive calmness. But when the silence began to grate on her nerves, she decided to address the subject head on.

"Is there something we need to do first?" She waved her hand in a nervous gesture.

Alexander was momentarily speechless in his surprise. "I was going to speak with ye and offer ye a wee bit of ale, but if ye wish to have me in your bed…" When his eyes darkened with an unreadable emotion, Sybella flopped back onto the bed and adjusted her pillow.

"I am nervous enough. This prolonged torture doesnae benefit anyone. Can ye please do what ye need to do?" She bit her lip in a nervous gesture.

A gentle chuckle answered her as her husband stood perfectly still beside the bed. "Do what I need to do?" He dropped down beside her, facing her, while she continued to stare at the ceiling. Draping his arm over her waist, he shook his head. "Ye donna want any wooing words before we—"

"Why would ye need to give me wooing words when I am already your wife?" she asked dryly.

"Look at me." When she turned her head, she saw a suggestion of annoyance in his eyes. "Ye are far too tense. Ye need to relax and calm yourself. This doesnae have to be unpleasant."

"Speaks the man with the..." Sybella gestured toward her husband's manhood and quickly added, "*cluigean.*" *Hanging thing.*

Her husband stared at her and then burst out laughing. When she started to grind her teeth, the amusement left his eyes. "Sybella, I only try to speak with ye to calm ye."

She huffed. "Ye have been doing naught but speaking. I donna think your words will change the end result, unless I am mistaken."

In one swift movement, he lowered his head and moved his mouth over hers. His kiss was surprisingly gentle. His tongue traced the soft fullness of her lips and then explored her mouth. He shifted and kissed the pulsing hollow at the base of her throat as blood coursed through her veins.

She became instantly awake.

Her husband's arms encircled her, one hand at the small of her back. She could feel his uneven breathing on her cheek as he held her close. The warmth of his arms was so male, so bracing. His mouth was warm and sweet on hers.

The mere touch of his hand sent a warming shiver through her, and she tingled from the contact. She felt transported on a soft and wispy cloud. Alexander's demanding lips caressed her, and his slow, drugging kisses were driving her mad.

With his tongue, he ravished her mouth. He released her briefly, only enough to breathe, and then repeated his ritual again.

Raising his mouth from hers, he gazed into her eyes. He slid the nightrail off her shoulders and down her arms, as she lay bare beneath his sultry glance. He tugged off his tunic and hastily tossed it aside.

Sybella gasped as bare skin met bare skin and she felt her breasts crush against the hardness of his chest.

Her husband picked up a lock of her hair and caressed it gently. "Ye are so verra bonny."

When he lightly kneaded her breasts with his rough fingers and teased her nipples into hard aching points, her mind was robbed of any coherent words. He lowered his head and kissed her taut nipples, rousing a melted sweetness within her. She found it difficult to remain still when he suckled the tips of her breasts.

There was a heated swelling between her legs, a moistness she did not understand.

When he slid his hand over her trembling stomach and then between her legs, she froze. He kissed her again and, with a few skillful strokes of his fingers, pushed back the shock of his personal touch. His finger thrust inside her, imitating the movement of his tongue in her mouth.

He felt so strong against her body that she was completely enthralled by his masculinity. The possessiveness of his touch did not lessen her awareness of the man in her arms. In truth, she sensed a sudden secureness, protectiveness, coming from him. Is this what it meant to be husband and wife? Her mind was so cluttered with thoughts that she wasn't exactly sure what she was experiencing.

Her husband's body moved to partially cover hers, his hands lifting her nightrail above her hips. She momentarily stiffened but quickly remembered Mary's words of wisdom.

❧

As Alex crouched over his bonny wife, he cursed the dim light. From what he could see, Sybella was exquisite. Her creamy breasts filled his hands and her slender hips ignited his passion. Frankly, she aroused him so swiftly that he was afraid he might not be able to take it slowly. That would be a definite challenge.

He reached down and loosened his kilt while he continued to drug her with passionate kisses. He knew she was more than a little nervous, so he would continue to distract her in pleasant ways.

Praise the saints. The lass was so wet and ready for him.

He eased himself inside her and, with one quick thrust, made her his.

Sybella gasped and he held himself up on his forearms, fighting to remain still. He tried not to breathe. His body shook with strain, and sweat beaded on his forehead. Damn, how he craved to move.

He wanted to give her body time to adjust to him, but the feel of her tight heat was almost his undoing. He placed his head to hers, maddened with need.

"Is that all?" she asked with rounded eyes.

He tried to stay the laugh that wanted to escape from him. "Nay, lass, there is much, much more." He grasped her by the calves and gently pushed her legs up until her knees were bent.

When he pressed deeper within her, she clamped her eyes shut and cried out, "Yan, Tyan, Tethera, Methera, Pimp, Sethera, Lethera, Hovera, Dovera, Dik—"

"What are ye doing?" he asked through clenched teeth, his chest heaving. When she hesitated, he thought she was about to answer him. But her eyes remained shut and she continued to chant—louder.

"Yanadik, Tyanadik, Tetheradik."

"God's teeth, Sybella!"

"I count sheep," she said, her voice cold and lashing.

His wife's emotionless words killed his ardor like a bucket of ice-cold water. When Alex pulled back, Sybella swiftly rolled to her side, tugging the blankets away from him. She became as quiet as a mouse, her behavior unsettling.

Momentarily taken aback by her change in attitude, he swallowed hard, trying not to reveal his anger. He'd tried to be patient with her, but when his *beloved* wife purposely ignored him and did not even stir, he'd had enough. He promptly stood and grabbed his kilt and tunic from the floor. With one last look at the bed, he glowered at the wily female and stormed through the adjoining door. Her actions were as cold and empty as the bed she would sleep in this eve.

When Alex reached his chamber, he contemplated what the hell had happened. His mind turned to their embrace on the parapet. The lass had given in freely to the passion of his kiss. He would love to know what had changed between then and when he'd left her bed only a short moment ago.

He'd never forget the expression on her face. With her eyes clamped shut, Sybella's look was one of pure torture. He was as gentle and careful as he could've been for her first time, but when his wife started to count sheep beneath him, that was the last straw. He would never forget the relief that crossed her face when he rolled onto his side. He wasn't a total arse. He was going to stay and offer her comfort. But from the look of things, she wanted no part of it—or him.

Whatever his wife's issues were, she had better get over them soon. He would be visiting her chamber often and would not think about leaving her alone until she became with child. He was disappointed in her. She had seemed so willing to start anew when he kissed her that afternoon, and for a brief time, he was foolish enough to believe they had an understanding.

He refused to dwell on his wife's odd behavior any longer.

At least the MacKenzies would be leaving in a few short hours. Maybe then, he could finally get everything and everyone around him back to normal. That had not been the case for so long that he needed to remember exactly what normal entailed. Nevertheless, he had one less problem to worry about. His clan would be fed; his union with Sybella taking care of that.

And poor Aunt Iseabail.

Perhaps once all of the commotion had ended and everything settled down, she would have time to rest. The festivities seemed to be taking their toll. Although his aunt obviously favored the companionship of William MacKenzie, the last thing Alex wanted was another of Sybella's pesky kin under his roof. By this time on the morrow, it would all be over.

❧

With a long, exhausted sigh, Sybella pulled herself to her feet and then quickly dropped back onto the bed.

Her body ached.

No wonder. But at least the toughest part was over and she now knew what to expect—although it wasn't nearly as insufferable as Mary had described.

Sybella rose from the bed, wanting to spend some time with Colin before he took his leave. When a feeling of loneliness washed over her, she willed it away. Everything would be all right. She would accept nothing less. Even though the last few days had unsettled her, she would smile and hold her head high when her clan left for home.

She pulled out her day dress and had turned to the bed when she noticed a spot of blood on the covers. Lifting her nightrail, she observed the same underneath.

Mary never mentioned blood.

Dear God.

Why was she bleeding? It was not her time.

There was a knock on the adjoining door. "Wife?"

The door cracked open and Sybella ran to close it,

barely missing Alexander's face. "Please donna come in here," she said in a rush of words.

Her husband's large hand gripped the door. "Why? What is amiss?"

She pushed again, but the door would not budge against the huge mass of her husband. "Please, Alexander. There is naught—"

He shoved the door open and walked through, stealing a glance around her chamber. "What is amiss?"

"'Tis naught," she said with as much innocence as she could muster. She whipped the covers up on the bed and bunched up her nightrail, holding it to the side. When his eyes narrowed, she was keenly aware of his scrutiny. She continued to stare at him, feigning indifference.

He let out a long, audible breath. "Did we nae discuss that I will nae tolerate lies between us? It has only been one day, and already ye forget my words." He leisurely walked over to the sitting area and pulled out a chair. "I will simply sit here until ye speak the truth."

When she lifted her brow, he returned the same gesture and waited.

Sybella paled at the enormity of the command. She had not forgotten the words they spoke on the parapet, but she was intensely humiliated. She sat down on the bed, her fingers squeezing the bridge of her nose. "Alexander—"

"I am listening." His tone was the same as if he were talking with a child. Pausing, he seemed to choose his words carefully. "I thought we had an understanding last eve. I expect the truth. Mayhap I wasnae clear in my purpose. When I ask something of ye, I presume ye would be honest. I told ye as much before. I donna tolerate lies."

Why would he make her speak of this? He folded his muscled arms over his chest and was not going to relent. Why did this come as no surprise? She had no choice but to yield to his command. She was forced to speak the truth, no matter how humiliating, but she certainly didn't have to look at him while she spoke.

"I bleed and 'tisnae my time," she said softly.

"What?"

Sybella repeated her words louder and closed her eyes. Footsteps stopped in front of her and a hand rested upon her shoulder. When she did not glance up, Alexander sat down on the bed beside her.

"Lass, 'tis normal for your first time. The reason I called upon ye this morn was to tell ye I ordered a bath for ye. It should help to ease the soreness ye feel. There is naught to be ashamed of, and ye donna need to hide such things from me. I am your husband. We are as one."

She was helpless to halt her embarrassment. "I… didnae know it was normal. When I saw the blood…"

He smiled warmly. "Didnae your mother speak with ye about such things?"

Sybella shook her head. "My mother became ill before she had the chance. There was only Mary."

A strange look passed over his features. "Mary?" When an unwelcome blush crept onto Sybella's cheeks, he grabbed her hand. "I am your husband. Tell me. What *exactly* did Mary say to ye about such matters?"

"Obviously, she didnae tell me about any bleeding."

He patiently listened while Sybella repeated most of what Mary instructed her.

"And the sheep?"

"As I already said, I am to remain perfectly still and close my eyes. When that *cluigean* goes in, I am to count sheep to ease the pain."

Alexander glanced sideways, and she swore he laughed and then covered it quickly with a cough. What was the matter with the man? He'd asked what Mary said, and Sybella had spoken honestly. After all, that's what he demanded.

"Nay worries. Is there anything else I can do for ye?" he asked, rubbing her shoulder.

She shook her head. The conversation had already gone too long. If this was any indication of how her day was going to go, she suddenly had the overwhelming urge to crawl back into bed and cower under the blankets.

He rose from the bed and kissed her on the top of the head. "Your bath will be here soon."

Sybella watched Alexander walk through the adjoining door. Closing her eyes, she sat bent over with her face in her hands. Among other emotions was a deep sense of shame. How could she not know what was happening with her own body? And worse yet, she'd needed a *man* to explain it to her. Her pride had been seriously bruised.

There was a knock at her bedchamber door, and the men carried in a tub as well as steaming buckets of water. What a welcome sight. As soon as the door closed behind them, Sybella quickly disrobed and sank into the hot bath. She moaned aloud and did not care who heard her. The hot water felt so comforting against her skin. She swore she had only shut her eyes for a moment when there was another rap at the door.

"Sybella, 'tis Mary."

Sybella groaned but not because of the soothing water. "Come in."

Mary walked into Sybella's chamber and closed the door. She pulled out her skirts and sat on the edge of the bed, but not before she spotted the stained nightrail thrown carelessly on the floor.

"I see ye are still in one piece. Are ye all right?" asked Mary.

"I donna know. I did what ye said and barely moved to ease the pain. I think the counting helped as well. It wasnae as bad as I thought it would be. Howbeit ye didnae tell me there would be blood."

"Aye, well, I didnae want ye to worry. Some women bleed more than others. Ye will be sore for a few days, but it will nae be as painful the next time." Mary smoothed her tresses. "The men are packing our belongings. After we break our fast, we will take our leave." She smiled down at Sybella. "I will miss ye, and I wish ye naught but happiness with your new husband."

"I will miss ye as well, Mary." Sybella pulled herself to her feet and Mary handed her a drying cloth.

"Ye can always come to visit. And besides, Anabel would welcome the sight."

"She has grown so fast. I can only imagine the young lass she will become by the time I see her again."

As long as the Highland weather permitted, Sybella often found escape in the confines of the village. Ever since Anabel was a bairn, she had been taken with Sybella—well, who was she fooling? Sybella had been taken with Anabel. The little girl's temperament was irresistible. In some aspects they were similar, always wanting to be included, to belong.

Refusing to give in to her spell of listlessness, Sybella dressed quickly. Mary helped to pin up her tresses, and even though her cousin-by-marriage frequently pushed her to the edge of sanity, Sybella would truly miss her. After all, Mary was the only woman companion she had in her life.

They walked into the great hall and Sybella gazed upon the faces of her kin, a difficult task knowing in a few short hours the room would be filled with nothing but MacDonells. When a flicker of apprehension coursed through her, it was almost as if Colin sensed her discomfiture and was immediately by her side.

"How are ye, Ella? Are ye all right? If he harmed ye—"

Sybella spoke with as reasonable a voice as she could manage. "Colin, I am fine. Truly."

A look of relief passed over his features. "I am glad to hear it. As I told ye before, ye only need to call upon me and I will come to ye."

"I appreciate your concern, but I will be fine, Brother. Much to my surprise, Laird MacDonell has been naught but kind to me."

When Colin saw Alexander sitting at the table on the dais, his eyes narrowed. "And that better nae change."

Sybella tapped her brother playfully in the arm. "Nay matter what, ye will ne'er stop being the overprotective brother. The man is now my husband.

I donna think he would harm me." She lowered her voice. "And besides, the sooner he trusts me, the sooner I can start to search for the stone."

"Remember what I said and donna rush things. And ye know, Ella, I will always worry about ye. I am your brother."

After heartfelt good-byes, Sybella watched the last of her kin ride through the gates. She closed her eyes and squared her shoulders. Her courage and determination were like a rock inside her. When Alexander approached her, she vowed to show the man how unconcerned she was about her clan's departure.

"Are ye all right?" he asked solemnly.

While her husband's words about being truthful replayed in her mind, she contemplated whether or not to speak honestly. But that nagging feeling would not cease. How would she ever get the man to trust her if she didn't speak the truth on some occasions? Against her better judgment, she decided to share her feelings.

"I will be. I feel somewhat saddened to see my clan take their leave, but I am proud to be your wife." Her words seemed to please him because he gifted her with a bright smile.

"I am proud to have ye as my wife."

"What do we do now?" When he raised his brow, she realized the meaning of her words insinuated something which she was not yet ready to repeat. "I mean to say—"

"I know what ye meant. Do ye wish for a tour of my home or my lands?"

He didn't need to ask her twice. With the sun

shining in her face, Sybella's decision was already made. She was about to speak when Alexander chuckled in response.

"I see it in your eyes, lass. Let me secure our mounts."

She followed him into the barn. Massive wooden beams were overhead, and the smell of hay tickled her nose. Her husband certainly knew his horseflesh because gigantic steeds occupied every stall. As soon as she passed one mount with its pawing feet, the next one would follow suit. The horses playfully threw their heads and nodded in greeting. The animals seemed anxious to run free in the open air, a feeling she knew all too well.

Alexander poked his head around the corner. "Come here and see the mount I have chosen for ye."

She walked to the very last stall where a gentle mare several hands shorter than the rest stood very still. The chestnut horse was so immobile that Sybella had to look twice to make sure the beast was not dead. "I donna know what to say."

"She is a verra quiet horse. I think ye two will get along fine." He patted the even-tempered creature on the neck and then looked at Sybella for approval.

"Where is my own horse?" she asked, glancing around the stable. When Alexander raised his brow questioningly, she added, "The one I rode from Kintail."

"Your father's men gathered him this morn, lass."

"My father took my horse?" Her voice unintentionally went up a notch.

"Ye donna like this one?"

If she was to spend the rest of her days under a

MacDonell roof, she could not hold her tongue all of the time. And this happened to be one of them. "'Tisnae that I donna like her, but mayhap she would be more suited for someone like Aunt Iseabail. I know how to ride, Alexander. I donna need a quiet mount."

He closed the distance between them until his imposing frame stood before her. She cast her eyes downward as her husband brushed past her. "Then tell me, Lady MacDonell, which mount would ye choose?"

After inspecting each available mount in the stable, she pointed to the most muscular of the bunch. "This one."

"*That* one?" Alexander glanced sideways in surprise. "The captain of my guard has his brother, lass. Those two are indeed a handful. I donna think he is suited for ye. Nay, pick another."

Sybella laughed to cover her annoyance. "Ye asked me which horse I would choose, and I made my decision. I am nae some fragile flower. I have ridden with Colin many—"

He threw up his hands in the air. "*Fine*. If he tosses ye onto your arse, I will be the first to say I told ye so." Alexander opened the stall door and mumbled under his breath. "What did I get myself into?"

She folded her arms over her chest. "Ye do realize I can still hear ye."

Her husband peeked around the stall door. "My apologies. Would ye rather I speak when I look at ye? I would be happy to repeat—"

When she realized that he was only jesting, she rolled her eyes. "Just cease and saddle the mount."

He pulled the animal from the stall. Without giving

her a chance to protest, he hefted her onto the horse as if she weighed as little as a bairn. If her mount's prancing feet and agitated movements were any indication, the horse was indeed a high-spirited beast. She knew she only needed to give the animal a firm hand and let him know who was in charge, similar to her own husband—although, she couldn't imagine Alexander willingly accepting defeat.

He swung up effortlessly onto his mount and grabbed the reins. "Are ye sure ye want to do this?" When her eyes narrowed at his repeated question, he shrugged his shoulders. "Come. I will show ye the loch."

They rode along the dirt path, with Sybella following her husband. When visions of Alexander in her bed replayed in her mind, she quickly replaced the wicked thoughts with the memory of his kiss upon the parapet. Although she had acted like a wanton fool in broad daylight, the touch of his lips had been quite enjoyable. Was she supposed to feel this way? She was so confused. She knew she had to betray him, but yet she still managed to find pleasure in his touch. How could that be? What was wrong with her? She thought the man would be...different. He definitely stirred something within her that she didn't understand.

Alexander was so confident in every move he made. That's why she couldn't help herself when her eyes became focused on his broad back and strong shoulders. She tilted her head to one side, stealing a slanted look at his solid frame. Her husband was rather pleasing to the eye, even though he was a MacDonell.

Dipping his head slightly, he asked, "Do ye like what ye see?"

Her mouth dropped. "What?"

He swung his head around and looked at her. "The loch, Wife."

"Aye. 'Tis verra bonny—the loch."

When they reached a small clearing, Alexander helped her down from her horse and tethered their mounts to a branch.

"There is something I wish to show ye."

He grabbed her hand and led her into the trees. They continued to walk, the smell of the loch and foliage overwhelming her senses. When they reached the edge of the tree line, it was as if a curtain had been opened on a window before her—the thicket cleared and they were surrounded by water on three sides.

"This is magnificent," she stated simply.

Glengarry sat imposingly in the distance, and the water looked like a silken blanket draped across the land. She closed her eyes as the small waves lapped against the sandy shore.

"I thought ye would enjoy it. If we have much rain, it will flood this land."

"Thank ye for sharing this with me. Truly."

"'Tis my pleasure, lass. I want ye to feel comfortable here. This is now your home, too."

Alexander peered at her intently, and she made it a point to concentrate on everything but him. Every time his gaze met hers, her heart turned over in response. She decided not to make eye contact until she could figure out what caused this unnerving reaction. Well, that was what she told herself until he turned her to face him.

There was a tingling in the pit of her stomach.

Laird Alexander MacDonell was so disturbing to her in every way. She tried to steady the dizzying feeling within her, but her husband portrayed a vitality that definitely captured her.

He stepped closer and clasped her body tightly to his.

God help her. She had no desire to back out of his embrace. Her eyes fell to his lips, and the anticipation was almost unbearable. She tried to calm her racing heart. She couldn't afford to be distracted by romantic notions—or whatever this might be.

He gently brushed a kiss across her forehead, and then his lips slowly descended to meet hers. His mouth covered hers hungrily, his tongue sending shivers of desire through her.

As his mouth grazed her earlobe, she drew his face to hers in a renewed embrace, succumbing to the forceful domination of his lips. For one insane moment, Sybella actually wanted him to crush her mouth in a hard, bruising kiss.

He was so warm and so very tempting.

When long, tickling tendrils brushed against her cheek, she couldn't help herself. She wound her hand in Alexander's thick hair and pulled him closer. Her soft curves molded into his lean body.

He tugged at her dress, exposing a creamy breast. His lips touched her nipple with tantalizing possessiveness, and he fondled the other with his rough fingers. The rosy peaks grew to pebble hardness.

And then he stilled…

Thundering hooves approached from a distance. Alexander hastily adjusted her clothing and she smoothed her skirts. Branches cracked and snapped behind them as someone trudged through the brush. A man as imposing as her husband emerged into the small clearing.

"John." The captain of Alexander's guard.

Sweat beaded on the man's brow and his breathing was labored. "Pardon the intrusion, my laird. 'Tis Lady Iseabail."

Seven

"WHAT'S WRONG?" ALEX'S HEART SANK, AND A worried expression crossed his brow. "I told ye to have someone look after her." He grabbed Sybella's hand and pulled her along behind him, not waiting for John's response.

"Aye, I had *Ian* keeping an eye on her," said John, following his laird through the brush.

Alex smirked and spoke with sarcasm. "Aye, because he did so well when ye asked him to look after…" He was about to say the MacKenzie's son, but thought it best to keep that knowledge to himself lest he found himself thrown from his wife's bed within a day's time.

When they reached their mounts, Alex lifted Sybella onto her horse and then turned to John. "Where was Aunt Iseabail last?"

"Nay one has seen her since she broke her fast. Ian thought she was in her chamber. I have men searching the castle and a handful of them wandering the grounds."

Alex placed his hand on the flank of Sybella's

mount. "I will ride with ye back to the stable and then I must take my leave."

"Does she wander off by herself often?"

"More so than I would like." He started to walk away and spoke over his shoulder. "The last time she did this, I found her in the woods where my men hunt. She forgot why she had left home."

"Then we must find her. I will assist ye in searching the grounds."

Shaking his head in disagreement, Alex mounted his horse. "The last thing I need is to worry about ye. Ye have yet to know my lands and ye ride a mount that isnae easy to handle." He thought he heard his wife growl at him, but the lass was the least of his worries.

They galloped on the dirt trail beside the loch, and his eyes continued to search the surrounding area. As they reached the end of the path, he slowed his mount and Sybella darted around him. He called after her, but the daft woman only increased her speed. The lass fled up the hill past the clan burial markers and ran her horse full speed into the forest.

John and Alex merely stared, tongue-tied. Alex had to admit that he was momentarily speechless with surprise at seeing his bonny wife handle her mount with the same skill as a seasoned Highland warrior. But that was no excuse to rush blindly into the woods with complete and utter disregard for her own safety. He quickly recovered his wits and nodded to John.

The men thundered up the hill after Sybella and cautiously slowed their mounts when they reached the tree line. Once Alex caught his witless wife, he would need a tremendous amount of strength not to throttle her. God's teeth! The woman's carelessness was going to get her killed.

They separated and he could still see John a few yards away through the foliage, but neither of them spotted Sybella.

A branch snapped to the right and Alex's horse shied.

"*Thalla dhachaigh! Mach a seo!*" *Go home! Get out of here!* Sybella screamed through the trees.

Alex turned his mount toward the sound of her voice. And then his breath caught in his lungs.

Sharp, white fangs were bared and saliva dripped from the wolf's mouth. A cool sweat dripped down Sybella's back, but she didn't have time to think about that. The animal stood his ground firmly between her and Aunt Iseabail.

The color drained from Aunt Iseabail's face, and the poor woman's eyes widened with fear. She took a step to the right just as the wolf turned his head, taking another predatory step closer to her shaking frame.

"Stay right where ye are," ordered Sybella in a low voice. The thought of the beast rending Aunt Iseabail's soft flesh tore at Sybella's soul.

The gray hair of the wolf's coat stood on end, and the animal let out a low, throaty growl. Sybella tried to keep control as the beast crept slowly closer, getting ready to make his move. Since screaming did not scare it off, Sybella realized she needed to do something else, quickly. For some reason, the wolf seemed…off. It was unusually hostile for being alone in the daytime.

Sybella was frantically searching the ground for anything to use as a weapon when she spotted a rock within reach. She bent down carefully, reaching for the stone with the tips of her fingers. Her eyes never left the wolf.

The animal took one step closer to Aunt Iseabail.

Sybella brought back her arm, throwing the rock with all her might and hitting the wolf in the back of the thigh. The animal flinched, whirled around, and then headed straight for Sybella with wild green eyes and sharp fangs bared.

Her husband rushed through the trees on his mount. "*Coimhead!*" *Look out!*

"Alexander!" Sybella jumped to the side as he hefted his broadsword and his blade struck down the wolf. As soon as the animal fell to the ground, Sybella ran to Aunt Iseabail's side. "Are ye all right?"

The older woman placed her hand over her chest. "Praise the saints that wolf gave me but a fright. If it wasnae for ye, my dear, I donna know what would have happened. *Mòran taing.*" *Thank you very much.*

Sybella smiled with compassion. "Ye donna need to thank me. Your safety is all that matters. Are ye sure ye are unhurt?"

Alexander approached and a swift shadow of something Sybella could not identify crossed his face. "Are ye injured?"

"*An gaisgeach,*" said Sybella with a smile. *My hero.* "The wolf wasnae right. I am sorry ye had to kill him, but the animal was sick."

He nodded in response. "Aunt Iseabail," he said with renewed patience, "how do ye fare?"

"Thanks to ye and your lady wife, I am fine," she said with relief.

"Ye had us all worried. Why didnae ye tell someone when ye took your leave of the castle? Ye could have been killed. Ye are verra lucky my wife found ye when she did." He ran his large hand over her gray tresses, and Sybella couldn't help but smile when her husband's aunt pushed his hand away in response.

"'Tis unfortunate I came across the wolf, but the last time I looked, Alexander MacDonell, I donna need to ask your permission to take a walk," she chided him.

"Of course ye donna, but ye could have told someone where ye were going."

"I was looking for ye, Nephew."

"And I am here. What was so important that ye needed to seek me out, Aunt Iseabail?"

When she did not respond, Sybella spoke kindly. "'Tis all right, Aunt Iseabail. We were worried about ye, and ye are now safe. 'Tis all that matters." She turned to her husband and nodded. "Mayhap ye can carry your aunt to your mount." He raised his brow and Sybella discreetly gestured to Aunt Iseabail's bare feet.

His eyes darkened with emotion.

When Sybella spotted Aunt Iseabail from the path walking into the woods, she hadn't given her actions a second thought. She'd made a mad dash up the hill, refusing to lose sight of the poor woman. The last thing Alexander needed right now was to be worried sick over his missing aunt. Besides, Sybella found herself developing a certain fondness for Aunt Iseabail.

When Alexander bent to pick up Aunt Iseabail, she

squealed. "Nephew, I am perfectly capable of walking on my own accord. Put me down."

"Ye have nay voice in the matter. I will carry ye to my mount." He walked back and lifted Aunt Iseabail onto his horse. Once she was secure, he spun around to assist Sybella, but then his eyes widened. "I would have assisted ye as well."

Sybella sat upon her mount and spoke in a somewhat annoyed tone. "I donna need your assistance. See to your aunt."

Alexander swung up behind his aunt and gave a brief nod to John. "Make sure ye call off the men." He paused and then quickly added, "And have words with Ian."

"It will be more than words. I assure ye," said John dryly.

They rode back silently to the castle, and as soon as they entered the bailey, Sybella quickly dismounted. She grabbed the first person she saw and had him order a bath for Aunt Iseabail. When she turned, Alexander had lowered his aunt to her feet.

"Alexander," said Sybella, reaching out and touching her husband's back. He turned around and she gave him a gentle smile. "I ordered a bath for Aunt Iseabail, and I will take her to her chamber. Donna worry. I will see she is cared for."

Closing what was left of the small distance between them, he glared down at her. "And after ye are finished, we will have words."

When he switched all of that intensity to her, she became confused. Why would the man be cross with her? He should be thanking her.

Refusing to agonize over his sudden change in behavior, she stepped around her wall of a husband and draped her arm around Aunt Iseabail. "Come, Aunt Iseabail. I ordered a bath for ye, and we will get ye cleaned up."

"Thank ye, my dear. Ye are so kind."

As Sybella turned her head, the captain of Alexander's guard forcefully shoved a man into the stone wall of the bailey.

She presumed the man was Ian.

Aunt Iseabail opened the door to her chamber and Sybella followed her in. For a moment, Sybella felt a pang of guilt for having been in the woman's bedchamber with Colin. Only by chance had they managed to escape unscathed and undetected. She couldn't imagine trying to explain her way out of that one. Colin's curiosity could have raised much discord between the MacDonells and MacKenzies, had the two of them been discovered. And her search for the stone would've been over before it had even begun.

The men carried in the heavy tub and dumped in the buckets of steaming water. Once they had departed, Sybella helped Aunt Iseabail undress and get into the tub.

Sybella reached for a rag. "Are ye able to lift your foot?"

"I think so."

As Aunt Iseabail lifted her foot, Sybella wiped the muck that was stuck to the bottom like a second skin.

"What happened to my foot? There is so much dirt," the older woman asked.

Sybella paused and then rinsed the rag. "Ye didnae

have anything on your feet when ye walked in the woods."

"Why would I walk in the woods without my boots?"

"I donna know, Aunt Iseabail. Ye donna remember going for a walk?"

"Aye, I remember taking a walk, but how could I forget to don my boots?" The poor woman lifted her other foot and gasped. "What was I into?"

Sybella scrubbed Aunt Iseabail's foot, not thinking her question needed a reply. "There. Ye are clean. Ye are verra fortunate nae to have any cuts or scrapes." She grabbed under Aunt Iseabail's arm, helped the woman to her feet, and handed her a drying cloth.

"Ye are a kind woman…" Aunt Iseabail's eyes glazed over.

"Sybella."

"Of course, my dear. My nephew is so lucky to have ye as his new bride." She stepped out of the tub and Sybella handed her a shift.

"Would ye like me to have a tray brought up for ye, or do ye think ye will be all right to join us for the midday meal?"

The older woman's eyebrows shot up in surprise. "I am nae dead, Sybella. I will join ye for the noon meal."

A giggle almost escaped Sybella when the words left Aunt Iseabail's mouth. Sybella remembered her own mother scolding her for asking the same question not long ago. "That would be delightful. Alexander hasnae really had a chance to show me much of Glengarry. I hear the gardens are extraordinary. Mayhap ye could escort me after the meal. I would love to see them."

Aunt Iseabail donned her day dress and then placed her hand on Sybella's forearm. "Let us have a bite to eat and then we will take a walk in the garden. I'm verra proud of my flowers."

Sybella sat next to Alexander during the midday meal. Leaning toward him, she lowered her voice. "Aunt Iseabail is fine. There was nay need to call for the healer. I was thankful she had nay cuts or bruises, especially on her bare feet."

He nodded in response. "Thank ye for seeing to my aunt. I will need to make certain she doesnae wander too far from the castle again."

"*Dè nì thu?*" *What will you do?* When her husband raised his brow, she quickly lowered her gaze. She didn't mean to question his authority. The last she wanted to do was upset him further. "*Tha mi duilich.*" *I am sorry.*

"Nephew," said Aunt Iseabail, "after the meal, I will take your new wife for a walk in the garden. Ye cannae keep her all to yourself, ye know."

"I have nay intention of doing so," he said dryly.

Sybella started to take a drink from her tankard but hesitated briefly when she heard her husband speak softly to her.

"Lass, I called after ye, and I know ye heard me. Ye ignored my command and blindly rushed into the forest riding a mount that was unfamiliar to ye. Ye could have been killed." When she remained silent and lowered her eyes, he quickly added, "Praise the saints. Ye arenae going to shed tears, are ye?"

She stiffened as though he had struck her, and then she whipped her head around. "It would take more than ye, *Alexander MacDonell*, to make me cry," she responded sharply. "I spotted Aunt Iseabail from the path, and by the time I would have pointed her out to ye, she would have been out of sight. Ye do realize that the wolf would've attacked her. And I didnae blindly rush into the forest. I have been hunting with Colin since I was a wee bairn, and I am a *superior* rider." She tossed her hair over her shoulder. "I will nae offer ye apologies for seeing to the welfare of *your* aunt."

∾

Alex's wife perplexed him. To be honest, Sybella's behavior had rendered him speechless. Earlier in the stables, the lass had insisted she could handle her mount—and she did. In addition, she had not hesitated to rescue his missing aunt. His wife was quickly becoming a pleasant surprise.

When he had met the young lass at the waterfall so many years ago, she was headstrong, reckless. But he would be the first to admit that he liked his women with some spirit. And he had a feeling Lady Sybella MacDonell had plenty.

Holding up his hands in mock defense, he gave her his wooing smile. "I donna want to spar with ye. I only show concern for your safety. I am now your husband and ye are my responsibility."

She nodded briefly and took a drink from her tankard.

Neither one of them spoke for the remainder of the meal. He had an underlying feeling that he had made her angry, but he was only concerned for her welfare.

Now that he had actually seen the lass handle the horse, perhaps he could learn to trust her words—in time. Until then, she was under his care and his protection, even if he had to protect her from herself.

"Aunt Iseabail, I shall accompany ye and my wife to the gardens."

"That would be delightful, Nephew. I am sure your bonny new wife would love to have ye in attendance as well."

Sybella nodded politely, but a blind fool could have seen the truth in her eyes. "It would be wonderful to have ye accompany us, my laird," she said with false sincerity.

"Alex."

A flash of humor crossed her face and she raised her brow. "Donna push me."

"I wouldnae think of it."

Alex escorted the women to the gardens. He often found solace on the walls of the parapet but had not wandered aimlessly along the garden paths for quite a while. He knew Aunt Iseabail prided herself on working in the garden beds, and her efforts were obviously rewarded. Most of the flowers were in full bloom, with red, yellow, and purple petals painting the sides of the garden path.

A breeze wafted the scent of roses through the air, and Sybella brought her finger to her nose as if to stifle a sneeze.

"What do ye think?" he asked her.

"The garden is quite lovely."

Aunt Iseabail smiled. "I have always enjoyed it. The flowers on Dòmhnall's grave are from here. I remember when we were children and my brother used to trample my mother's garden with his swordplay." She shook her head. "As we grew older, I think Dòmhnall began to appreciate the beauty."

"The flowers for the celebration were verra bonny," said Sybella.

"Ye were fortunate most were in bloom. Ye will have to schedule carefully so that the petals are in bloom when your bairn is born."

When Sybella's mouth dropped, Alex could not stay the chuckle that escaped him. "Now ye know 'tis nearly impossible to schedule such an occasion, Aunt."

She cast a wicked smile. "That doesnae mean the two of ye cannae be trying in the meantime."

Sybella colored fiercely and he gestured to a bench. The two of them sat while Aunt Iseabail pulled weeds from the garden beds.

"She seems to be doing much better," said Sybella.

Alex hunched over, his arms resting on his thighs. "Her mind comes and then it takes its leave with little or nay warning. I think the celebration added excess worry, but now that we are wed, I hope she can rest." He sat up and gave her a warm smile. "I must thank ye again for seeing to her. She is my responsibility. I donna expect ye—"

"Donna be ridiculous. We are wed. Your burdens are nay longer your own. Aunt Iseabail is kin."

"I thank ye for your words, but I will nae have ye hurt. Ye faced the wolf alone. Had ye waited for me… Ye are also my kin, my *wife*, and I will nae have ye injured by being so reckless."

She closed her eyes. "Alexander, I told ye before

that Aunt Iseabail would've been injured or worse had
I waited for ye. And before ye judge me, I would ask
that ye give me a chance. Take me hunting and ye will
see. Your concern is misplaced." Remembering her
brother's words, she quickly added, "Ye need to learn
to trust me. As ye said, I am your wife."

He suppressed a sigh. "We shall see."

"'Tis all I ask."

"Since ye are now the lady of the castle, if anything
isnae to your liking, let me know. Please make any
changes that ye need. The household staff has been
instructed to heed your command."

Sybella nodded. "I cannae see myself making many
changes. Aunt Iseabail has done wonderfully."

"Nephew, could ye please come here and pull this
dastardly root?" asked Aunt Iseabail, her hands placed
on her hips.

"Pray excuse me." He rose from the bench and
approached his aunt. "And pray tell, where is this
dastardly root?"

She pointed to the menacing plant, and he bent
over and tugged at the stem. When he turned his
head toward Sybella, she hastily lowered her gaze.
He wasn't blind. He didn't miss his wife's obvious
examination and approval. For some reason, he was
pleased that she had softened somewhat toward him.

❧

Sybella promptly lowered her gaze. She wouldn't give
the rogue the satisfaction of knowing how much she
favored his appearance. There was a maddening hint
of arrogance about Laird Alexander MacDonell, and

once again she found herself drawn to him. She found it somewhat hard to believe that this man was from the same clan that her kin grew up despising. From what she had seen thus far, Alexander's family was nothing but kind. In fact, the heartfelt tenderness her husband showed toward his aunt warmed Sybella's heart. Perhaps this marriage would be easier than she had anticipated. But that would make her true purpose much harder to carry out.

"Be warned. When Aunt Iseabail asks ye to take a walk in the garden, her purpose is to make ye pull weeds," said Alexander in a jesting tone. He sat back down on the bench and they shared a smile.

"'Tis perfectly fine with me. I would rather have my hands in the dirt than sit idle."

"And yet, that doesnae surprise me."

He patted her leg and her skin tingled when he touched her. She cleared her throat in a nervous gesture, and almost as if her husband knew how he affected her, he fingered a loose tendril of hair on her cheek. She was by no means blind to his attraction, and his nearness made her senses spin. It was far too easy to get caught up in the way he looked at her.

As Sybella moistened her dry lips, he quirked his eyebrow questioningly. He reached out and caught her hand in his. It was an odd sensation, but once her fingers touched the warmth of his hand, she felt…safe.

A devilish look came into his eyes and he slowly lowered his head to kiss her.

"God's teeth, Alexander! Are ye two just going to sit there all day, or are ye going to help me pull these overgrown weeds?"

Sybella brought up her hand to stifle her giggles, and Alexander managed a choking laugh.

"Your timing is impeccable, Aunt."

Eight

THE DAY HAD NOT TURNED OUT THE WAY ALEX HAD planned. He'd wanted to gently woo his wife and slowly stir her passion. He had not expected to be disrupted in the middle of a tryst with his wife to hunt for Aunt Iseabail and strike down a wolf with his broadsword. This eve, he was determined not to be interrupted again and held from his purpose.

Before long, Sybella would be with child and he would have fulfilled his duty to the MacDonell clan. Of course, that was if he could undo the damage of Mary's outlandish words to Sybella. Nothing killed his ardor more than having a woman with clenched eyes beneath him counting sheep.

This eve, he had given the lass more than enough time to prepare for him to come to her. Alex opened the adjoining door to Sybella's bedchamber and gently closed it behind him. One bedside candle remained lit and he almost cursed the darkness. Selfish as it might be, he wanted to see all that the lass had to offer.

As he approached the bed, he could see his wife's golden locks tumbled carelessly over her shoulders.

Her full, rosy lips were parted in gentle, rhythmic breathing. He brushed his fingers through her hair and softly caressed her cheek. When she let out a little snort and then rolled over onto her side, he could barely contain the chuckle that escaped him.

A perfect ending to a less than perfect day.

Not having the heart to wake the sleeping beauty, Alex sought his own bed and tried unsuccessfully to stay the memory of his wife's luscious flesh. How could he forget the rosy peaks of her breasts as they grew to pebble hardness? He had given every part of her body the attention it deserved—from her taut stomach to her creamy thighs to every fold in between.

When he realized his body's normal reaction to his impure thoughts, Alex took his hand to himself, taking care of his own desires lest the lass bolt like a scared rabbit the next time from all of his pent-up frustration. The last thing Alex wanted to do was frighten Sybella from his bed. For now, he would sate his own needs; tomorrow was another day.

Alex awoke in the morning to blankets that were knotted and pillows that were thrown from the bed. He sat on the edge of the bed and shook his head, realizing that at times like these, he usually would seek out the skillful Doireann. His leman's expert touch had cured his urges and satisfied all of his desires. Granted, this was the same lass who had tried to shackle him into marriage, but there had never been any expectations between them. He could merely take his leave from Doireann's bed—or from his study wall or the stables—and not think twice. Now that he had a wife, it was a little more complicated.

Out of respect for Sybella, Alex would stay true to his vows. But he knew he was going to have to do a lot more wooing to have his wife trust him enough to willingly let him share her bed. Granted, he could simply wake her up and demand his marital rights, but he was not that kind of man. In any event, this was definitely a first. He'd never had to woo Doireann; she'd freely shared her favors with him—among others. In truth, he wasn't sure how to woo his new wife, but he had an idea about how to start.

Alex rose from the bed and rubbed his hand through his hair. He donned his kilt, threw on his tunic and boots, and went to the garden.

❧

Sybella sat up and stretched her arms. For the first time since she could remember, she felt rested. She threw the covers from the bed and momentarily paused.

Alexander had not come for her.

She briefly wondered why her husband had not sought her bed the night before. She wasn't exactly sure how such things worked, but perhaps it was too soon after their initial encounter. When another disturbing idea popped into her mind, she wasn't sure how she felt.

What if Alexander had a leman?

Not that she was by any means an expert on the subject, but she knew from her own clan that some married men kept a harlot on the side. She was fairly sure Angus didn't have one. Sybella would have to be a fool not to notice how much the man worshipped Mary. If Alexander had one of these women, Sybella prayed that he would have enough sense to keep his leman hidden from sight. Something within Sybella stirred at the thought of sharing him with another woman. She couldn't help but ponder whether or not Alexander touched his leman as he touched her.

"Sybella, cease your thoughts. Ye are being ridiculous," she said aloud to herself. She approached the stand and splashed cool water on her face. When the morning haze cleared, she donned her day dress and slippers. She swung open the door to find her husband standing against the wall.

"Good morn." He pulled his arm from behind his back and handed her a bunch of roses tied together with a ribbon.

Sybella stood momentarily frozen. When she reached out to take the flowers, a prickly thorn pierced her skin. She brought her finger to her lips.

"Be careful. The roses have thorns on the stems," he said, pointing to the jagged edges.

She wasn't about to tell the man that the thorns were to be removed. And she sure as hell wasn't going to tell him that the flowers were to be cut, not pulled out by the roots. Sybella carefully held the thorny roses out in front of her as clumps of dirt hung from the bottom of the roots. She could barely stay the giggle that wanted to escape her, and she tried desperately not to laugh. After all, Alexander had tried to make her feel special, and the flowers were a thoughtful gesture.

"The roses are verra bonny. I truly thank ye. Give me but a moment and I will place them in some water."

He waited for her outside the door. "Are ye ready to break your fast?"

"Aye." Sybella walked out of her bedchamber and closed the door.

"Did ye sleep well?"

She nodded. "I actually did." She was hesitant to ask, but it was only polite. "And ye?"

"As well as could be expected."

They walked to the great hall and took their seats upon the dais. Sybella had just reached to take a bite of oatmeal when Aunt Iseabail stormed into the hall. With reddened cheeks and a fiery look in her eyes, the woman cursed the entire way to her seat. Whipping out a chair, Aunt Iseabail sat down and clenched her teeth.

Sybella reached out and touched the woman's arm. "Is everything all right?"

"Nay, 'tisnae all right."

"Tell me what is amiss and mayhap I can assist ye," Sybella said in a compassionate tone.

"Nae unless ye can repair the damage to my flowers," Aunt Iseabail replied with a snappish tone.

"Pardon?"

Aunt Iseabail clutched her tankard until her knuckles turned white. "Some daft fool pulled out a large portion of my new roses. They were just starting to bloom, and instead of cutting them, the idiot pulled out all of the roots. I am afraid they are destroyed."

Sybella bit her bottom lip and turned her head slightly toward her husband. Alexander sat as still as a stone statue, keeping his eyes on his trencher.

"How do ye know it wasnae a deer or a rabbit?" asked Alexander.

"Nephew, I am nae daft. The animals chomp at them. They donna pull them out clean by the roots."

He nodded. "Rest assured, Aunt Iseabail, if I find the miscreant, he shall be punished."

"I should hope so, Alexander. Ye know how much I favor the garden."

Sybella looked at her husband and his eyes widened. "Nae a word," he said under his breath.

Sybella managed a reply through stiff lips. "I value my life."

He chuckled in response.

 ✌

Alex didn't try to speak with Sybella until he was sure he was clear of Aunt Iseabail's ire.

"Ye said ye like to hunt."

She nodded and swallowed what was left of her oatmeal. "Aye, verra much. If ye havenae figured it out yet, my laird, I love to be out in the fresh air."

"'Tisnae that difficult to discern. After the meal we will test your skill with a bow."

She lifted her brow and gave him a mischievous grin. "Why, Alexander? Ye donna trust me to hunt beside ye?"

"Before I give ye a bow and a verra sharp arrow, I want to be sure ye know how to use them. I am nae willing to take a chance alone with ye in the woods lest ye hit something of most importance." He glanced down at his manhood and then gave her a wry grin. For some reason, he enjoyed jesting with her.

Sybella paused, clearly weighing her response. "Donna worry, my laird. 'Tisnae that big of a target."

Alex choked on his wine, and his wife abruptly changed the subject to the matter at hand. "There is nay need to give me a bow. I brought my own."

"Of course ye did. I wouldnae want to give ye one which wasnae familiar to ye. That would be a complete disadvantage. Why donna ye fetch your bow and I will meet ye behind the stables?"

"Verra well."

He watched Sybella's hips sway as she walked out of the great hall, thinking that her frequent displays of insolence made him smile.

Alex made his way to the stable. He took a couple of bales of hay from the loft and set up a mock target in the back. After setting the last bundle in place, he had just brushed his hands when a voice spoke from behind him.

"Ye cannae be serious."

He whipped his head around and lifted his brow. Sybella wore the same gown as in the morn, with her bow thrown casually over her shoulder. Her mouth was set in annoyance, and her eyes narrowed in disapproval.

"What is the matter now?" he asked.

She lifted her palm, gesturing at the target. "Ye truly want to test my skill with a bale of hay. Is that how ye train all of the wee lads, then?"

Without giving him a chance to respond, she reached for an arrow, raised her bow, and barely took time to aim. The arrow whizzed low behind Alex's backside and landed in the hay. He scarcely moved his arse in time. He turned his head and studied the placement of the arrow, dead center. Shaking his head, he turned to his wife, and personal triumph flooded through her.

She tossed her blond locks over her shoulder. "I see

I have rendered ye speechless, my laird. They say there is a first time for everything."

Alex winked when he caught her eye. "Verra well done...for a lass." He paused long enough on the last word to intentionally irritate his wife.

Sybella was opening her mouth to protest when he quickly closed the distance between them. Wrapping his hand around her back, he pulled her close. He continued to plant kisses on her lips between each of her scolding words until she stood mute. Only when she finally succumbed to the forceful domination of his lips and he felt her soften and return his kiss did he gently pull away.

His eyes caught and held hers.

❧

The look on Alexander's face mingled eagerness and tenderness. Sybella wasn't sure which dominated. She was without words as he lightly brushed his thumb over her jaw and they shared a smile.

"I told ye I was good." When his eyes rounded, she quickly added, "A good shot."

He bobbed his head in agreement and then backed away from her. "Come, Wife. I have something to show ye."

"Nae now, Alexander. I have already seen it," she said dryly.

He lifted his brow and Sybella followed him into the stables. He searched the stalls and stopped when he found what he was looking for. The magnificent creature stood tall, pawing at the ground. And the animal was exactly as she remembered from last eve.

"*Dè do bheachd air?*" *What do you think of him?*

Sybella reached out and patted the horse's muscular neck. "I told ye before. He is a verra fine beast."

"And he is yours."

She stared wordlessly, her heart pounding. "Truly? I donna know what to say."

"Since ye have nay suitable mount, I wanted to give ye one which I know ye can handle. Ye proved that more than enough last eve with Aunt Iseabail, lass. I only ask that ye have an escort when ye ride. Do we have an understanding?"

Between the roses this morn and now the shock of his generous gift, words wedged in Sybella's throat. The MacDonell was actually a thoughtful and caring man. But she wished he'd stop doing things like this. Her feelings were becoming confused.

Sybella walked toward him and smiled. "Aye, of course." Standing on the tips of her toes, she brushed a soft kiss on his cheek. "He is a magnificent horse. I truly thank ye for your kindness, Alexander."

"Then grant me a boon."

She froze. That's what had gotten her into trouble with him in the first place. Why deals were never made in her favor was beyond her comprehension. She did not like this, but against her better judgment, she nodded in agreement.

"Please call me 'Husband' or 'Alex.' Surely 'tisnae that difficult for ye."

Breathing a sigh of relief, Sybella smiled. "I suppose I could call ye that."

"And I will call ye Ella."

She didn't know what to say. Colin was the only

person who called her Ella. He'd been calling her that since she was a wee bairn. It was his own special name for her, and to be truthful, she wasn't sure she wanted to share something so personal with the man she was destined to betray. She was perfectly aware that the closer she allowed herself to get to him, the more difficult her task would be. Agreeing to search for the stone had been a lot easier when she believed Alexander was nothing more than a cur. Then again, she still barely knew him. Their only history consisted of the waterfall and their wedding.

As Alex sensed her hesitation, the corner of his mouth curved in exasperation. "Do ye nae permit me to call ye Ella?"

Her voice wavered. "'Tisnae that…I just…Why do ye wish to call me Ella?"

His face lit up with surprise. "Why? I heard your brother say as much to ye. I want ye to feel at home here, Sybella. Glengarry is now your home. I thought to call ye something by which ye are accustomed in order to make ye feel more comfortable here…with me."

Sybella briefly closed her eyes, feeling like a complete dolt. The man was clearly trying to welcome her and surprising her at every turn. And here she was, acting like an arse. She quickly chastised herself, although she was generally resentful of the entire situation.

"Please accept my apologies. I meant nay disrespect. Ye only caught me unaware since my brother is the only man who calls me Ella. It would please me greatly if ye would call me the same." She gave Alex a polite smile and his expression lightened.

"How about we saddle our mounts and take our leave for a wee hunt?"

"That would be delightful. I would wish to change first." As she turned on her heel, her husband spoke.

"Ella."

She turned around and raised her brow.

"The name suits ye."

Smiling at Alexander's compliment, Sybella sought her chamber and changed her gown. Her father would be proud. In a matter of days, she was able to see a subtle difference in her husband's behavior toward her.

He was starting to trust her.

When she returned to the stables, the horses were already saddled. The animals whipped the reins with their muscular heads and pawed at the ground. Sybella approached the new gift her husband had bestowed upon her and shook her finger at the prize horseflesh.

"I am only going to say this once. We can do this the hard way or the easy way. Ye obey me and we will get along fine. If ye donna, trouble will find ye and there will be nay special treats."

A warm voice came up behind her. "Do ye think that really works?" asked Alexander, his mouth twitching with amusement.

She shrugged. "It doesnae matter. It makes me feel better."

"Are ye ready?"

She raised her brow. "Are ye?"

"Are ye going to spar with me if I offer to assist ye onto your mount?" he asked.

"If it makes ye feel better, I will let ye assist me."

Alexander paused and then lifted her onto her horse. "Thank ye...Alex."

His smile was boyishly affectionate and he patted her thigh. He turned and mounted his horse, giving her a brief nod when he was ready. They left the bailey and followed the same path she had traveled on her way to Glengarry.

Sybella turned in the saddle and looked over her shoulder. "The first time I saw your home, I thought the view was quite impressive."

"I am pleased Glengarry suits ye, lass. Ye can be comforted that 'tis now your home as well." His smile broadened in approval.

Alex turned his mount from the main path and entered the woods. The rays of the sun were immediately blocked by the tall pines and foliage. Sybella loved the smell of fresh pine. Unfortunately, her nose did not.

When she let out a loud sneeze, her mount took off in a startled rush through the forest. The frightened beast scraped her leg on a tree trunk as she pulled back on the reins and spoke in soothing tones, trying to calm her skittish horse.

Her husband rode up beside her. "Are ye all right?"

Refusing to rub her bruised leg, she forced her head high. "I am fine. I see the look in your eyes. It was only a sneeze. I can control him."

He guided his mount back onto the trail. "I didnae say anything."

"Ye didnae have to," she said under her breath.

They traveled deeper into the wooded land and Alex stopped his mount. "We will try to hunt here. I have had much luck in the past." He dismounted and raised a brow when he turned around to assist her.

Sybella's feet were already planted on the ground. "We are away from prying eyes, my laird. There is nay need for such propriety."

He shook his head and tethered their mounts to a tree. They grabbed their bows from the side of the saddles and walked a few yards into the forest. Careful not to disturb the area, they continued stealthily into the brush.

Nothing moved.

Alex gestured with his bow that he would widen the distance they hunted and moved quietly to Sybella's far right. As she had practiced so many times with Colin, the hope was that he would encircle any small animals and flush them out toward her. She waited patiently for something to cross her path. To be truthful, she wanted to prove to her husband that she could hunt as well as any man.

Sybella glanced around and could no longer see Alex through the trees. Taking advantage of a moment to herself, she bent down and partially lifted her day dress. She spotted a trace of blood from the scrape on her leg. Damn. Leaning her bow against a tree, she licked her thumb and was bending down to wipe the blood when something whizzed over her head.

She bolted upright and came face to face with an arrow that penetrated the tree. Praise the saints. Her husband's jesting was completely out of control. It was one thing to pretend to take aim at the man's arse but entirely another to take aim at her head. If the arrow had struck her, she would've been seriously injured or…dead.

Pulling out the arrow with a purpose, Sybella went in search of her husband. "Alex! *Alexander!*" she bellowed. Fury almost choked her, and curses fell from her mouth.

As her husband approached her, she threw words at him like stones. He stared at her, puzzled, while she continued her rant.

She slapped the arrow into his chest. "How dare ye! Nay matter how skilled I am, I would *ne'er* take aim at someone else's head. What the hell is wrong with ye?"

The man simply stood there, blinking with confusion. "Ella, what are ye talking about?"

Sybella pointed to the arrow he held in his hands. "I donna appreciate ye taking aim at my head nay matter how amusing ye think 'tis. If I would have moved, ye could have killed me."

Alex stood to his full height and his eyes narrowed. He turned his head slowly from side to side and then lowered his voice. "Ella, 'tisnae my arrow."

Nine

SYBELLA'S EYES WIDENED. "WHAT DO YE MEAN, 'tisnae your arrow?"

A chill ran up Alex's spine as he turned and escorted Sybella firmly by the elbow. "The hunt is over. Walk quickly back to your mount. Now." With senses heightened, his eyes darted around the trees, brush, anything that held even the slightest of movements.

"Ye are making me nervous. If that isnae your arrow, do ye think someone deliberately took aim for my head?"

He increased his gait. "I donna know and I will see ye safe before I find out."

The lass almost had to run to keep up with him. "Why would someone want to…I know your clan wasnae exactly thrilled to have me as your wife, but I thought my dowry would more than make up for their uncertainties."

The woman needed to learn when to keep her opinions to herself. How typical of a MacKenzie to blame a MacDonell. And who said the arrow was shot by one of his kin? When he did not respond, Sybella's face clouded with uneasiness.

"I didnae mean to accuse your—"

"Then donna," Alex simply stated.

When they reached their mounts, he lifted Sybella onto her horse and handed her the reins. "I think the man is nay longer here, but I cannae be certain. Ye ride behind me, close, and as fast as ye can. I will nae chance another shot. Do ye understand?"

She nodded wordlessly and he left her no room for debate.

They rode through the forest cautiously, and when they reached the main path, Alex gave his mount his head. They traveled hard and fast on the trail back to Glengarry, with Alex looking back several times to make certain his wife was safe. Not much surprised him about her. The lass had managed to hold her seat throughout their hastened journey home. And she followed his commands like a seasoned warrior, without question.

As they thundered into the bailey, Alex called to John, who stood upon the parapet. Alex quickly dismounted and walked over to Sybella. He lowered her to the ground and then gestured to one of his guards.

"Escort my wife to her chamber." He turned and placed his hands on Sybella's shoulders. "Go to your chamber and donna come out until I come for you. *Feumaidh mi falbh*," he said sternly. *I must go.*

"*Glè mhath*," she said, eyeing him with concern. *Very well.* "Be safe, my laird."

Alex watched the lass take her leave and then he whirled on John. "Someone took a shot at my wife."

"What?"

Alex walked over to his mount and pulled the arrow out of his bag. Handing the arrow to John, he said, "Luckily, the lass had bent over, but it barely missed her head."

John took the arrow and studied the feathers. "I donna recognize it."

"Before the trail becomes cold, seek our best tracker and I will take ye to where we hunted."

John's eyes widened in surprise. "Ye took your new wife *hunting*? That was your brilliant idea to woo her?"

Alex shrugged. "The lass seemed to enjoy it before someone took aim at her head."

As if Alex's words brought John back to purpose, the captain of the guard took his leave. Alex mounted his horse and impatiently waited for his men to return, his mind racing.

Who the hell would want to take a shot at his wife? Granted, she was a MacKenzie, but she was merely a lass. The whole circumstance did not make sense. If his clan had wanted to do harm, they would've attempted something while the MacKenzie was underfoot. He shook off the idea. It was not his clan. The MacDonell men were loyal to a fault.

When John returned with Ian, Alex exchanged a carefully guarded look with John. Although Alex was reluctant to admit it, Ian was their best tracker. However, Alex could not ignore how careless the man had been with his duties of late. Between not keeping a watchful eye on the MacKenzie's son and letting an aging woman slip through his grasp, Ian was currently not held in a favorable light. This was the man's last chance at redemption.

The men mounted their horses, clomping hoofbeats storming through the gate. Alex led John and Ian to the same area where he and Sybella had tethered their mounts. The men dismounted and Alex nodded over his shoulder.

"We only walked but a few yards into the trees."

John and Ian followed him into the brush, and then Ian stopped. "Did ye walk away from Lady MacDonell here and walk that way?" asked Ian, pointing to Alex's right.

"Aye, that is my trail and the lass walked this way," said Alex, gesturing to the left.

Ian continued to survey the path along which Sybella had walked. "Lady MacDonell stopped here." He searched the small area and rubbed his fingers over the bark of the tree, discovering where Sybella had pulled the arrow out. "From the placement of the arrow, the shot was taken from over there. In order to nae compromise the signs, it would be best if ye remained here, my laird. I will encircle this section and try to pick up on the man's trail."

Alex nodded and watched Ian study the ground for clues to guide them.

"Who do ye think would want to take a shot at your new wife's head?" asked John, leaning his sword against the tree.

"I donna know. Our known enemy is the MacKenzie, but God's teeth, I wed the man's daughter. If it was the MacKenzie, surely the daft fool would take aim for my head and nae that of his own daughter. I donna like it."

"Alex, I donna know what ye are thinking, but our clan would ne'er plot something against a lass—even if she was a MacKenzie."

Alex ran his hand through his hair. "And I know as much. That is what troubles me. If nae the MacKenzies or the MacDonells, then who?"

"My laird," said Ian, returning with a disgusted look upon his face. "There is nay trail."

Alex raised his brow in surprise. "What do ye mean?"

"There are nay signs of another man."

⁓

Sybella sat confined in her bedchamber for hours. She paced, sat, slept, and paced some more. How much longer would she be made to suffer? She couldn't for the life of her discern who would intentionally try to injure her—or worse. Granted, she wasn't sure of the number of enemies her father had managed to gather over the years, but it couldn't be that many. A sudden thought popped into her mind and she stilled.

Praise the saints.

She was under the roof of her father's enemy. Could a MacDonell have enough hatred for her that he would want to kill her? That made no sense. Alex's clan had already benefited from her dowry. Her death would serve no purpose—unless, of course, her husband found her out and wanted her removed as his wife, permanently. Sybella heard herself swallow.

What was she going to do? She was trapped here. She closed her eyes and silently prayed that Colin would hear her thoughts. Perhaps even come for her. She couldn't imagine sleeping another night in this bed. She'd have to sleep with one eye open.

When there was a knock at her door, she stiffened.

"Ella, 'tis me," said Alex.

Sybella slowly opened the door and let him in. He had a strange look on his face that she couldn't quite figure out. If he'd discovered her purpose, he did not say. When she closed the door, he turned and hesitated. In her nervousness, she blurted out the first words that came to mind.

"What did ye find out?"

He ran his hand through his hair. "Naught."

"What do ye mean?"

"I donna understand it. Ian is my best tracker. He found my trail when I broke off from ye, and he found your trail where ye stopped by the tree, but there is nay evidence of another man. It was as if he wasnae there."

She folded her arms over her chest. "I didnae shoot the arrow at myself, Alex."

He reached out to touch her, and she gently pulled away from him. "I am nae saying ye did. I am saying there are nay signs of another. Do ye know of anyone who would want to see ye harmed, lass?"

"Besides ye?" Sybella couldn't help herself. The words were out of her mouth before she had a chance to stay them.

Alex's eyes narrowed. "*Me?*"

"If ye donna want me as your wife, I—"

He quickly closed the distance between them, and her last words were smothered by his lips. He forced her mouth open with his trusting tongue, and she succumbed to the domination of her husband's kiss. Blood pounded in her brain, leapt from her heart, and made her knees tremble. If not for his hands supporting her, she would have fallen.

The caress of his lips on her mouth set her aflame. He was so warm. Hot. She couldn't miss the musky smell of him as he pressed her closer.

She tried to deny the pulsing knot that had formed in her stomach and her wildly beating heart, which was the only sound audible.

His shoulders heaved as he breathed, and his closeness was so male, so bracing. Her mind told her to resist, but her body refused to listen.

He swept her, weightless, into his arms and carried her silently to the bed. Her head fit perfectly in the hollow between his shoulder and neck.

He eased her down onto the bed and reclaimed her lips, pressing himself on top of her. She was made to endure the cruel ravishment of his mouth. His kiss became punishing, as if he scolded her for the words she had attempted to speak.

When he pulled back, Sybella tried to swallow the lump that lingered in her throat. His eyes searched her face, reaching into her thoughts.

"I would ne'er cause ye harm, Sybella." He brushed back the hair from her face. "I am proud to have ye as my wife."

Before she could respond, Alex reclaimed her mouth with savage intensity. She'd never dreamt that she could crave one man's touch with so much eagerness. The wicked sensations left her burning with fire. For someone who had wanted to kill her, he certainly went out of his way to give her pleasure.

He pulled down her dress over her shoulders. She could barely sustain the gasp that escaped her as his thumb began stroking small circles over the sensitive tip of her breast. She closed her eyes, allowing the pleasure to crash down upon her. If she was going to die, praise the saints, this was the way she wanted to meet her maker—in the arms of her enemy.

His lips trailed a path down her neck, and her body turned to liquid fire, heavy warmth pooling between her legs.

"Ye are so beautiful." Alex's voice was tight with strain.

When his hand slid under the edge of her skirts, Sybella's breath caught as his fingers trailed their way up along her thigh, then higher still.

She froze and could no longer return her husband's kiss. She couldn't think about anything other than his hand and where it was going to touch her.

"'Tis all right, Ella," he whispered against her ear.

Nothing could have prepared her for the sweet rapture of his finger brushing against her tingling flesh. Over and over, he swept against her. She knew she should be shocked. This had to be a sin to feel so wonderful.

"God, ye are so wet for me."

She writhed in sweet agony. Instinctively, she lifted her hips against his hand, wanting more. As if he sensed her impending need, he finally slid his finger inside her. God's teeth! What was happening to her?

Her breathing was coming hard and fast, and she squeezed her thighs against her husband's hand.

"Alexander..."

"Just come for me, sweet Ella."

"Alex..."

She tensed as the force of her release hit her and Alex

continued to rub her most sensitive spot. Her body ached for his touch. She could no longer control the outcry of delight as she shattered into a million pieces.

She called out his name again and he let out a guttural moan. He hastily released his kilt and moved his hard body atop hers as she caressed the length of his back. His lips brushed her nipples, and when he suckled her breast, she thought she'd died in bittersweet rapture.

Sybella snuggled against him as their legs intertwined. Sweat beaded upon his brow. Everything was so hot. So wet. And with one quick thrust, they were as one.

He slowly moved inside her and she waited for the pain to come. To her surprise, a spurt of hungry desire spiraled through her instead. She could feel the heat of his body course down the entire length of hers.

His hardness caused her whole being to flood with passion, and she was again roused to the peak of desire. She'd never dreamt she could feel so warm and secure in her husband's embrace.

"I beg ye nae to count sheep," he said through gritted teeth.

She spoke in between breaths. "I have nay intention…of counting…sheep."

As if he sensed the awakened response within her, he moved faster and she completely surrendered to his masterful seduction. She wanted to yield to the burning sweetness that seemed captive within her.

Passion rose within her like the hottest of fires, clouding her brain. They both came together, exploding in a downpour of fiery sensations.

And she gasped in sweet agony—again.

As Alex lay next to Sybella, both of them spent, he briefly contemplated at what point he had lost all self-control. When Ian had assured him there was no trail, many thoughts had raced through Alex's mind. Frankly, bedding his wife was not one of them.

The lass had stood defensively before him, blatantly accusing him of wanting to harm her. She had made him angry, and Alex wanted to do nothing more than teach her a lesson. He had meant every word when he spoke his marriage vows, so he was bound by duty to protect her. How could the daft female think he would deliberately cause her harm? For the first time, he had wanted to be with her—and not because it was his duty. Whether he wanted to admit it or not, he was starting to care for her, and he hoped his actions showed her that.

Sybella nestled her bottom against his groin, and he wrapped his arm around her waist. "Are ye all right?" he asked softly.

"I donna know. Mayhap ye should pinch me to make certain I am nae dead."

He chuckled in response.

She turned over, facing him. Lifting her hand, she brushed the hair from his cheek. "Ye told me before that ye want honesty between us." Sybella looked him directly in the eye and paused. "Did ye really want me as your wife?"

Praise the saints. The question was like a double-edged sword. No matter what he answered, he was doomed to suffer a most unpleasant fate. Granted, he was the one who had lectured the lass and demanded she spoke the truth. And he couldn't very well expect her to speak openly with him if he didn't follow his own advice.

Damn. Damn. Damn.

Alex swallowed his pride and shifted his manhood away from her. "Nay. Howbeit it was naught against ye, lass. I didnae want to settle myself with any wife." He silently reflected a moment. "After my father's passing, Aunt Iseabail made me realize I needed to continue the MacDonell line. In order to accomplish that, I needed a wife. Your father offered your hand and I think the fates stepped in. MacKenzie or nae, ye are my wife, Ella. I am glad 'tis ye."

For a moment, he sensed an odd twinge of disappointment and then she quickly masked her expression. "I donna know of anyone who would want to cause me harm. Ian didnae find anything?"

"He found the tree where the arrow struck, but there were nay signs of anyone besides the two of us. I donna know of any man who can cover his tracks without leaving a trace of something. It troubles me. Ye are well protected within the walls of Glengarry, lass. There is nay sense worrying upon it. And if ye take your leave from the castle, ye will have an escort."

Sybella sighed. "Aye, but I donna like the idea of the stone walls closing in on me like a prisoner, trapped within my own home."

"Until we find who is responsible for—"

"Taking aim at my head?"

"Cease your worried thoughts. 'Tis my responsibility to see ye safe. I will protect ye, Ella, and ye have naught to worry upon."

There was a knock at the door.

"Aye?"

"My laird, there is a messenger at the gates."

"I will be there in a moment," said Alex.

He rose from the bed. As he grabbed his kilt from the floor, Sybella stood and straightened her dress. Her bonny locks were tousled and she looked...enchanting. They looked at each other and smiled in earnest.

Alex placed his hand on her shoulder in a possessive gesture. "I hope this time was much more pleasant for ye."

Sybella flushed miserably. "It wasnae...unpleasant."

He lifted her chin with his finger and his eyes narrowed. "It will only get better." When she licked her lips, he gave her a kiss she would surely remember. "Ye donna have to stay within the walls, but donna leave the gates."

As he walked toward the door, she called after him. "Alex, thank ye." She wrung her hands. "I truly didnae think ye would want to kill me. At least, I hoped ye didnae."

"Ella, we have only been wed a few days. Give me time." A smile played on his lips and he closed the door behind him.

He walked into the bailey and approached the messenger.

"My laird, a message from Laird Ciaran MacGregor of Glenorchy," the man said, holding out the missive.

Alex read the penned note and smiled. Aunt Iseabail would be pleased. Dismissing the messenger, Alex tapped the letter in his hand and went in search of his aunt. The last place he looked should've been the first.

As he approached the garden, the sight before him was most definitely not what he had expected to see.

He stopped and watched his lady wife, who was down on all fours. She dug around the bottom of a bush and then rose to her feet, pulling at the dense branches. When the bush didn't budge, Sybella squatted low to the ground and her legs encircled the unruly shrub. She tugged several additional times, and on the last attempt, she let out a loud moan and fell flat on her arse with the bush splayed in her lap.

Alex couldn't control the rumble of laughter that escaped him. "I am betting the bush won," he said as he approached her. He reached out and lifted the shrub, which had her pinned to the ground. He tossed the unruly plant to the side and then extended his hand to pull her up.

Of course when the lass fell to the ground, he couldn't help but come to her rescue. Her tresses were tousled, and she had a smudge of dirt on her nose, cheeks, and forehead. About the only spots not covered in soil were her rosy lips. When her hazel eyes stared back at him, his heart hammered in his ears. He could've just stood there watching her—that was until Aunt Iseabail spotted him.

"Alexander, come and look what happened to my roses." Aunt Iseabail pointed to the empty spot in the garden.

He carefully guarded his expression as he studied the dirt. "I am sure ye will find something else to plant there, Aunt."

"I suppose, but I cannae believe my roses were destroyed by an idiot."

A giggle escaped his wife, and she promptly turned her head away from him when he gazed in her direction. He needed to change the subject, fast.

"A messenger arrived from Glenorchy."

Aunt Iseabail's eyes lit up in surprise. "Glenorchy? And how are Rosalia and her bairn?"

"I donna know. Ye can ask her when she arrives within a sennight."

His aunt clapped her hands and then embraced him. "Nephew, that is wonderful news. We must prepare for a bairn under our roof."

Praise the saints. He knew it was coming. It should only take a moment.

"Speaking of which…"

And there it was.

To his surprise and gratefulness, his wife interjected. "Who is Rosalia?"

"My apologies. I should have explained," said Alex. He walked over to Sybella and sat down beside her. "Rosalia is my cousin from Glenorchy. 'Tis a rather long tale. Are ye sure ye wish to hear it?"

"Aye, please continue."

"A long time ago, Aunt Iseabail's son left the Highlands and wed an English woman. This woman refused to wed him unless he agreed to live in England. At the time, he thought he truly loved the lass and gave up everything—his clan and wealth—and moved to Liddesdale, which is between the English and Scottish borders.

"They had one daughter, Rosalia. Lady Caroline Armstrong, Rosalia's mother, had a taste for treasures that were beyond her means. So much, in fact, that the clan coffers were emptied by her lavish spending. In order to replenish the coin, Rosalia's parents arranged for her to wed an unsavory English lord. My cousin simply refused and they beat her horribly for her insolence."

Intense astonishment touched Sybella's pale face. "That is terrible."

"Rosalia took matters into her own hands and fled Liddesdale. With only her mount, she was trying to reach Aunt Iseabail here in Glengarry."

"*Alone?* Through the Highlands?"

"Aye. Laird Ciaran MacGregor of Glenorchy found her and offered her protection. The MacGregor was to escort Rosalia to Glengarry and he did—only to be wed. The two of them were clearly a love match, and my cousin's bairn is almost a year old now."

"Alexander, is that all ye're going to tell the lass? What about your daring rescue?" asked Aunt Iseabail.

Apparently, out of all Aunt Iseabail's ailments, her hearing was unaffected. "Sybella doesnae need to hear it."

His wife winked at Aunt Iseabail and smiled. "Come now, Husband. I would love to hear of your *daring* rescue." Her eyes twinkled with amusement.

He rolled his eyes. "It wasnae that daring." Alex turned his head over his shoulder at the sound of approaching footsteps.

"Pardon the intrusion, my laird. There is a MacKenzie at the gates."

Ten

Sybella followed her husband into the bailey.
Her bond with Colin was strong. Perhaps her brother
had sensed her initial unease and come to her rescue
after all. She would be sure to tell him his concern was
unwarranted. But as she approached the man standing
in the bailey, her mind spun.

She walked hurriedly to the MacKenzie man's side
and reached out her hand in a comforting gesture. "*Dé
th'ann?* Ennis?" *What is it?* "What has happened?"

Alex lifted his brow, puzzled, but Sybella was more
troubled by what Ennis was doing there.

"*Gu meal sibh ur naidheachd. A h-uile latha sona
dhuibh.*" *Congratulations to both of you. May all your days
be happy.* "I didnae mean to worry ye, lass. We were
unable to attend the celebration because my wife was ill
and couldnae make the journey. Howbeit there was a
wee lass that wouldnae let her papa rest until she could
give ye a proper farewell." Ennis turned toward the
stables and whistled. "Anabel, *mach a seo!*" *Get out here!*

The young girl's fiery red tresses bounced around
the corner, and her eyes widened when she spotted

Sybella. She ran and threw her tiny body into Sybella's arms. "Sybella!"

Ennis cleared his throat. "Anabel, Lady MacDonell."

Sybella smiled. "'Tis all right." She dropped to her knees and wrapped her arms around the wee lass, her heart filled with warmth and love. "Anabel, I cannae believe ye came all this way to see me. I am verra honored."

Anabel looked at Alex, and he winked when he caught the little girl's eye. She pulled out of Sybella's embrace and then encircled her mouth with her hand to whisper in Sybella's ear. *"Cuir an aithne 'cheile sinn."* *Introduce us*.

Sybella stood and brushed off her skirts. "Laird Alexander MacDonell, pray allow me to introduce ye to—"

Alex bent over and gently took Anabel's hand. "Lady Anabel." He brushed a brief kiss on the top of her hand.

Anabel gave him a small curtsy and then her voice softened. "I am nay lady, Laird MacDonell."

Alex spoke in a compassionate tone. "Now that simply is nae true. Any lass as bonny as ye would surely be born of noble birth. Of course ye are a lady."

Ennis gave Alex a slight bow. "Laird MacDonell."

"Any man of my wife's clan is welcome at Glengarry."

"We will nae be any trouble, and I will try to keep Anabel out from underfoot. We will take our leave on the morrow."

"And who is this bonny creature?" asked Aunt Iseabail, strolling into the bailey.

Sybella turned, and before she had a chance to speak, Anabel curtseyed. "'Tis a pleasure to make your acquaintance, m'lady. *Is mise* Anabel." *My name is Anabel.* The little girl lowered her voice and whispered, "Is that right, Sybella?"

"Aye, ye are doing verra well." Sybella rubbed her hand over Anabel's curly locks.

"'Tis my great honor to meet such a well-mannered lass," said Aunt Iseabail, beaming with approval.

"Ennis and Lady Anabel will be our guests for the eve, Aunt."

Aunt Iseabail clapped her hands in excitement. "That is positively delightful. I will have the maids ready your chambers. If ye follow me, I will show ye to your rooms."

"My lady, please donna trouble yourself. Anabel and I can sleep in the stable. We donna have to sleep in the cas—"

Aunt Iseabail shook her head in disapproval. "Donna be ridiculous. Come."

While Anabel and Ennis followed Aunt Iseabail, Sybella studied her husband. With his hands clasped behind his back, he stood tall, domineering. She wished she could become proficient at reading his mind. "Alex, I hope ye arenae angry that Ennis and Anabel would pay a visit."

He reached out and placed his hand on her shoulder. She was shocked at the impact of his gentle grip. "Ella, it would take much, much more to fire my ire than to have a wee bonny lass under my roof for an eve. How could I be angry now that I am gifted with two such beauties? Anabel is from your village?"

Relief passed over Sybella's face. "Aye, I would often take walks with Mary to spend time with Anabel. The poor lass has two older brothers who sometimes arenae too kind to her."

Alex stood to his full height. "Do ye want me to have words with them? Some men say I am a verra fierce laird."

"Aye, I can see how fierce ye are with Aunt Iseabail and it truly frightens me," she said with a more relaxed tone.

His voice was low, alluring. "Now Ella, ye know ye cannae yet speak openly of my prowess, except perhaps in our bed."

❦

Alex watched Sybella's cheeks turn crimson. Although she was now his wife, he loved to see that he could still get a reaction from her. The woman held up better than Alex had expected. Granted, their marriage did not have the best of beginnings—between Aunt Iseabail's jaunt into the woods and someone taking aim at Sybella's head. But at least the lass was not cowering in the corner somewhere in tears. She was strong, and he actually found that quite refreshing.

John approached Alex in the bailey. "Who is the MacKenzie man? I donna recognize him."

"He comes from Sybella's village," said Alex.

"So soon after the MacKenzie departed?"

"The man said his wife had fallen ill and couldnae travel to the celebration. The lass and Sybella are close, but I donna believe in chance occurrences. This MacKenzie man arrives shortly after someone tries to harm Sybella. My wife may trust him, but I donna. Have someone other than Ian keep a watchful eye on him. He might speak in truth, but I will nae leave anything to chance."

Alex couldn't help but notice the strange look upon John's face. "What?"

John shook his head. "'Tis naught. I am only relieved to see ye still hold some sense and donna fully trust the MacKenzies. Your new wife doesnae yet hold your bollocks in the palm of her hand, and I am glad to see it."

"Your words provide me with much entertainment," Alex said dryly. "Make sure the men stay alert." He gave John a brief nod and then walked through the bailey.

Another blessed night with another MacKenzie underfoot. Ennis and his daughter appeared harmless enough, but Alex had had his fill of Sybella's kin. He stopped himself mid-thought. The lass probably felt the same way about the MacDonells, and soon enough the MacGregors would be in attendance as well.

As he prepared to sup, Alex couldn't stay the nagging feeling in the pit of his stomach. How could there be no trace of the man who had tried to kill Sybella? That was practically an impossible feat. In fact, he didn't know a single man who could be so skillful at hiding his trail. That was something he would surely contemplate. Perhaps the MacGregor could shed some light.

Alex entered the great hall to see that his wife and aunt had already taken their seats on the dais with Ennis and Anabel. He greeted his guests and took his seat beside Sybella. He couldn't help but notice the lightened expression on the face of his wife as she conversed with the young lass.

"Can I give it to her now, Papa?" asked Anabel. When Ennis nodded his head in agreement, Anabel's eyes glowed with enjoyment. She handed Sybella a small cloth bag. "'Tis a gift for your wedding."

Sybella opened the bag and pulled out a handkerchief embroidered with tiny flowers around the edges. "Anabel, I absolutely adore this. Thank ye."

"Mother made it, but I told her to put on the flowers since ye like the garden so much."

"I shall treasure it always." Sybella wrapped her arms around Anabel and kissed the top of the girl's head. "It was a verra thoughtful gift. And how is your mother feeling?"

"She was in bed with a fever, but she is doing much better," said Ennis, taking a drink from his tankard.

"I am relieved to hear it."

Alex leaned forward. "Tell me, Lady Anabel, do ye have any lads that favor your company?"

Anabel crinkled her nose. "The only lads are my brothers. They donna let me play with them, but 'tis all right. I play by myself and can do things a lot faster without them anyway. Who needs *lads*? Besides, Sybella told me I donna need a prince to be a princess."

Alex choked on his ale.

❧

Ennis pretended to be fascinated with his meal and Alex coughed. Sybella believed a quick change of subject was in order.

"If ye are finished with your meal, Anabel, do ye want to see the gardens?"

"If ye see the dolt who pulled my roses, tell me, Sybella," said Aunt Iseabail, waving her finger. "Who knows what that beast will target next!"

"I will be sure to let ye know if I see him, Aunt." She looked at Alex, and his eyes widened.

He leaned in close. "I thought she would have forgotten by now," he whispered.

"I donna think that is going to happen anytime soon." Sybella stood and held out her hand to Anabel. "Come, Anabel, and I will show ye Lady Iseabail's bonny flowers."

The girl jumped out of her seat. "Aye! I would love to!" She turned toward her father.

"'Tis all right, but ye stay close and listen to Lady Sybella."

"Aye, Papa," said Anabel, exasperated. Turning like a whirlwind, she shook Sybella's hand. "Let us take our leave."

Sybella walked leisurely through the garden hand in hand with Anabel. When the girl swung their hands, Sybella couldn't help but smile. What she wouldn't give to be that young and innocent again. Her biggest concern would've been spying on Colin. A little voice pulled her from her musings.

"Do ye like it here, Sybella, or do ye want to come home?" asked Anabel with a serious look on her face.

Sybella smiled warmly. "I will always miss ye and Kintail, but Glengarry is now my home."

"But donna ye miss us?"

Sybella knelt down, turning Anabel to face her. "Of

course I do, but I am now wed and my place is beside my husband." Something in that statement gnawed at Sybella's gut. She continued to speak in a soothing tone while she rubbed Anabel's arms. "I told ye before I wed that doesnae mean ye cannae come to visit and that I cannae come to visit with ye. Ye arenae that far away. Do ye understand?"

The young girl became thoughtful for a moment and then she nodded. "Do ye love your husband? I heard Papa say that Laird MacDonell was our enemy before. Why? What did he do?"

"Anabel, ye shouldnae be worried about such things. Ne'er get involved in the ways of men. Who knows what goes on in their minds? Look at your brothers."

Anabel giggled. "Aye, they are naught but a bunch of arses."

"Anabel! Those arenae proper words for a young lady to say. Where did ye hear that?"

Anabel covered her mouth with her hand. "My apologies, Sybella. I heard ye call *your* brother that."

Sybella stood and brushed off her skirts. "Well, I'm sure it was naught that wasnae deserved," she mumbled under her breath.

The young girl ran from flower to flower, sniffing, touching, and spinning around. She was a bundle of pent-up energy. A dark cloud rumbled overhead, signaling that a change in weather was certainly going to curtail the moment. The first drop of rain hit Sybella's brow, and she had just opened her mouth to speak when the skies blackened and buckets of rain pelted her in the face.

Anabel bolted around the corner of the flower bed

and fell on the ground at Sybella's feet. Sybella helped the poor girl stand, her dress covered in mud. In the middle of the storm, Anabel looked down at her ruined clothes and started to cry.

"Papa will be so angry at me for soiling my dress," Anabel sobbed, holding out her skirts.

Anabel's troubled expression pulled at Sybella's heart as she stood in the middle of the garden with her dripping hair hanging in her face. Without giving it a second thought, Sybella bent over and picked up a handful of mud, wiping muck over her own dress.

"What are ye doing?" asked Anabel with widened eyes.

"He cannae be angry at us both. 'Tis only dirt." She grabbed Anabel's hand and they ran for shelter, slipping and sliding on the soggy ground.

They sprang into the great hall, a welcome site, and their breathing was labored. Sybella looked at the watery trail left behind them and called for a maid.

"What the he...Er, what happened?"

Sybella lifted her eyes to see Alex standing there, flanked by Anabel's father. With both hands on her hips, she confronted them. "We were caught in the rain."

"And what? Fell in the mud? Ye two are covered in muck," said Alex in a partially scolding tone.

She thought she detected laughter in his eyes, and then he winked at her broadly.

Anabel lowered her head. "'Tis all my fault, Laird MacDonell. Please donna be cross with Syb...er, Lady MacDonell. I fell in the mud and knew Papa would be angry with me, so Lady MacDonell put mud on her dress, too. I beg ye nae to scold her. I should be the one who is punished."

Sybella was about to speak when Alex knelt in front of Anabel. "Lady Anabel, ye should be commended for your bravery in speaking the truth. Know that I could ne'er punish a lass for speaking honestly, nay matter what the circumstances. Your word is your bond. When ye are truthful, ye are respected for your honesty. When ye donna tell the truth, ye are deceitful and donna earn the right of respect. And I most certainly respect ye for all of your honesty, Lady Anabel."

He stood and patted the girl on the shoulder. "Now the two of ye get to your baths."

Ennis escorted Anabel to her room, and as soon as Sybella lifted her muddied skirts, Alex leaned in close. "We will discuss your punishment later, Ella." There was an invitation in the depths of his eyes, and Sybella was enthralled by what she saw.

"Aye, my laird, I have been verra, verra bad," she said in a sultry voice.

Her intent was to give her husband a taste back of what he always insinuated. What she did not expect was to see his eyes darken, a muscle tick at his jaw, and his kilt tent in apparent arousal. Praise the saints. Why was her mouth suddenly so dry?

"Pray excuse me while I seek my bath." She nervously stepped around him.

"Do ye need me to wash your back?"

She froze and then turned, merely lifting her brow.

༄

Alex watched the muddied temptress walk away. His wife was indeed still a child at heart, and even her walk had a sunny cheeriness. His smile broadened in approval. The woman he'd married was compassionate enough to ruin her own dress to save the feelings of a little girl. He began to think perhaps he was wrong about the dreaded MacKenzies—well, one of them in particular.

"Alexander, there ye are. I have been looking everywhere for ye," said Aunt Iseabail. She looked flustered.

"I have been here."

"I can see that now, Nephew. I wanted to tell ye something…" She tapped her finger to her lip. "It seems to have slipped my mind again. Damn, Nephew. Donna get old. Ye will nae like it."

Alex wrapped his arm around Aunt Iseabail's shoulders. "Ye arenae old. I told ye before. Ye will more than likely outlive us all."

"'Tis bothering me. I know I had something of importance to tell ye."

"Donna think upon it. I find that if I think upon something else, my first thought will come back eventually."

"I suppose. Where is the bonny little lass?" she asked, looking around the great hall.

Alex chuckled and rolled his eyes. "She and Sybella were caught in a storm, and the mud got the best of them. They are seeking baths as we speak."

"Annie is such a bonny lass. I hope ye and Sybella soon have enough bairns to fill our table for the noon meal."

"Anabel is quite lovely. I'm sure in good time when the gods are willing to bless us with a—"

"And I told ye, Nephew. Donna leave it to the gods. Are ye at least trying to get your wife with child?"

If Alex had to discuss his coupling habits with his aunt one more time…

"My laird, pardon the intrusion. A moment, please," said John, walking into the great hall. Water dripped from his soaked frame.

"I will leave ye lads to your business then." Aunt Iseabail walked back toward the kitchens, and Alex breathed a sigh of relief.

"I must commend ye on your most appropriate timing." He playfully wiped his brow.

John chuckled. "She wants a bairn under her roof before she dies."

"Donna remind me. What was it ye wanted?"

"I had Ian tracking in the woods and he was still unable to find a trail. Now that we have rain—"

"Any trail there was is now dead."

"Aye."

"Sybella stays inside the castle walls and doesnae journey outside the gates until we find who is responsible. My cousin and the MacGregor arrive within the sennight. The man is verra wise in battle and may have a few ideas. Keep alert. I am by nay means lowering our defenses."

John nodded. "Aye. Seòras watches the MacKenzie man and there hasnae been anything amiss."

"Good. Make sure it stays that way. I will nae have a threat under my own roof."

"I will leave ye to your *duty* then, my laird," said John with a wry grin.

"'Tis quite enough that I hear it from Aunt Iseabail. I donna need to hear it from ye, ye bloody arse."

Alex headed to the parapet to seek a brief reprieve.

The heavy weather had passed, and he loved the smell of the air after a hard rain. He stood upon the darkened parapet with only the torchlight to illuminate the glistening walls. He lifted his face, feeling a light mist spray his cheeks.

Some of his men walked the walls and some sought shelter, conversing by the gate. In the time since his father's death, Alex had managed to secure an alliance with their enemy and make certain the clan would be fed for several winters to come, and now he had a wife. He hoped his father was proud. If he could only solve the mystery of who would want to take aim at his bonny wife's head, Alex could rest. Now he knew why he had waited so long to take a wife. The fairer sex was nothing but trouble.

Eleven

SYBELLA KNELT IN THE DIRT AS AUNT ISEABAIL STOOD over her shoulder in the garden. It was hard to believe that almost a sennight had passed since Ennis and Anabel took their leave. Sybella already missed her kin, and her beloved husband wasn't paying her much attention. The wooing part of their marriage was undoubtedly over or had been abruptly halted. Either way, something had obviously changed. And God help her, she missed her husband. Whether she wanted to admit it or not, she had developed a certain fondness for him that weighed heavily on her heart.

Alexander had not visited her bed since she'd been cursed with her monthly courses over the last few days. She had the impression that the man was either brooding because she wasn't with child or was unable to bed her due to her womanly time, or perhaps both.

Sybella shook her head as she pulled a stubborn weed. She was somewhat disappointed that they hadn't gotten the chance to spend more time together before he resumed his daily duties as laird. But he hadn't taken long before recommencing his swordplay with the men in the bailey and seeing to the accounts. She wondered if she was ever in the man's thoughts.

"I might be losing my mind at times, but I am nae deaf. If ye have something to say, speak your mind and cease your mumbling, lass. 'Tis driving me mad," said Aunt Iseabail.

"My apologies."

"I know my nephew can be infuriating, but—"

Not wanting to create unnecessary worry for Alex's aunt, Sybella shook her head. "'Tisnae Alexander troubling me."

"He had better nae be troubling ye," said a familiar voice.

Sybella's eyes lifted and then she flew to her feet. Hefting her skirts, she jumped over a bush and ran straight into her brother's arms. "Colin, 'tis so good to see ye." She held him in a tight embrace, not wanting to let him go.

He kissed her on the top of the head. "And ye as well, Ella. I see naught much has changed since ye became a MacDonell. Ye still look much the same, covered in dirt."

She pulled back and playfully tapped his arm. "What are ye doing here?"

Before he could answer, Aunt Iseabail cleared her throat. "I will leave ye to your visit, then."

Colin gave Aunt Iseabail a slight bow. "Lady Iseabail, 'tis a pleasure to see ye again."

"Aye, be sure to tell William I wish him well," she said with a slight blush on her cheeks.

"I will, m'lady."

As Aunt Iseabail walked away, Sybella hugged her

brother again. "I cannot believe ye are here. I have missed ye so." She pulled away and smiled. "Ennis and Anabel came to visit—"

"Aye, I heard all about it. The wee lass couldnae stop speaking of it. She had a good time with ye and I think she misses ye." Colin hesitated. "I need to have words with your husband, and then we will spend time together before I take my leave."

Sybella had a difficult time keeping the whine from her voice. "Must ye take your leave so soon? Ye just arrived. In truth, I was hoping ye could remain for a few days. Alexander's cousin should be coming from Glenorchy any day now, and it would be nice to have another MacKenzie around."

Colin smoothed her tresses. "Come now, lass. Ye seem to be adjusting to your new life just fine."

Sybella glanced over his shoulder and spotted the captain of Alex's guard. He stood alert, keeping them both under heavy scrutiny. She leaned in close. "They donna trust us, Brother. He watches ye with the eyes of a hawk."

"It doesnae matter if they donna trust the MacKenzies. 'Tis important that they trust *ye*, Ella."

"I heard there was a MacKenzie at the gates," Alex said as he walked up behind them.

Colin turned around and extended his arm. "Laird MacDonell, I come on behalf of my father. There are matters which we need to discuss."

"Come to my study." Alex clasped Colin's arm, nodded, and then turned and gave Sybella the same gesture. "Wife."

"Husband." The man behaved no differently toward

her than toward her kin—although Colin received an
actual physical greeting, whereas Alex hadn't touched
her in days. Men were truly a mystery that she did not
have the patience to figure out.

Sybella resumed her purpose in the garden, not
able to stop herself from pondering. Why would her
brother request an audience with her husband? Had he
heard her mumbling to herself? Surely he didn't think
Alex had mistreated her. Perhaps she should intervene.
Her husband wasn't really treating her poorly. And
the last thing she needed was to be the start of another
battle between the MacKenzies and the MacDonells
before she had a chance to look for the stone. Besides,
she needed to tell her brother that Alexander was not
the man he thought he was.

She ran to catch up to him. "Colin!"

Her brother turned around and smiled. When her
eyes darted nervously back and forth, Colin sensed her
unease. "I need only but a moment, Ella. 'Tis naught
that concerns ye."

His wife looked like a frightened rabbit. What the hell
did she think? That he would pull out his sword and
run a MacKenzie through in the middle of the bailey?
What kind of man did she take him for? Alex couldn't
focus on his wife's odd behavior because right now,
he needed to find out what another damn MacKenzie
was doing under his roof.

Alex escorted the MacKenzie's son to his study
and closed the door. He gestured for Colin to sit. He
grabbed two tankards and pulled out MacGregor's ale,

pouring them each a healthy dram and placing one of the cups in front of Colin. "Ye look as though ye could use a drink."

"Thank ye. And how is my sister?" Colin took a drink of ale.

"She enjoyed having Anabel visit, but there is something of importance that I must ask of ye."

"Aye?"

"Is there anyone who would want to harm my wife?"

Colin stirred uneasily in the chair, and tense lines appeared on his face. "Nay. Why do ye ask?"

There was a heavy moment of silence.

"We were in the woods and someone took aim at her. She bent over just in time as an arrow struck the tree above her head."

Colin placed his tankard on the desk and sat forward on the edge of his chair. "My father has many enemies," he said solemnly.

"And I was one of them, but I spoke my vows and I am a man of my word."

"I am nae accusing ye."

"Before ye even think of saying the words, my clan wouldnae harm her. I need to know who else would benefit from seeing her injured—or dead."

Rubbing his hand over his brow, Colin sighed. "Mayhap now is a good time to tell ye the reason for my visit."

"By all means, enlighten me," said Alex dryly.

"The MacLeod attempts to raise arms again on Lewis. His Majesty will most definitely nae be pleased. King James's men havenae traveled this far north, but 'tis only a matter of time before they do. Our men still remain on Lewis, and my father requests a score of your men to help keep the MacLeods under control. When they see the MacKenzies and MacDonells have joined forces, the MacLeod men may think twice before picking up arms against us. We wouldnae want word of the MacLeod starting another uprising to reach His Majesty's ears."

Alex tapped his fingers on the desk. "I have heard rumblings about the MacLeods, but I have also heard words of MacKenzie men taking the lives of the innocent." His eyes studied Colin. "I want to know what ye did to the MacLeods that they attempt to raise arms against ye again. Before I send my men into a battle that isnae our own, I will have the truth."

"The battle with the MacLeods became your fight once ye wed my sister." Colin's response held a note of impatience.

"Be that as it may, I will have the truth." Alex sat as still as a stone statue, refusing to budge.

Colin sat back in his chair and glanced around the study, his expression becoming somewhat guarded. "My father is a verra determined man."

"I knew that from his attempts to steal our cattle," Alex said with sarcasm.

"If His Majesty travels north, all of the power that he bestowed upon the Highland lairds—"

"Ye can spare me the details. I am aware of political matters."

"We did what was necessary to have the MacLeod surrender."

"Did ye spill the blood of women and children?"

Colin hesitated and could barely look Alex in the eye. "Aye."

Curses fell from Alex's mouth. "Do ye think mayhap the MacLeod wishes to harm Sybella after ye killed his own?"

"It would make sense, but we havenae received word of any MacLeods taking their leave from Lewis," Colin muttered uneasily.

"Aye, but ye arenae certain."

"I am nae certain."

Alex wondered if there would ever be a time when the MacKenzies were not a thistle in his arse. As far as he was concerned, the MacKenzie was no different than the villain who had taken his cousin a few years ago. Then again, Archibald Campbell, the seventh Earl of Argyll, certainly had gotten his recompense. Perhaps it was only a matter of time before the MacKenzie got his.

Clearly dismissing his wife's brother, Alex stood and downed the last of his ale.

"And what of the men?" asked Colin.

"I will arrange for a score of my men to assist ye in keeping the peace with the MacLeods. Howbeit they will be under my orders nae to kill innocents. That might be the way of the MacKenzie, but 'tisnae the way of the MacDonell."

Colin ignored his words. "May I have a few moments with my sister before I take my leave?"

"By all means."

❧

Sybella washed up in her chamber and opened the door to find Colin waiting for her. His expression was grim and he looked tired, worn.

"There is something we need to discuss, Ella." He brushed past her into the room and gestured for her to close the door. He pulled out a chair in the sitting area and sat down.

"What is amiss?" She sat down on a chair beside him.

"Your husband says someone took a shot at ye with a bow."

"Aye. The arrow barely missed my head. Praise the saints, I havenae had to look over my shoulder since I have remained inside the castle walls. I pray there isnae anything more to worry about, given that naught untoward has happened since, but I am still verra unsettled. I donna know who would want to kill me."

"Father has many enemies. I donna know who—"

"Donna be so quick to judge our father, Colin. More than likely the MacDonell has also made a few foes along the way. And whatever ye do, please donna concern Father with this. My husband has me verra well protected. There is naught Father can do that Alexander hasnae done already."

"I give ye a word of caution nae to walk outside the castle gates alone."

"Cease your lectures. I have already had my fill of them. Howbeit I will make sure that I have an escort," said Sybella with an appeasing tone.

"We donna know who is responsible for taking aim at ye. I will have your word that ye will be careful, even within your husband's gates."

"Ye have my word." She raised her hands in mock surrender.

Colin reached out and grabbed her hand. Unspoken pain was alive and glowing in his eyes.

"What is it, Brother? I have a feeling there is something more that ye arenae telling me."

A gentle smile played on his lips. "Ye know me too well." He sat back in the chair, looking uncomfortable. "We have battled so many years with the MacDonell."

Sybella squeezed her fingers over the bridge of her nose. "How many times must we have the same conversation?"

Ignoring her words, Colin continued. "There has always been reiving between us. We take something, they take something. We burnt the MacDonell's stable to the ground, and in retaliation, they burnt our church." When she remained silent and didn't question him further, Colin stood and walked over to the stone fireplace. He placed his hand on the mantel, and for a moment, he was quiet, searching. She'd never seen her brother quite so unnerved.

"There are certain matters of politics which I have sheltered ye from for your own protection." He remained still, weighing his words. "His Majesty's forces make their way to Lewis, and Father wants ye to find the stone within a sennight. If the king's men arrive at Lewis and find the MacLeods arenae under control, His Majesty will strip Father of his power over the isle and mayhap even his position in the Highlands."

She sat back, momentarily rebuffed.

When Colin spoke again, his voice was calming. "Our conquest on Lewis was the last our seer foretold. Father doesnae want to take the chance of making another move without the seer's sight and doing something to permanently seal the fate of our clan."

"Colin, who is this seer?" Sybella stood and approached him.

"I told ye before, it doesnae matter, and for your own safety, 'tis better that ye donna know." When Sybella scrunched up her face in annoyance, Colin continued. "I know I told ye to wait until ye earned your husband's trust, but we nay longer have time on our side. Ye can nay longer leave Glengarry without an escort and are now given the perfect opportunity to search for the stone within the walls of the castle.

"Take it room by room, one at a time, and leave naught unturned." He made a circle with his hands. "Remember the stone is of brown color and about this big around with a hole in the middle. 'Tis also small enough to keep in a jewelry box, a desk drawer, or a hollowed-out book. Search every chamber, everywhere and everything."

She took a deep breath and straightened her spine. "Colin, ye and Father are wrong. Alexander is a good man, and I've seen naught to tell me otherwise. He is kind and has a verra compassionate soul. Ye should see the way he cares for his aunt." Sybella shook her head. "I cannae deceive him, MacDonell or nae. And frankly, I have had enough secrets between us. I am taking my leave with ye to Kintail. And *I* will speak with Father. I will nae do this." She opened her trunk at the foot of the bed and pulled out her sack.

Colin whirled around, his mouth set in annoyance. "When will ye open your bloody eyes, Ella, and see the truth of our father's ways? *Father* is the one who sent me here to make ye search for the stone! If ye didnae wed the MacDonell, your beloved sire was going to ship ye off to Lewis to marry the damn MacLeod on that desolate isle!"

She threw up her hands in the air. "Lies…Ye speak naught but lies. Father *told* me he would ne'er wed me to the MacLeod. Why would ye say such hurtful words, Colin? Ye are my brother. I donna understand why ye are doing this. Are ye angry because Father entrusted me to find the stone?"

He looked offended and lowered his voice. "I would ne'er do anything to hurt ye, Ella. Whether ye realize it or nae, I have always protected ye. Father wants the seeing stone returned to us and will do anything to recover it. Ye *must* find it. Ye donna have a choice. Ye cannae travel to Kintail and tell Father ye will nae do this. Trust me, ye simply cannae. Ye seem to have developed a certain…fondness for your husband. The MacDonell doesnae have to know ye look for the stone. Ye can be discreet. For if ye donna, Father will plot something against the MacDonell and I will nay longer be able to hold our sire at bay."

When she sat down on the bed with the sack on her lap, she tried to mentally rein in her temper. She never thought she would see the day when a MacKenzie killed another MacKenzie under the roof of a MacDonell.

There was sourness in the pit of Sybella's stomach. "I am such a fool. Ye must help me. I know I agreed to search for the stone, but things have…changed."

Colin's expression was almost regretful. "I see ye care for him." When she did not respond, he continued. "I want ye to think upon my words. Father will ne'er let ye continue with your new life—nae until ye recover the stone and return it to our clan. I donna want to see ye hurt by refusing our father's command. Ye have nay idea what the man is capable of. Ye have to do this whether ye like it or nae. Once ye are alone with your thoughts, ye will see reason."

When she scowled at him, he quickly added, "Ye are a MacDonell in name only, and MacKenzie blood runs thick through your veins. I have faith that ye will do as our father commands."

Sybella was so angry that tears welled in her eyes. *"An diobhail toirt leis thu. Mach a seo!"* The devil take you. Get out!

Colin merely walked out and closed the door behind him. Fury almost choked her. Her marriage was nothing more than another MacKenzie scheme. If Alex ever found out, there would be a bloody war. And reiving would no longer be an option. It would be man against man, sword against sword, to see who could shed the most blood between them.

She closed her eyes.

Sybella had spoken the sacred vows that bound her and Alex as one. MacKenzie blood or not, she was now a MacDonell. She had pledged her troth. Tears slowly slid down her cheeks. Her misery was like a weight upon her shoulders, a stab of guilt buried deep in her breast. How was she supposed to get herself out of this situation? Alex had preached words of honesty and trust. Perhaps she could find a way to speak with him without making him angry and without blood being shed. She wasn't exactly sure what she'd say, but she'd figure it out. She always did. She had started this marriage under a false pretense, and now it was clearly time to right that wrong.

Sybella wandered aimlessly through the halls in search of her husband. She would need to proceed cautiously and think about her words before they escaped her lips, lest she find herself on the pointy end of Alex's sword.

She reached Alex's study and was lifting her hand to knock when raised voices sounded from within. She had to admit that she was curious if Colin had taken his leave or if he had again sought out her husband.

Sybella looked around and then placed her ear to the door.

"'Tis good to have ye again under roof, MacGregor. I grow tired of the damn MacKenzies."

"Ye still donna trust them?" asked a deep voice.

Alex smirked. "As much as ye trusted the bloody Campbell."

Twelve

"AND YE MUST BE LADY SYBELLA MACDONELL, MY cousin's new wife."

Sybella bolted upright, her eyes widening in surprise as she tried to mask the guilty look on her face. The woman speaking had chestnut tresses and wore a dusky rose dress that hugged her full-figured frame. She carried a bairn with curly brown locks and azure eyes that stared back at Sybella.

"My apologies. I was searching for my husband to tell him that my brother had taken his leave. I didnae know ye had arrived, my lady." Sybella approached the woman and smiled. Running her hand over the bairn's head, she said, "'Tis a pleasure to make your acquaintance, Lady MacGregor. And who have we here?"

The woman's face lit up. "Please call me Rosalia. And this is my son, Lachlann."

"Only if ye call me Sybella. And if ye donna mind me saying so, your son is a handsome laddie."

"Thank ye. He is almost one year now and has already been taking steps and getting into trouble.

Granted, he staggers like his Uncle Declan when he is in his cups, but my wee lad does try his best."

"He is a lad. Of course he is getting into mischief," said Sybella with a giggle. "Have ye seen Aunt Iseabail yet?"

"Nay, we only walked through the gates a moment ago, and Alexander stole Ciaran away to his study."

"Then come. Ye have had a long journey. Let me offer ye something to eat and drink, and we will find your *seanmhair*." *Grandmother*.

Sybella walked with Rosalia and Lachlann by her side when she wanted to do nothing more than crawl back into bed and lift the covers over her head. And to think she had almost been foolhardy enough to speak the truth to her husband! How many times had Alex preached to her about truth and honesty—yet she still couldn't fathom the words that she'd heard escape his lips. If he couldn't follow his own advice, how could she be expected to honor him with the same courtesy?

She bit her lip to stifle her outcry. Alex didn't trust her. Not that she had given him any reason to place his faith in her, but the thought gnawed at her gut. How was she supposed to search for the stone now? Something must have shown upon her face because Rosalia interrupted her thoughts.

"We didnae arrive at an inopportune moment, did we? Ye look troubled, my lady."

Sybella forced a smile. "Nay, and please call me Sybella."

As they sat in the great hall, Sybella couldn't stop her racing heart. Her face burned with the memory of Colin's words. Her father would never let her rest until she found that dreaded stone. And here she was, placed in a dangerous position that required her to betray her husband and his clan. Then again, how could she possibly deceive Alex when he had never trusted her to begin with?

"So how do ye find being wed to Alexander?" asked Rosalia, bouncing Lachlann gently on her lap.

"'Tis something we are both yet getting accustomed to."

"Your clan must be fairly close if your brother was able to pay ye a visit."

"My clan is from Kintail. 'Tis about a day's ride from Glengarry."

Rosalia lowered her voice. "Alexander wrote in his missive that my *seanmhair* isnae doing well. Her memory is fading."

Sybella sighed. "I notice it more when she becomes upset, but aye, she is sometimes forgetful. The day after Alex and I wed, we found Aunt Iseabail walking in the woods in her bare feet. She came across the path of a lone wolf. If Alex hadnae arrived when he did…She said she was searching for Alex but didnae remember her purpose and didnae realize she wore nay boots."

"My poor *seanmhair*. 'Tis one of the reasons we came to Glengarry. We havenae seen her since Ciaran and I wed. And she has yet to lay her eyes upon Lachlann."

At that moment, Aunt Iseabail walked into the great hall with outstretched arms. "My dearest Rosalia. How lovely to see ye again."

Rosalia stood with Lachlann and embraced her

seanmhair with one arm. "'Tis so wonderful to see ye." She pulled back and smiled. "*Seanmhair,* I have someone I would like ye to meet. This wee lad is your great-grandson, Lachlann."

Aunt Iseabail's eyes glowed with enjoyment. "Ye have brought me the greatest gift of all, Rosalia. He is absolutely bonny. And he looks just like his sister, Anabel."

Rosalia paled.

❧

Alex sat in his study with the MacGregor, grateful for another generous gift of ale. No sooner had Sybella's brother walked out of the gates than MacGregor had appeared. The man's timing couldn't have been more perfect. Now that Alex knew about some of the MacKenzies machinations against the MacLeods of Lewis, he sought MacGregor's counsel. He would have time to visit with his cousin later, but at the moment, Alex was more curious to see if the MacGregor had any sound advice to offer him.

"So the MacKenzie's son told ye that they killed innocents?" asked MacGregor, shaking his head in disgust.

"Aye. I cannae think of anyone else who would want to kill my wife."

"'Tis a logical choice to think the MacLeod would want to avenge his clan by taking aim at your wife."

"Aye, but I have ne'er known of a man who could cover his tracks so well. My most skilled tracker couldnae find the trail."

"Mmm…'tis difficult to say, but we donna know

what the MacLeods do on that savage isle. And ye say naught has happened since your wife has remained inside the walls of the castle?"

Alex nodded in response.

MacGregor had a look of concentration on his face. "My men are verra skilled. I will send a few of them out with your men to scout. Mayhap they can pick up something."

"Thank ye."

"Donna worry, MacDonell." MacGregor gave a brief nod. "Ye helped save my wife. I will help to save yours. Rosalia will be cross with ye for stealing me away for so long." He stood and downed the rest of his drink. "Come. Let us find our women."

Alex walked with the MacGregor to the great hall where the women were gathered around Aunt Iseabail at the table. Rosalia's eyes lit up when she spotted her husband. When Alex offered Sybella a smile, her eyes darkened and she quickly lowered her gaze.

MacGregor placed his hand on Rosalia's shoulder and bent to kiss her on the top of the head. "Wife." He turned and kissed Aunt Iseabail on the cheek. "'Tis wonderful to see ye again, my lady."

Aunt Iseabail smiled. "Your husband hasnae changed. He is still a verra fine looking man, Rosalia."

MacGregor's face reddened slightly.

Rosalia stood up from the bench and embraced Alex. "Cousin, marriage suits ye. Ye look well," she said with a grin.

Alex raised a brow. "I could say the same for ye, Rosalia. And this young lad must be Lachlann. Congratulations to ye both." He ruffled the bairn's hair and was rewarded with a smile. Alex stood behind Sybella and placed his hand on her shoulder. He didn't miss how she tensed under his fingertips and then abruptly stood. "And this is my wife, Lady Sybella MacDonell."

"'Tis a pleasure to make your acquaintance, Laird MacGregor. My husband speaks of ye highly."

"Please call me Ciaran."

"Verra well. I am Sybella. Ye have journeyed far. Please sit and I will get ye something to drink."

"Nephew, did ye see their strapping young bairn? How much longer do ye think it will be before ye have one of your own? I am nae getting any younger, ye know."

Alex shook his head. Rosalia giggled, MacGregor smirked, and Sybella paled. "Give it time, Aunt. Ye cannae schedule such things."

To Alex's relief, Rosalia came to his rescue. "Ye cannae rush the gods. When they bless Alex and Sybella with a bairn, they bless them."

"I suppose ye are right, but I find that the more time passes, the more impatient I become."

"Ciaran, Lachlann is falling asleep in my arms. I think I will go to our chamber and lay him down," said Rosalia, repositioning the bairn.

MacGregor held out his arms. "Nay, give him here. I will take him. Ye stay and enjoy the company of your kin."

"Thank ye."

The fierce MacGregor laird departed the great hall, carrying his bairn in a way that was as gentle and nurturing as the caring father that he was. Alex remembered when the man's blade had struck down Archibald Campbell, the seventh Earl of Argyll. It was hard to believe that a warrior so adept on the battlefield could be a loving, devoted husband and father. Alex didn't miss seeing how the man doted on his wife and child. Perhaps one day he himself might know the feeling of holding his own son, his heir.

Rosalia and Sybella resumed their seats flanking Aunt Iseabail, while Alex sat down on the other side of the table. "And how is life at Glenorchy? If I were to guess by that smile upon your face, Cousin, I would say life is treating ye well."

"Everything has been wonderful. Ye probably received my missive that Declan and Liadain are wed. And Aisling and Aiden are expecting another bairn."

"Ye will have so many MacGregors underfoot that your husband could start his own army."

Rosalia giggled. "Donna give him any ideas. And what of ye, Alexander?" She leaned forward and smiled at Sybella. "My cousin is treating ye well?"

Alex didn't fail to notice Sybella's slight hesitation. "Aye, he is verra kind."

"I am sure my *seanmhair* would have words with him if he wasnae."

Aunt Iseabail nodded. "'Tis true, Nephew."

"I am so sorry to hear of your father's passing. He still seemed hale the last time we were here," said Rosalia in a soft tone.

"His health slowly faded."

"He was a good man."

"Aye."

Rosalia leaned in close to Aunt Iseabail. "And how

have ye been enjoying having another woman within the walls?"

Aunt Iseabail clapped her hands. "I simply love it! Sybella is quite lovely company."

"And I feel the same for ye," said Sybella, her eyes distant.

"Have ye heard word of your mother, Rosalia?" When Rosalia's lips thinned, Alex gave her an apologetic smile.

Rosalia shifted on the bench. "Nae since her English lover's fate joined that of the bloody Campbell."

❧

"Who is the bloody Campbell?" asked Sybella. If she was being compared to this man, she wanted to know who he was.

"He was Archibald Campbell, the seventh Earl of Argyll. And his lands bordered the MacGregor. He was the right hand of the King, but his greed got him killed," said Alex with a trace of bitterness.

Sybella's eyes widened innocently. "So I take it he wasnae a man to be trusted."

"Trusted? I wouldnae trust him alone with a dog. He held my cousin against her will in order to force MacGregor to break King James's command. The man got what he deserved. He had nay honor."

Alex had said that he trusted the MacKenzies as much as Ciaran trusted the bloody Campbell. Granted, the words Sybella overheard had been spoken with a heavy wooden door between them, but did Alexander truly think her clan had earned the same fate as the bloody Earl of Argyll? Something clicked in her mind:

she believed the Campbell had met his demise upon the blade of Ciaran's broadsword. Is that truly how her husband felt?

Rosalia cleared her throat. "Can we nae speak of the bloody Campbell? The man has been buried for some time, and he still manages to anger Ciaran. Please donna even whisper the earl's name."

"Aye, there is much to celebrate," said Aunt Iseabail.

Alex smiled. "Of course there is, Aunt."

"After a long journey, I would love to walk. Why donna we all walk down to the loch?" asked Rosalia. "I am nae sure how long Lachlann will sleep."

"I would rather ye nae leave the gates. Why donna ye walk to the parapet? I will join ye after I escort Aunt Iseabail to her chamber. Ye look weary, Aunt."

Aunt Iseabail looked startled by Alex's suggestion. "Aye," she replied hesitantly. "If ye insist."

Rosalia rubbed Aunt Iseabail's arm. "'Tis all right, *seanmhair*. Ye rest and we will have plenty of time to spend together."

While Alex cared for his aunt, Sybella found herself walking the halls of Glengarry once again with Rosalia when all she wanted to do was retire to her empty chamber. She desperately needed an end to this brutal day. She continued to struggle with the memory of her husband's words and the duty she felt to her clan. This was all one big nightmare, and honestly, she wasn't sure what to do.

They stepped out onto the parapet, and Rosalia gave Sybella a knowing look. "Now ye can tell me the true reason why Alexander doesnae want us to walk to the loch."

Sybella rubbed her fingers over the stone wall. "Ye are verra observant."

"Aye, well, when ye live with Ciaran and his two brothers, ye donna miss too much. Tell me. What is amiss?"

Sybella became increasingly uneasy under Rosalia's examination. Frankly, she was tired. Her clan wanted her to betray her husband; her husband didn't trust her; and now she was standing here with her husband's cousin, who wanted answers.

"I can see it in your eyes." Rosalia paused. "Listen, if it wasnae for the company of my sisters-by-marriage, I would be daft. We are all kin. Ye can tell me anything that is troubling ye. I am a verra good listener."

Sybella rubbed her brow. She was somewhat reluctant to speak, but she gathered that Rosalia would find out the truth eventually. "Someone aimed an arrow at my head while I walked in the forest with Alexander."

Rosalia gasped. "Are ye all right?"

"I am fine. Naught untoward has happened since Alexander has confined me within the walls of the castle. His men still scour the woods."

"What enemies has my cousin made to warrant such an act?" asked Rosalia in a tone indicating that she did not necessarily require an answer.

"What makes ye think the man is an enemy of my husband?"

Rosalia shook her head. "I find most often that women are only pawns in the games of men."

"Be that as it may, my clan was the only known enemy of Alexander. But we are wed and our clans are now joined. I donna know of anyone who would want to cause me harm."

"Alexander must be worried about ye something fierce."

Mixed feelings consumed Sybella. Her husband worried for her safety simply because it was his duty. He was her sworn protector. It wasn't as if he actually cared about her. He'd basically said so himself. When Sybella didn't answer, Rosalia tapped her arm.

"I know this may nae sound too comforting at the moment, but donna worry about it. Ciaran and his men are here and will help my cousin capture the miscreant. Ye are safe. Your husband will protect ye."

"Rosalia's right, ye know."

Sybella whipped her head around as Alexander approached them on the parapet. The gentle breeze blew a piece of his hair onto his face, and his words didn't register on Sybella's dizzied senses. Her feelings toward him were so mixed up that she mentally chided herself.

"Why are ye women speaking of this? Do ye nae have womanly subjects to discuss such as raising a bairn or stitching tunics or the like?"

Stitching tunics? Sybella was about to open her mouth when Alex's cousin spoke before she had the chance.

"I think someone taking aim at your wife's head is more important to discuss than talking about stitching tunics, Cousin," Rosalia said in a scolding tone.

Alex draped his arm over Rosalia's shoulder. "I donna want ye causing Sybella more worry."

"Aye, let her be mute. That will surely fix all of

your problems." When Alex's eyes darkened, Rosalia murmured softly, "Pray excuse me." Rosalia lifted her skirts and simply walked through the parapet door.

Sybella was somewhat surprised that Alexander's cousin spoke her mind. In fact, she liked it very much. She hadn't often found a lass who would stand up to a brawny Highland laird.

"I meant what I said. There is nay need for ye to be worried about such things. Now that MacGregor is here, we will find the man responsible. Did ye have a pleasant visit with your brother?"

At the mention of Colin, Sybella nervously wiped her sweaty palms on her day dress. She suddenly had the feeling that she was one of Anabel's brothers caught doing something he shouldn't. She stood to her full height. "It was nice to see him again."

Sybella was drawn to the sound of pounding hoof-beats below. She looked over the side of the wall to see a score of armed MacDonell men heading out the gate. "Where are they going?" Surely Alex wouldn't send that many men to search the forest again.

"My men travel to Lewis."

Her eyes shot up in surprise. "Lewis?"

"Aye."

"This wouldnae have anything to do with the MacLeod, would it?"

His expression became guarded. "And what do ye know of the MacLeod of Lewis, lass?"

She lowered her gaze. "Naught but that the man is verra uncivilized."

Alex remained perfectly still. When she looked up, he gave a brief nod. "Ella, these arenae matters for ye to be concerned with." When she looked away from him uneasily, his fingers reached out and grabbed her chin. "Are ye all right? Something seems amiss."

"'Tis naught." She reached up to remove his hand and became aware of the warmth of his touch. Damn. She was more shaken than she cared to admit.

"If something is troubling ye, tell me. I told ye this before, lass."

Sybella searched anxiously for the meaning of his words while attempting to keep her fragile control. The man was unnerving. If she hadn't heard his words through the study door, she would've sworn he actually cared how she felt. Praise the saints, the man was good. She would give him that.

She gently tapped his hand away. "I would tell ye, Alex. As I know ye would tell me if something was amiss."

A smile played at the corners of his lips. "Before long, ye will be able to travel beyond the walls. Ye have my word. We will find the man. Until then, ye need to have faith in me and nae worry."

Sybella laughed to cover her annoyance.

Have faith in him…

If she remembered correctly, Alex was the one who said he trusted the MacKenzies as much as the MacGregor trusted the bloody Campbell. He clearly didn't trust her, but she was supposed to "have faith in him." How typical. Now the brute wasn't even paying attention to her. He gazed over the wall and she stared at his broad back. He didn't even turn around. Her anger could no longer be controlled.

"Ye expect me to—"

Without warning, Alex turned, his expression darkened, and he shoved her hard into the stone wall with a heavy thump.

Thirteen

As soon as Alex turned, he heard the whizzing arrow coming straight toward them. His only thought was to block the arrow from reaching Sybella. He hammered her forcefully into the parapet wall, his only purpose to keep her safe. His battle-hardened senses reached full awareness and he jumped to his feet. He leaned over the side of the wall and yelled for John.

"Archer!" Alex pointed in the general direction, and John and his men ran out of the gate, swords in hand.

Sybella moaned as she lay sprawled on the stone floor.

Alex knelt by her side and supported her head in his arms. "Ella, are ye all right?" When he pushed her hair back from her face, her eyes were heavy, searching. "Ye need to answer me. Are ye all right?"

When she didn't answer, a pang of guilt gnawed at him. He hadn't meant to harm her. Perhaps by protecting her he'd rammed into her a little harder than he initially thought. While Sybella breathed in shallow, quick gasps, a knot formed in Alex's stomach.

He noticed that she was unresponsive and that the color had drained from her face.

He gently tapped her cheeks. "Wife."

A hot tear rolled down her cheek. "Alex…I cannae…catch my breath."

"Shhh…donna speak." He sat down beside Sybella and pulled her against his chest. "The air has been knocked out of ye. Give it but a moment until ye feel it return."

"My body aches. I feel as though I was run over by a stampede of horses. Why did ye do that?"

He lifted his hand and smoothed her hair. "An arrow shot from below."

Holding her ribs, Sybella slowly pulled herself into a sitting position. Intense astonishment touched her pale face. "Ye saved my life."

"It was naught."

"Ye risked your own life to shield me. Ye placed yourself in harm's way for me, a MacKenzie."

"Of course I did. I am your husband, and lest ye forget, ye are now a MacDonell." When she tried to stand, Alex stood and pulled her to her feet. When she swayed, he bent down and lifted her into his arms.

"Ye donna need to carry me."

"Ye can barely stand." He kicked open the parapet door with his foot and descended the stairs. When he reached the bottom, he saw Rosalia carrying Lachlann and walking toward them with long, purposeful strides.

"Alexander, what is happening? What is wrong with Sybella?"

He spoke as he carried Sybella through the hall to

her chamber. "The archer took another shot. John and my men seek him out."

"Aye, Ciaran took off with a purpose with his men as well. Let me get the door." Rosalia repositioned Lachlann on her hip and opened Sybella's bedchamber door.

As Alex gently lowered his wife to the bed, she let out a grunt and grabbed her ribs. "God's teeth, MacDonell. Ye pack a strong wallop."

"What happened?" asked Rosalia.

"We stood upon the parapet and an arrow shot through the air toward Sybella. In trying to protect her, I pushed her into the wall."

Sybella rubbed her head. "More like rammed."

Rosalia sat down on the edge of the bed with Lachlann. "Are ye all right? Alexander is a big man. That had to hurt."

"It wasnae verra pleasant, but the man saved my li—"

"MacDonell!"

Alex hastily swung the door open to find MacGregor. Sweat beaded on the man's brow and his breathing was labored.

"We found the man."

❧

Sybella's head throbbed and her body ached, but nothing would keep her from seeing the man who had tried to take aim at her head. After Alex departed with Ciaran, Sybella told Rosalia that she wanted to rest. Her words weren't totally untrue. She did want to rest, but there was no way she was going to miss what was happening in the bailey.

She made her way down the steps, and as soon as she stepped out the door, she found an unoccupied wall and stood quietly. She couldn't see a damn thing. A mountain of men encircled something, but she wasn't able to make anything out.

Sybella walked slowly along the edge of the wall, trying to get a better view. Was it just her opinion, or were all Highland men extremely large? She stood on the tips of her toes, but broad shoulders blocked her ability to see the archer who had tried to kill her—twice.

Ciaran moved, and she saw Alexander raising his arm and striking the man who knelt before him. Sybella bent over and watched through the legs of the Highlanders as the man fell to the ground. She had to restrain herself from walking over and pushing the men aside to see the miscreant who had tried to harm her.

Someone pulled the man to his feet, but she still couldn't see his face. Ciaran asked the archer a question, and when the man didn't answer, she watched in awe as her husband punched the arse forcefully in the gut. The man bent over briefly, but Alex's guard promptly pulled him upright. The archer could barely stand, with his legs bent and about to collapse. She gathered that the only reason the bastard remained standing was because two men held him up by his arms.

"Ye will answer me!" bellowed Alexander.

The archer must have spit in Alex's face because the men gasped as Alex wiped his face with his arm. Ciaran balled his fist into the man's face, and Sybella cringed as she heard something crunch beneath the forceful blow. No doubt the MacGregor had broken the man's nose or face. Frankly, she wasn't sure which. Perhaps both.

"Who sent ye?" asked Alex in a raised voice.

Perhaps she could get a better look from the other side. She tried to circle along the wall unnoticed. The way Alex and Ciaran's men surrounded the man, she didn't think anyone would pay much attention to a lady—well, at least she hoped not. She could just make out the top of the man's head while she approached the other side of the bailey.

One of the guards shifted, and she managed to get a view of a black, yellow, and red tartan, the clan colors of the MacLeod of Lewis. Praise the saints. Rosalia was right. Sybella was nothing more than a pawn in the game of men. She knew her father had disputes with the MacLeod of Lewis, and now the MacLeod was coming after her for her father's ways.

"Throw his arse in the dungeon," Alex ordered his men. "We will find a way to make him talk. *An diobhail toirt leis thu.*" *The devil take you.* Alex turned to the captain of his guard, and something unspoken passed between them.

When John grabbed the man's arm, Sybella was finally able to get a clear view of the man who had attempted to kill her.

As she took a step forward, her eyes widened and her jaw dropped.

༄

Alex rubbed his knuckles, which stung and bled. In truth, the blood was of little consequence; of far more importance was whatever he would be able to gain from this savage MacLeod. Alex was sure there was valuable information to be had, if only the man would talk. The archer had made a grave error in judgment by keeping his mouth shut. John could be very persuasive, for Donald had taught him well.

"Let him rot in the dungeon. He will eventually speak the truth. And if he doesnae, there are ways in which he can be persuaded," said MacGregor. He looked over Alex's shoulder and his eyes narrowed. "Wash the blood from your hands. Your wife watches ye."

Alex turned to see that Sybella's face was paler than normal. Damn. He didn't mean for her to see him beating the man. However, she should understand that he would do anything to keep her safe. He wiped his hands on a rag and then walked toward her. She remained perfectly still.

"Ye were supposed to be abed."

Sybella paused. "Aye, but I wanted to see the man who tried to kill me."

"He is a MacLeod, but he will nae speak. 'Tis only a matter of time before he does. Once he confirms his orders, I will deal with the MacLeod."

"Ye are keeping the man in the dungeon, but ye donna keep him guarded below?" she asked as John and his men returned to the bailey.

"He cannae escape. When my father built the Rock of the Raven, he made certain there was nay means of escape for any prisoner. Ye are safe, Ella."

"I am relieved to hear it."

Alex noticed the tremor in her voice. "Come

inside. Ye have had enough excitement for one day."
He placed his arm around her shoulder and guided her
into the great hall.

MacGregor was already there, speaking with Rosalia
and Aunt Iseabail. Upon Alex and Sybella's approach,
Rosalia walked over to Sybella and embraced her.
"Ye must be so relieved that the man was caught. At
least ye nay longer have to fear," said Rosalia, giving
Sybella a compassionate smile.

"Aye. And I must thank ye, Laird MacGregor, for
all ye have done to assist my husband."

MacGregor nodded. "Ciaran. And there is nay need
for thanks. Your husband did the same for Rosalia."
MacGregor wrapped his arm around his wife and
kissed her on the cheek.

"That's what kin are for," said Rosalia.

Sybella smiled, but she looked tired, worn. "If ye
will pray excuse me, I think I need to rest."

"I will walk ye to your chamber," Alex said.

"Nay, I will be fine. Truly."

"All right, but I will be in to check on ye later, Ella."

Alex watched Sybella take her leave and knew from
her wobbly stance that her body was still sore from
where he had thrown her into the wall. At least she
was not permanently injured and no longer had to fear
for her life. She would be well enough in a few days.

"Alexander, ye caught the man responsible for
trying to harm your wife. Your father would be proud.
I am somewhat surprised it was the MacLeod's doing.
We've always had trouble with the MacKenzies, and
now it seems that we have a new enemy among us,"
said Aunt Iseabail.

"Some of my men traveled to Lewis to support the MacKenzie's efforts. The MacLeod will be dealt with."

"I should hope so after he tried to harm your wife."

"Pray excuse me," Alex said to her.

He needed to clear his head. He walked to his chamber and poured some water into the bowl. He washed his hands and then bent over and splashed water over his face. As he reached for the drying cloth, he sighed. Something had unsettled him, and he could not quite place his finger on it. It would come to him eventually. Thoughts like this always did.

He tossed the cloth on the bedside table and approached the adjoining door. He lightly tapped on the door and opened it quietly in case his wife slept.

"I'm awake, Alex."

He walked through the door and closed it behind him. Sitting on the edge of the bed, he gave Sybella a smile. "How do ye fare?"

"My body aches, but I'm sure I will be fine."

"Would ye like me to order a bath for ye? The water may help to soothe the soreness ye feel."

She reached out and touched his arm. "Nay, but if ye donna mind, I shall sup in my chamber this eve and seek my bed early."

He smoothed her hair. "I donna mind. 'Tis probably best for ye. Is there anything else I can do for ye?"

"Nay, I only wish to rest."

"Then I will leave ye be." Alex stood and kissed Sybella on the top of the head. "Ye can sleep well this eve, knowing ye are safe. Donna hesitate to call upon me if ye need anything—anything at all."

"Thank ye. I will."

Alex walked out into the hall and closed the door. Sybella would rest, and she would feel better with each passing day. As soon as he spotted the arrow, his first thought had been of his wife. At that moment, he realized that Sybella meant more to him than he had been admitting, even to himself. He'd known from the beginning that there was something special about the lass.

He briefly wondered how John fared with the MacLeod's whelp in the dungeon and knew there was only one way to find out.

Sybella waited until the darkened hours of the night. She threw on her black cloak and walked out into the hall, softly closing the door behind her. With the main torches extinguished, she could easily keep to the shadows and find her way to the dungeon. The guards would be watching the wall, not concerned with anyone inside the castle. At least, that was her hope.

Fortunately, Alex had left her alone and she had gotten just enough rest to see to the task at hand. Even though her ribs still pained her, nothing would keep her from her purpose. Once she had seen the man in the bailey, her thoughts became more puzzled by the moment. She needed answers. She needed to know why.

She had taken a step forward when she spotted a guard who sat against the wall. Damn. She quickly backed up. When the man let out a snort, she realized he slept. Surely she could sneak by him unnoticed. She proceeded cautiously toward him but had to walk quickly to not be spotted by other men who might be wandering about. She cast the man a hastened glance, and even in the shadows of the night, she thought the man looked like Ian.

If Alex found out that Ian had neglected his duties yet again, he would…She wasn't exactly sure what he'd do, but she knew that Ian's fate would not be pleasant. Yet she silently thanked the guard who slumbered because his lack of attention definitely worked in her favor.

Sybella descended the stairs to the dungeon. Her heart was beating fast, and she had to stop briefly to rest against the darkened wall. She took a deep breath, realizing that she had made it this far. It was too late to turn back now.

When she reached the last step to the dungeon, she stopped. There was an eerie chill that hung in the air, sending a shiver down her spine. She lit the candle she had confiscated from her bedchamber and illuminated the unsavory pit of hell. Some kind of unidentifiable muck lay upon the ground. Sybella held the candle in one hand and hefted her cloak with the other. There was no time to study where her feet placed her. Frankly, she didn't want to know. Her senses were overwhelmed with the smell of sweat, blood, and only the gods knew what else.

Heavy stone walls and iron bars lined what she could only refer to as a center path. She inched her way to the first door and held the candle between the bars. She waited a moment until the flickering light stilled. She felt somewhat relieved that the cramped quarters were empty.

As Sybella made her way to the second door, she gasped when some kind of vermin ran over her boot. Her entire body stiffened in shock, and it was virtually impossible to steady her erratic pulse. She had no trouble hunting animals, but for some reason, rats unnerved her. There was no time to be fainthearted. With an unsteady hand, she again lifted the candle between the bars, this time to see shackles lining the wall. She couldn't help but cringe. When she heard a moan, she quickly walked to the next door and raised the candle.

She jumped.

White eyes stared back at her from a blood-smeared face. The archer sat shackled to the wall, and blood also covered most of his kilt. The putrid stench from within the chamber smelled of unwashed bodies, urine, and decay.

Sybella stood momentarily speechless and resisted the urge to gag.

"Who are ye?" she whispered through the bars. The man merely smiled and displayed empty spaces where his teeth should have been. No doubt Alex's guard had removed them.

"Why have ye come here, Lady Sybella? This is nay place for a lady."

She gasped. "Ye're my father's man. I thought I recognized ye in the bailey."

The man spit and blood splattered from his mouth. "Aye. Better run along, lass. Off with ye now."

"Why are ye here? Why are ye dressed in the MacLeod tartan?"

"'Tisnae your concern, my lady. Ye best seek your bed before your husband finds ye missing."

"But ye wear the MacLeod tartan. Ye donna understand. My husband will *kill* ye. Tell him ye are a MacKenzie and spare your life."

"That isnae part of the scheme, my lady."

Sybella's jaw dropped. "Part of the scheme? What scheme? I demand answers, and ye will give them. *Now*."

The man laughed. "Och, lass, MacKenzie blood still flows hot through your veins."

"I'm waiting."

"Look around, lass. I donna think I'm going anywhere soon."

"Ye will speak to me before the guard comes. Tell me what this is about. I will nae ask again."

He paused. "The MacKenzie wants his stone back."

"What are ye talking about?" she asked with exasperation.

"I shot the arrow in the woods to force the MacDonell to keep ye inside the castle walls so that ye could hunt for the stone." He shifted, wincing at the painful movement. "Your father was giving ye ample opportunity to search for the stone. I assume ye havenae had any luck."

"*Ye* shot the arrow? Ye barely missed my head." She wasn't about to tell the man she hadn't begun to search for the damn rock.

He chuckled in response. "I am a good shot, my lady. Besides, I had to make it appear real enough that the MacDonell would try to protect ye. I succeeded, did I nae?"

"Ye could have killed me."

"But I didnae."

"I still donna understand. Why are ye wearing the MacLeod tartan?"

"Your father is a verra cunning man. Your husband would ne'er suspect the MacKenzie now that he has wed ye. The daft fool even sent a score of his men to Lewis to keep the MacLeod under control. The MacLeod tartan colors suit our purpose, solving two problems with one solution, so to speak."

Sybella seethed with mounting rage—mainly at herself for being such a fool. And with the MacKenzie man's declaration, she found herself clenching her teeth. She knew that when she was crossed, her temper could be almost uncontrollable. God help her. Her chest was going to burst. The MacKenzies may want the stone, but they also had another goal: to destroy Alex. They wanted him to purposefully destroy the MacLeod. Her marriage was a mockery, only a pretense to do her father's bidding. And having the truth confirmed before her very eyes…This was not what Sybella had agreed to.

She felt as if her breath was cut off. Her own father. Colin was right. The man would do anything to get back this stone. Had she been blind all of these years? She'd believed her father was a true and just man. She shuddered when she thought of what her poor mother might have thought of this situation. The woman would be so ashamed. For the first time in her life, Sybella was thankful for her mother's passing because this whole scheme would surely have broken her heart.

Although Sybella did not currently hold Alex in a favorable light, she could not stay the feelings that he stirred within her. Whether she wanted to admit it or not, her husband was right. He didn't trust the MacKenzies, and in truth, her clan was no better than the bloody Campbell that Alex had talked about.

She was furious and her nostrils flared with anger. But she had come here with an intention, and she would get all of the answers she sought. A pulsing knot within her demanded more.

"Ye said that ye shot at me in the woods so that the MacDonell would keep me within the walls of the castle. He did. I donna understand why ye would take another shot at me upon the parapet."

"Your father was making it easier for ye to find the stone. And I didnae say I was aiming for ye upon the parapet, my lady."

Fourteen

Before Alex broke his fast, he sought the captain of his guard in the bailey. The words John spoke were not exactly what Alex had expected to hear first thing in the morn. When his eyes widened, John confirmed what Alex already knew.

"He is dead," repeated John. He leaned back casually against the wall. "Ian found him this morn."

"Did he say anything about the MacLeod or anything at all?"

"Nay."

"'Tis of little consequence. Break your fast and then gather some men. We travel to Kintail. When I tell the MacKenzie of the threat upon his daughter, I will use our alliance as a means to take the MacLeod's head. The MacLeods of Lewis will nay longer be a problem to the MacDonells or the MacKenzies. And King James will be pleased that there will nay longer be constant turmoil on Lewis."

John turned and walked away as MacGregor approached Alex. "Any word?"

Alex shook his head. "The man is dead."

"Verra unfortunate."

"I didnae need for the archer to speak to know his orders were given by the MacLeod. Even though the MacLeod wars with the MacKenzies and I donna agree with the way the MacKenzies killed innocents, the MacLeod made a grave error in judgment by aiming to kill *my* wife. Sybella is a MacDonell, and I protect my own. We ride to Kintail to speak with the MacKenzie. One way or another, I will have the MacLeod's head."

"I will ride along with ye. I donna necessarily want to leave Rosalia and Lachlann to travel to Lewis, but I will support ye in any way I can," said MacGregor.

"Ye have my thanks. Let's break our fast and then I'd like to leave with much haste."

Sybella was already seated at the table when Alex walked into the great hall. He took his seat beside her and noticed that she played with her food. She sat with a worried expression on her face, and he sensed that she was disquieted from last eve.

"How do ye fare this morn?"

"I am a wee bit sore but nae nearly as bad as yester eve." She kept her eyes down on her trencher.

"MacGregor and I travel to Kintail after we break our fast. My cousin will be able to assist ye if ye need anything."

Her eyes widened and her expression darkened with an unreadable expression. "*Kintail?* Why?"

"There are matters I need to discuss with your father." He took a drink from his tankard and could feel Sybella's stare drilling into him. When he turned his head, she continued to keep him under silent scrutiny.

She leaned in toward him and lowered her voice. "Ye cannae travel to Kintail."

"What do ye mean, I cannae travel to Kintail? Why? Will ye miss me, Ella? I know it has been a while since I joined ye in your bed." He scanned her critically and beamed approval.

Biting her lip, she looked away. "Please, Alex. I donna…feel safe with that man in the dungeon. Ye leave me alone and unprotected."

"Ye nay longer need to worry about him, lass."

A shadow of alarm touched her face. "What do ye mean?"

"He's dead." She flinched and seemed to have trouble looking at him. "Listen to me. There is naught more to fear. I will try to return this eve, but I must ride to Kintail and speak with your father about the MacLeod."

She paled.

ॐ

Alex continued to speak, but Sybella only half listened as she struggled with her conscience. She stirred uneasily in the chair, and the nagging feeling in the back of her mind refused to be stilled. She would have to guard her own actions as well as his. One wrong move and her father might make another attempt on her husband's life. She had no choice. There was no time to falter. She needed to decide quickly where her loyalties lay.

As she sat at the table, her nervousness slipped back to grip her. She tried desperately to force her emotions in order. No matter what her husband's feelings or her own were toward the MacKenzies at the moment, she and Alex were as one—husband and wife. She only knew one thing for certain: she was determined to make her mother proud. And deep down Sybella couldn't live with herself if she knew her mother wouldn't approve of her actions.

Nervously, Sybella moistened her dry lips. "Alex, when ye see Colin, would ye be so kind as to deliver a message for me?"

"Of course." He placed his elbow on the table and leaned in close. "And what message might that be?"

Uncertainty made her voice harsh and demanding. "Could ye tell my brother that I will do as he asks?" She paused. "He asked me to make something for Anabel."

"Aye. Is everything all right? Ye seem...troubled."

"Nay worries, Husband." Giving him a slow, secret smile, she understood exactly what she had to do.

Sybella, Rosalia, and Aunt Iseabail walked the men to the bailey. Sybella watched in awe as Ciaran lifted his hand and caressed his wife's cheek. He lowered his head and his lips pressed against Rosalia's, tender and passionate. It was somewhat hard to believe that this was the same man who supposedly killed the Campbell laird. She mentally corrected herself: the bloody Campbell.

Ciaran pulled away and tucked a piece of hair behind Rosalia's ear. "*Tha gaol agam ort.*" *I love you.* He ruffled Lachlann's hair. "I will return with much haste. And ye, my little lad, will see to your mother." When he stepped away, he winked broadly at Rosalia.

"Ella."

Sybella's private musings were quickly interrupted. She surprised herself when she turned and embraced Alex without any hesitation. "Please be careful, Husband. And donna forget to tell Colin what I told ye."

Alex's strong arms continued to hold her, and she briefly closed her eyes. She was hesitant to admit it, but his touch felt wonderful. Sybella breathed in his spicy scent and sighed. She couldn't understand how she could feel comforted by the very man her kin wanted to destroy. This was the same man who had been a sworn enemy of the MacKenzies for so long. And from what she had seen, there was no justification whatsoever for that stance. Alex portrayed nothing but kindness and compassion, whereas her own kin…She was disgusted at the thought.

Her family had woven so many words into their verbal web that Sybella wasn't sure what was right or wrong anymore. She could only trust the one person she had always depended upon—herself.

Sybella pulled away, and for a long moment, she simply looked back at her husband. She suddenly felt like the breathless girl at the waterfall. Her eyes portrayed what she already knew she felt in her heart. Praise the saints. She was falling in love with him. She wasn't sure when it had happened, but the admission was dredged from a place beyond logic and reason. And the worst part was that she gave the man no reason to trust her. His own wife.

She had to try to make amends.

Alex wrapped his arms around Sybella's waist. "I should return by this eve. I will try to make haste."

His voice lowered and his mouth curved into an unconscious smile. "And I will deliver your message to your brother." He paused longer than necessary, and she wasn't sure if he wanted her to say something. He looked around uncomfortably, and then his eyes met hers. "I will miss ye, Ella."

Before she could respond, she watched his broad back turn and he swung up onto his mount.

"Aunt Iseabail, I leave it to ye to make sure my cousin and my wife donna get into mischief."

Aunt Iseabail waved Alex off. "Those two are the least of your worries. Ye should be worried about what trouble I get them into, Nephew."

He again met Sybella's gaze, and a deep, unaccustomed pain formed in her breast. "*Dia leat,*" she said under her breath. *God be with you.*

She had to find that bloody stone.

Sybella quickly made her excuses to Rosalia and Aunt Iseabail. She opened the door to Alex's chamber, thinking her husband's room might be a good place to start. When a pang of guilt washed over her, she immediately pushed the feeling aside. In order to have a future, she reminded herself that she needed to correct the past.

She walked over to the stone fireplace and lifted the portrait of Alexander's father. A chill shot down her spine when she touched the painting. If a bolt of lightning had struck her where she stood, she wouldn't have been surprised. She rubbed her fingers along the rough stone wall where everything felt solid, secure. Nothing shook in its place.

She approached the giant bed with its tall corner

posts and ran her fingers over the blankets. Every time she had been close with Alex had been in her own bed, and she wondered what it would be like to sleep—or not sleep—in his. He was a powerful laird. She couldn't help but remember him as he touched her, satisfied her. She hungered from the memory of his mouth on hers. In spite of the task at hand, thoughts of him intruded.

She shook her head, hurtled back to earth as reality struck.

"Find the stone, Sybella," she said out loud. She lowered herself to the floor and felt for an indentation or anything that moved under the bed. "Find the stone and put an end to this madness once and for all."

She stood and brushed off her skirts. "Of course this couldnae be an easy task," she said, tapping her finger to her lip. "Where would ye keep something like that, Husband?"

Sybella looked around the room but nothing stood out at her. She moved the table by the bed and even looked underneath. She opened Alex's trunk and searched through his clothing. Absolutely nothing. If he wouldn't keep the stone in his chamber, where would he keep it?

She remembered Colin's words.

The library.

Placing her ear to the bedchamber door, she first listened for anyone who might be in the hall. She stepped out and closed the door. With hastened steps, Sybella made her way to the library. Colin was probably right. A hollowed-out book was a great place to hide the stone.

She made it to the library undetected and quickly closed the door. The last thing she wanted to be was disturbed. She approached the first shelf and picked up a book, fingering through the pages. It was just a book. She pulled out the next one and unfortunately had the same result. By the time Sybella had searched through some of the larger tomes, she realized she should have given up some time ago. The stone was obviously not in the library.

Something clicked in her mind.

Surely Alex wouldn't hide the stone in the dungeon. The last place she wanted to be was there. She kept that revelation stored in the back of her mind. If she had no choice, she would be forced to check there—as a last resort, with all options exhausted. She cringed at the idea of returning to that unsavory pit of hell.

Sybella rubbed her brow. There was a lot of space to cover in this castle, and worse yet, she searched by herself. What if she couldn't find the stone? She refused to think about that and hastily made her way to Alex's study, his private domain.

With its masculine touches, the room reminded her of him. The MacDonell crest hung on the wall behind a large wooden desk, and a shield with matching swords hung on the opposite wall. When she spotted another shelf lined with books, she held hope that maybe her luck hadn't run out yet.

She picked up the first book and flipped through the pages. She was so frustrated that she wanted to scream. All of the books were simply that. Books. She ran her fingers behind the MacDonell crest and didn't feel anything out of the ordinary. At this rate, her search was going to take forever. She walked to the opposite wall and ran her hand behind the shield and swords, hastily pulling back her finger when a sharp blade cut her.

Damn! Sybella sat down in the chair behind the desk and looked for something to wrap her finger. Why were the smallest cuts always the worst? She placed her finger to her lips and rifled through Alex's desk. What was this? She pulled out a flask and sniffed the contents. Her suspicion was correct. She briefly wondered if this was the infamous MacGregor ale that her husband had spoken about. There was only one way to find out.

She brought the liquid to her lips and let the fiery concoction burn its way down her throat. Plagued with a coughing fit, she replaced the ale in the drawer. Let the men have their drink. Her stomach could barely tolerate it. She pressed both hands over her eyes as if they stung with weariness. Praise the saints. What if she had overlooked something where she'd already searched? Her task was quickly turning into a nightmare.

Leaving Alexander's study the way she had found it, Sybella walked out into the hall. Time was most definitely not on her side. It was almost time to sup, which meant Rosalia and Aunt Iseabail would be in the great hall. Sybella suddenly found the perfect opportunity to act like a thief in the night.

Sybella reached Rosalia's room and knocked on the door. When no one answered, she ducked inside. Seeing Lachlann's little tunics made Sybella cringe.

What kind of person had she become to resort to this? She was not this type of woman, and guilt slowly crept back to plague her.

If she didn't find the stone, Alexander would not be safe. Once she delivered the stone to her father, the man would have no choice but to call off his minions. She still found it hard to fathom that her sire had tried to kill her husband because she had yet to deliver the stone. With a steely resolve, she realized there was no question. She had to do this. Failure was not an option.

Following the same ritual as in Alex's chamber, Sybella searched under the bed, checking for any-thing that moved or was out of place. She moved the table, checked behind the tapestry, examined the stone fireplace. Not a damn thing. With frustration mounting, Sybella opened the door and stepped out into the hall.

She jumped.

"What are ye doing in my chambers, Lady MacDonell?"

❧

"It seems nae long ago when I rode by your side to free my cousin," said Alex.

MacGregor rode up beside him. "I was thinking the same. Why do ye think these cowardly men target our women, MacDonell? The bastards have nay honor and donna fight like men. They hide behind the skirts of a lass and use our women as pawns."

"Things arenae as they once were. I wonder if His Majesty will eventually send his men into the

Highlands. The MacKenzie seems to think that if the MacLeods arenae brought to heel, the king's guard will travel to Lewis. I donna understand how there can be peace when clans such as the MacLeods of Lewis and the bloody Campbells are about."

"We are Highlanders. We administer justice the way we see fit. That is the way of it. And the MacLeod will be judged verra soon. The king cannae see fault with that."

"I hope ye're right. I grow tired of men who would do anything only for the purpose of political gain."

MacGregor chuckled. "I donna think that will ever change. 'Tis verra much the way of it."

As Alex rode to Kintail, his mind kept turning to Sybella. The woman was everything he'd desired in a wife, except the MacKenzie part, of course. She was kind, especially to Aunt Iseabail. And the lass was definitely not afraid to put him in his place. He found her honesty refreshing. Even when the MacLeod's man had tried to harm her again, the woman hadn't cowered in the corner in tears.

He was also particularly thankful that Sybella no longer counted sheep beneath him. In truth, he'd rather enjoyed their last couple of encounters. Who would've thought? He knew he had started to favor the lass, and perhaps his bonny wife was actually softening toward him as well.

John reined in his mount beside Alex. "The last time we dealt with the MacKenzie, ye shackled yourself with a wife. I cannae help but wonder what ye will bring home with ye this time, my laird."

Alex glowered at his friend. "I like ye better when

ye donna speak. I think ye forget your place. Mayhap I need to remind ye."

John laughed. "Aye, I would love to see ye join us in our swordplay. Howbeit it seems ye have been practicing your swordplay more with your bonny wife than your own men."

"Aunt Iseabail expects an heir."

"Aye, but ye donna fool me for one minute, Alex. I see the way ye look at the lass as of late."

"I looked at Doireann that way, too."

"My apologies. What did ye say? I couldnae hear through your complete load of hogwash."

Their conversation was quickly cut off as five MacKenzie men thundered toward them. When the men stopped, Alex recognized his wife's brother.

"MacDonell, what are ye doing here?" asked Colin.

"I come to speak with your father."

Colin nodded. "Then come. I will escort ye and your men."

As the MacKenzie men escorted them to Kintail, Alex looked at the sight before him. With MacKenzies and MacDonells riding side by side, he realized that not long ago, swords would've been drawn and fights would've ensued. MacKenzie and MacDonell tartans would have been ripped to shreds, the men with even bigger scars of their own.

When they reached the castle, Alex dismounted and handed his mount to the stable hand. With MacGregor and John by his side, Alex followed the MacKenzie's son into the great hall. The space was somewhat larger than what he had expected. And although he was hesitant to admit it, the room was more extravagant than Glengarry. Fine woven tapestries, as well as painted portraits of past MacKenzie lairds, hung on the walls. A large stone fireplace took up the center wall, and the MacKenzie clan crest was imbedded in the middle. Alex slowed his pace and read the words carved from stone.

Luceo non uro. I shine, not burn.

If MacGregor was surprised by the MacKenzie's apparent wealth, he didn't say so, not that Alex thought he would. They continued into the MacKenzie's study where the man looked up from behind his desk in surprise. The room was filled with dark furnishings, and two bookcases lined the stone walls. Two broadswords were mounted above one bookcase and a shield on the opposite side. When the MacKenzie turned his head and looked at MacGregor with further uncertainty, Alex spoke.

"Laird Ciaran MacGregor of Glenorchy, my cousin's husband."

The MacKenzie gestured the men to the chairs as Colin stood again by his father's side. "Please sit. Ye are a long way from Glenorchy, are ye nae?"

"My wife visits with her *seanmhair*."

"Ye are also the one who killed the hand of the king."

MacGregor's eyes darkened. "It was naught that wasnae deserved."

The MacKenzie quickly turned his attention to Alex. "Laird MacDonell. And how fares my bonny daughter?"

"Sybella is the reason for my visit."

The MacKenzie turned around and pulled ale from the shelf. "Can I offer ye and MacGregor a drink?"

"Nay, we will return to Glengarry."

"Verra well." The MacKenzie sat back casually in his chair. "I know my daughter is willful and rarely minds her tongue, but if ye give her time to adjust—"

"The MacLeod tried to kill her. Twice," Alex blurted out.

The MacKenzie sat forward and folded his fingers on his desk. "What do ye mean?"

Alex continued. "The first time was when we walked in the forest. An archer took aim at her head and barely missed. I had my most experienced tracker search the trail, and it was if the man had simply disappeared. The man was good and left nay trace. I confined Sybella within the walls of the castle and there were nay other attempts."

"But ye said there were two attempts," said the MacKenzie.

"Sybella and I stood upon the parapet, and the archer—"

"God's teeth!" The MacKenzie pounded his fists on the desk. "What are ye doing to protect my daughter? I placed her in your ca—"

Alex interrupted the MacKenzie's words vehemently. "We found the man."

The MacKenzie's face clouded with uneasiness. "Ye did?"

"Aye. He wore the MacLeod tartan but wouldnae speak."

"Where is he? Ye let me speak to him."

"He is dead," Alex simply said. "I donna know all of what went on between ye and the MacLeod of Lewis, but now the man has attempted to kill my wife. I demand justice."

"What do ye propose?" asked the MacKenzie.

"I will travel to Lewis with some of my men. I will either bring the MacLeod before King James to pay for his crimes or dispense my own Highland justice— sword against sword, man against man. I havenae yet decided. One way or the other, I will have the man's head."

The MacKenzie nodded. "Give me three days to arrange your passage to Lewis. I will have a few of my own men at your disposal as well. After all, the man attempted to kill my own daughter. We shall place his head on a pike together."

Alex stood. "I will return within three days."

MacGregor and John stood, following Alex to the door. Damn. Alex had almost forgotten and turned in midstride.

"Colin."

Sybella's brother looked at Alex in surprise.

"My wife wanted me to tell ye that she will do as ye ask." For an instant, Colin's gaze sharpened. Alex added, "Ye asked her to make something for Anabel."

"Aye. Thank ye for letting me know."

❧

As soon as the door closed, Colin attempted to speak but his father held up his hand to silence him. The MacKenzie stood from the chair and disappeared into the hall for a moment. When he walked back into the study, he closed the door behind him.

He chuckled with a dry and cynical sound. "Och, the MacDonell is naught but a daft fool."

"What do ye mean?"

"The MacLeod archer was my own man, Fearghas MacKenzie. 'Tis a shame I lost a good man, but he accomplished what he set out to do, unlike ye. By the time the MacDonell figures out what is afoot, it will be too late."

Colin started to pace and ran his fingers through his hair. "Father, what the hell are ye talking about?"

"Fearghas took the first shot at Sybella in the woods. And just as I figured he would, MacDonell confined her within the walls of Glengarry. Had ye done as ye were told, your sister would have already found the stone and it would already be back where it belongs."

Colin was breathless with rage. "Ye had a MacKenzie take aim at Sybella? Ye could have *killed* her! What if he had missed? 'Tis one thing to use your daughter to hunt for the stone and entirely another to take aim at the lass's head! When I talked with her and she told me about the archer, I didnae realize the man was our own kin! Ye didnae even give her time. She would have found the stone."

"Colin, spare me your excuses. Ye do your tasks at one pace, always have. By the time my stone is returned, I will be an old man. I told ye I need that stone before the king's men travel to Lewis."

"I donna understand. The MacDonell said two shots were made. If the MacDonell kept her within the walls, why would ye have Fearghas take another shot?"

His father's response held a response of impatience. "Fearghas obviously missed. The second shot was meant for the MacDonell."

"When the bloody hell did ye decide to kill the MacDonell?"

His father shook his head and waved Colin off. "It doesnae matter now. Sybella searches for the stone. Things couldnae have worked out more perfectly, if I say so myself. Now I just have to simply sit back and donna have to do a damn thing. The MacDonell will take care of our problem on Lewis by killing that blasted MacLeod, and King James will nay longer bother us. 'Tis only a matter of time before we MacKenzies rule Lewis."

Fifteen

Sybella fumbled for a plausible explanation and her voice broke miserably. "Rosalia...I was searching for ye. I thought mayhap ye were trying to put Lachlann to sleep so I opened the door."

"My *seanmhair* watches him, and I came to see if ye were going to join us or if ye wanted me to bring ye a tray."

"I will join ye and Aunt Iseabail to sup. The walls of my bedchamber have started to close in upon me." Sybella led Rosalia away from the door, trying desperately to mask the guilty expression on her face. She said a silent prayer of thanks when Rosalia followed her and appeared to believe the words that had hastily escaped her lips. No matter, Sybella recognized that she needed to be much more cautious.

When they entered the great hall, they saw Aunt Iseabail sitting at the table and holding Lachlann on her lap. With a bright smile upon her face, she bounced him gently on her knee. As Rosalia and Sybella approached the dais, Aunt Iseabail looked up.

"My great-grandson is quite a delightful lad."

Rosalia giggled. "Give him but a few minutes, *Seanmhair,* and he will be back to his ways. Just like his father."

"Be that as it may, until then, I shall enjoy him."

Rosalia pulled out her chair and sat down beside Aunt Iseabail. "Would ye like me to take him now? I know he can become quite heavy after a while."

Aunt Iseabail kissed Lachlann on the head. "Nay, I am having a wonderful time with him. He loves his *seanmhair.*"

Sybella sat down at the table and smiled. "Of course he does. He is a wise lad." She reached for a piece of bread and took a bite. All of this searching did wonders for her appetite.

"How do ye fare, my dear?" asked Aunt Iseabail.

Sybella nodded, wiping the crumbs from her chin. "I am much better, thank ye. I am surprised Alexander and Ciaran havenae returned yet. Do ye think it will be soon?"

"I wouldnae expect them until later this eve. They did ride the entire way to Kintail, ye know. And leave it to the men. Once they start talking amongst themselves, time passes and they pay it nay heed. Unless, of course, it's time for the midday meal or time to sup."

Sybella and Rosalia couldn't help themselves as they burst out laughing. This was definitely one of Aunt Iseabail's clearer days. The woman was pure delight. In truth, Sybella hated to see Aunt Iseabail's mind falter. And not only because of how Aunt Iseabail's decline affected Alexander. Naturally Sybella felt sympathy for her husband, but Aunt Iseabail was the type of woman that simply grew on a person. Sybella truly cared for her.

Aunt Iseabail waved her finger. "Ye laugh, but ye best remember that ye two havenae been wed all that long. I've had years to discover the ways of men."

Rosalia leaned in toward Aunt Iseabail and gave the woman a conspiratorial wink. "It doesnae take that long to figure out our men. I think Sybella and I already understand what ye mentioned, though. Food is definitely the way to a man's heart."

Without missing a beat, Aunt Iseabail responded. "Well, that or tupping."

Rosalia brought up her hand to stifle her giggles while Sybella was half laughing, half crying from Aunt Iseabail's blunt declaration. The woman was obviously in rare form this eve.

"What are ye two laughing at? I may be old, but I am nae dead."

Sybella sat back, watching the jesting between Rosalia and her grandmother. She couldn't help it when her mind drifted back to the many conversations with her own mother. Sybella realized she'd been far too long without female companionship—even crazy Mary. In truth, Sybella simply enjoyed hearing laughter, any laughter. Something she'd sorely missed as of late. Everything around her had quickly become far too serious.

When a thought of Colin popped into her mind, Sybella hoped her husband had remembered to deliver the message. Hopefully, she'd bought herself more time before her father decided to do something rash—again. Praise the saints. Her nerves were on edge. She wasn't masterful in the ways of deception and didn't like it at all. She'd almost been caught rummaging through Rosalia and Ciaran's bedchamber.

When the meal was finished, Rosalia placed a sleeping Lachlann in bed while Sybella retired with Aunt Iseabail to the ladies' solar—another place Sybella had yet to search. Perhaps she could find an opportunity to discreetly hunt for the stone.

The room was similar to the one at Kintail, with dainty pictures of the fairer sex wearing delicate gowns. At least the conversation was better than the same boring subjects at Kintail. When Sybella thought of the many times that Mary had reprimanded her for her stitching, a shudder passed through her. Surprisingly, life at Glengarry was becoming more like home.

Rosalia returned with a wine sack. "Finally, Lachlann is asleep. I brought us something to relax."

"What is that?" asked Aunt Iseabail.

"My husband's ale."

Aunt Iseabail held her hand over her heart. "My dear, are ye trying to kill me? That ale will knock me out for days."

"Come now, *Seanmhair,* a drink will nae hurt ye. In fact, it might be exactly what ye need. 'Tisnae only a man's drink. Can ye grab some cups from the shelf, Sybella?"

Sybella grabbed three cups and placed them on the table. She sat down beside Rosalia, who poured a healthy amount of MacGregor's ale into each cup and handed one to each of them.

"Before we drink, let me make a toast," said Rosalia. "To kin."

"To kin," answered Aunt Iseabail and Sybella in unison.

Sybella took a mouthful, clamping her eyes shut as she swallowed. The liquid burned down her throat like the hottest of fires. When she opened her eyes, Rosalia had already poured the women another.

"'Tis your turn to make a toast, *Seanmhair*."

Aunt Iseabail lifted her cup. "To my bonny Lachlann, the dearest lad in all the land."

"Aww…Who couldnae drink to that?" asked Sybella. She took another mouthful and closed her eyes again as she swallowed. The liquid was warm as it traveled down her throat but not quite as bad as the first time—or in Alex's study.

Aunt Iseabail placed her cup back on the table. "That is it for me, Rosalia. I am off to bed."

"Ye cannae take your leave just yet. Sybella hasnae made a toast."

Aunt Iseabail sighed. "All right. One more, and then I go to bed."

Rosalia refilled the cups and then nodded to Sybella. At this rate, Sybella would not be able to search for the stone. She'd be surprised if she could make it to her bed on her own accord. Perhaps Aunt Iseabail had the right idea and Sybella should flee while she had the chance.

Lifting her cup, Sybella smiled. "To new beginnings."

"To new beginnings," Rosalia and Aunt Iseabail said in unison.

Aunt Iseabail stood. "I am walking to my chamber before I am unable."

"Do ye want me to walk ye?" asked Rosalia.

"Nay, enjoy your eve while ye wait for your men to return."

Aunt Iseabail bent and kissed Rosalia on the head. "I love ye, my sweet lass."

"I love ye too, *Seanmhair*."

Aunt Iseabail walked over to Sybella and also kissed her on the head. "It warms my heart to see ye make my Alexander so happy, dear Sybella."

Sybella reached out and grabbed Aunt Iseabail's hand. "I am glad to be here, Aunt Iseabail." To be honest, Sybella meant what she said. The MacDonells were quickly becoming family. Home.

⁓

Alex was tired, but at least he'd received the answer he sought from the MacKenzie. The man had arranged passage for him to Lewis and agreed for Alex to bring back the MacLeod's head. A good day's work, if he did say so himself.

As they approached Glengarry, the sun started to set below the horizon, casting Alex's home in an orange glow. The castle looked warm, welcoming. He thought of Sybella and wondered if she would be the same. He was particularly fond of how the sunlight reflected on her golden locks, and he could not easily forget her skin of rose and pearl. Not being able to stay his thoughts, Alex shifted in the saddle. His wife was a rare beauty. And frankly, he missed her.

The men rode into the bailey, and Alex hoped that Cook had kept them something for sup, or he and his men would surely be raiding the pantry. The stable hand took their mounts, and Alex entered the great hall with MacGregor and John. They were starting to make their way toward the kitchens when the clanking sounds of metal against metal rang throughout the hall. Without hesitation, the men unsheathed their swords, running toward the sound of men in the heat of battle—under Alex's own roof no less.

They abruptly came to a halt.

What the hell?

The commotion came from…the ladies' solar. If Alex had not witnessed the sight before him with his own two eyes, he would never have believed it. His cousin and his bonny wife wielded their daggers while the men stood in the hall and merely gaped.

"I am the fierce Laird Ciaran MacGregor of Glenorchy. And I *will* be obeyed," slurred Rosalia, her voice deep.

"Give me but a moment while I fix my hair." Sybella held her dagger under her arm while she placed an unruly lock of hair behind her ear.

Rosalia laughed. "Aye, my cousin would say that."

The men lowered their weapons and sheathed their swords.

With his laugh barely contained, John said, "They are your problem. I go to eat." And with that, he waved Alex and MacGregor off, ambling to the kitchens.

MacGregor stepped in the door and folded his arms over his chest. "I donna sound like that, Wife."

Rosalia looked up and smiled, blowing her loose tresses from her lips. She stumbled over to MacGregor and placed her hand on his arm. "Ye are back." She turned to Alex and almost fell into him.

"Cousin, ye need to take care of your-r-r-r wife." Rosalia lowered her voice to a whisper. "She is in her cups."

MacGregor chuckled. "Sybella isnae the only one."

Rosalia looked offended. "I am nae drunk. Remember, Ciaran, I am used to your ale."

MacGregor looked at Alex and rolled his eyes. "Aye, I can see that. Come. I will take ye to bed."

She threw herself into MacGregor's chest and wrapped her arms around his neck. "I would *love* for ye to take me to bed, Ciaran." She stood on the tips of her toes and placed her lips to MacGregor's.

The man tapped Rosalia playfully on the bottom and then quickly scooped her into his arms. "Time for bed, Rosalia."

Before Rosalia had the chance to protest, MacGregor carried her down the hall, but not before Alex heard her say, "But we were having so much fun."

Alex stepped in the door and shook his head. Sybella stood before him with a look of pure innocence on her face. Her eyes were glassy and she swayed on her feet. She approached the table and put down her weapon.

"When I had the dagger made for ye, I didnae expect ye to be practicing swordplay with my cousin."

"Rosalia is in her cups. I was merely trying to keep her entertained."

"Aye." He walked over and pulled his wife into the circle of his arms.

"I missed ye, Alex. And I am so relieved to see my *beloved* father let ye return to me in one piece."

He detected censure in her tone, but her speech

could've been due to the ill effects of the ale. He rubbed his hands over her back, and she was so warm. Frankly, she felt damn good in his arms.

Sybella pulled back and brought her hand gently to his cheek. "My dearest Alexander, please tell me ye remembered to give Colin my message."

He kissed the palm of her hand. "Of course I did."

A look of relief passed over her face. "Why donna ye get something to eat? I want to remain here for a bit longer and then I will go to bed."

"That, Ella, isnae a good idea. Come, I will escort ye to your chamber." He placed his hand at the small of her back and gestured her forward. She took two steps and then turned around to face him.

"But there are things I must do—"

"And they will be here on the morrow. Off to bed with ye. Come." When she didn't move, Alex bent and lifted her into his arms. "I see ye are going to be difficult."

Sybella kicked her feet. "Alex, put me down. I am perfectly capable of walking on my own accord."

He chuckled as he walked out the door. "I donna think so, lass."

Alex carried his wife to her chamber, kicking open the door with his foot. He'd never heard her talk so much in his life. She'd chattered nonstop up the stairs, and he wasn't even sure of half the things she'd said. Gently placing her on her feet, he turned her around. He assisted her with her gown and helped her into bed.

"I donna want to go to bed. I am nae tired."

He rubbed his hand over her hair, smoothing her

tresses. "Ella, go to sleep." He bent over and kissed the top of her head.

"Why do ye nae share my bed to sleep? I donna mind."

Alex stood and ran his hand through his hair. "I donna know. I suppose I ne'er really thought about it."

"Do ye love me?"

"Ella, go to sleep. Ye know nae what ye speak. I go below stairs to sup." He pulled up the blankets to her chin and tucked her in. "Sleep well, Wife."

When she closed her eyes, Alex walked out and blew out the breath he'd held. He leaned up against the closed door and rested his head back. Sybella's question unnerved him. Did he love her? He obviously cared for her but *love*?

He needed a drink.

By the time Alex made his way to the kitchens, he was alone. John had already departed, and who knew what the hell MacGregor was doing. He quickly shook off that thought.

Cook had left Alex a tray on the table. He sat down and poured himself some mulled wine while Sybella's question continued to hammer at him. Why would she ask him that? Their marriage was certainly no love match, the wedding being arranged and all. Women should not ask questions they did not want to know the answer to. Love? Lust? Who was to say? He only knew one thing for certain: it was damn hard to remain coherent when she was close to him.

Alex finished his meal and sought his bed, needing to put an end to this day. He closed the door to his bedchamber and approached the adjoining door. Not wanting to wake Sybella, he placed his ear to the door. When nothing stirred from the other side, he took it as a good sign.

He undressed and walked to the bed in his naked form.

And then he jumped.

❧

"Dh' fhuirich mi riut." I waited for you.

Alex's eyes widened. "God's teeth, lass."

Sybella leaned up from the bed on her elbows. "Come now, Laird Alexander MacDonell. I thought ye were a fierce Highland laird."

"Aye, but I didnae expect someone to be lying in my bed in wait. *Tha e anmoch.*" It's late.

She held a private invitation in the depths of her eyes. "Then ye must forgive me." Praise the saints for the ale because she would've never had the courage to be so bold. She lifted the blankets, consciously exposing her bare body. "I will take my leave."

Alex jumped on the bed and grabbed Sybella's wrist. *"Chan fhaod."* No, you may not. When she raised her brow, he quickly added, "Stay. Please."

Sybella stared with longing at him, and he returned an appreciative glance. In truth, there was no place else she would rather be than in her husband's bed, crushed in his embrace. Her body ached for his touch and she was powerless to resist.

He eased her back down onto the bed, and she wrapped her arms around his neck. His eyes met hers and it was too easy to get lost in the way he looked at her.

"Tell me ye donna want me," she whispered.

His lips brushed against hers as he spoke. "I cannae. I told ye. There are nay lies between us."

The stubble of his beard burned her cheeks as his mouth came over hers. He forced her lips open with his thrusting tongue, shattering her calm with the hunger of his kiss. His hands pulled her closer, demanding a response. And she was more than willing to respond.

Her hands roamed brazenly and traced the muscles of his hard body. She tried desperately to mold their bodies as one. He cupped her with his hands, skimming his way down to her taut stomach and hips. He lowered his head and his mouth was delightfully warm as he sucked her nipple, sending a bolt of awareness through her.

She ran her fingers through his hair as his tongue whirled and nipped until the tips of her breasts formed hardened peaks. Heat flooded her body and her senses were drowning in pools of desire.

Her hand moved from around his waist. She didn't realize she had brushed the swollen tip of his erection until her instincts took over and she moved her fingers back to encircle him.

He was so hard.

"Careful, lass. Ye donna want this to be over before it has even begun."

She brushed her finger over his lips. "Alex…" She wasn't sure what she wanted to say, but the huskiness in her husband's voice made him so very male. Her thoughts spun.

God help her. She wanted him. *Now*.

She sank back deeper into the bed. He lowered his hand and entered her gently with his finger. She closed her eyes and tilted her head back with the pleasure that he gave her.

Before she knew what he was about, he'd drugged her with kisses down the entire length of her body. He moved and withdrew his finger, planting a kiss between her thighs. When she tried to push him away, he only widened her legs and continued to suck and lick her...there.

Sybella let out a cry of delight at the delicious sensations he brought her. She was going to come apart. And he sensed it.

He rose to his knees and entered her with a single thrust. Her nails bit into his arms and her hips rose to meet him, taking him deeper. She wanted it harder.

"Alex..."

"Come for me, Ella."

He lowered his hand and rubbed her most sensitive spot as he thrust in and out. Their bodies were in exquisite harmony with one another. Desire inched through her veins, rousing her to the peak of desire. She wanted to yield to the sweet burning sweetness that was captive within her.

The passion of his ardor mounted, and she finally abandoned herself to the whirl of sensations. Love flowed into her like warm, molten honey, shattering her into a million glowing stars.

But Alex wasn't done with her. He was unrelenting.

While she writhed in bittersweet agony, he forced her to a second release. Hard. Fast.

She hadn't even known that was possible.

Sybella lay drowned in a flood of liberation of mind and body. She was drawn to a height of passion she had never known before. Satisfaction pursed her mouth and she felt a bottomless peace. Tonight there were no shadows across her heart. This was where she knew she belonged. By her husband's side. In his bed. As his wife.

Alex placed his arm around her waist and nuzzled her neck. "Ye may sleep in my bed anytime ye wish."

She giggled in response. "May I ask something of ye?" She brushed the tiny hairs on his arm with her nails.

Alex stiffened. "Aye."

"I hope when ye share my bed that your only purpose isnae to get me with child." She didn't dare look at him because he paused. In fact, there was a heavy moment of silence and she thought at one point he may not even respond.

"'Tisnae the only reason I share your bed, Ella."

And that was all he said. Nothing more. Nothing less. The next thing she heard was a snort in her ear as her husband slept. She rolled onto her side and faced him. Placing her head to his chest, she breathed in the scent of him and sighed.

"Oh, Alex. *Tha gaol agam ort.*" *I love you.*

Sixteen

SYBELLA'S UNRULY LOCKS TICKLED ALEX'S NOSE. HE wiped them away and then opened his eyes. This was most definitely not a dream. His bonny temptress of a wife lay nestled into his chest. For a moment, he did not move and simply watched her. She looked peaceful, like an angel who'd spread her wings and embraced him, touching his very soul.

She stirred in his arms. "Are ye awake already?"

He rubbed her shoulder tenderly. "Shhh…Go back to sleep, Ella."

She draped her arm over his waist and sighed. "Ye feel so warm and wonderful."

"As do ye."

"Do we have to leave this bed?"

He chuckled in response. "I love the thought of keeping ye here all day, but I'm afraid there are things to which I must attend."

Sybella groaned. "I suppose Aunt Iseabail would wonder where we were." She lifted her head and smiled. "*Madainn mhath*."

His finger traced her jaw. "Good morning to ye as

well." He kissed her tenderly and then sighed. "Ye know ye do make it nearly impossible to leave this bed."

"Then donna."

"Ye tempt me too much, Wife."

She buried her face in the corded muscles of his chest. "I do?"

Alex suddenly had the feeling that the bonny siren lying in his bed had a burning desire, an aching need, for another kiss. "*Thig an seo,*" he growled. *Come here.*

"What?" Her voice was a mask of innocence.

Alex pulled her up, sliding her body against his. Parting her lips, Sybella raised herself to meet his kiss. His mouth continued to explore her soft ivory flesh. She was so incredibly tempting. He seared a path down her neck, her shoulders. He nibbled on her earlobe. And then he pulled back and gave her a peck on the top of the head.

"If I donna stop now, I will keep ye chained to this bed all day. I really enjoyed being with ye, but I must get dressed and prepare for travel."

She raised herself up on her elbow. "For *travel*? Where? When?"

"Your father has arranged passage for me to Lewis—in three days."

Sybella paled.

❧

Three days. Sybella had three days to find that bloody stone.

Fear and anger knotted inside her. If she didn't discover that dreaded rock by then, she would be forced to tell Alexander the truth. He was entering into a war that was not his own, caused by her father, no less. Not only had her sire made an attempt on Alex's life, but now her husband would be marked as an enemy of the MacLeods for killing their chief—who had never tried to kill her to begin with.

God help her. Alex would never trust her once he learned the truth. Frankly, she wasn't sure what he'd do, and for the first time in her life, she was afraid. Her only hope was to find the stone, deliver it to her father, and pray the man would do the right thing and stop Alex from going to Lewis.

She rose from the bed and wrapped herself with a blanket. "I will do anything I can to assist ye."

Alex stood and donned his kilt. "Thank ye, but there is naught ye can do. I must meet with John and MacGregor. While I travel to Lewis, MacGregor will stay behind. He will see to your welfare."

She walked around the bed and faced him. "I donna want Ciaran to look after me. I want ye."

"Ye flatter me, lass, but I have nay choice. I must travel to Lewis."

All Sybella could manage to do was nod.

"Donna look so troubled. I will return before ye know it." He sat on the bed and put on his boots. "As ye said, I am a fierce Highland laird."

She smiled but knew the smile did not quite reach her eyes.

He moved in an instinctive gesture of comfort. "Ye worry overmuch. I will be fine. Why donna ye take a walk to the loch? I am sure my cousin and Aunt Iseabail would love to go with ye." He bent his head and kissed her lips. "I shall meet up with ye later."

She watched her husband close the door and then she pivoted on her heel. Sybella practically ran into her chamber, splashed cold water on her face, and dressed. For a moment, she thought about not breaking her fast, but she knew that if she didn't show up, someone would come looking for her. She would just eat quickly and resume her purpose. Curse her father and brother. In truth, she wasn't sure how many more times she could.

Sybella walked to the great hall, running over her mission in her head. She'd already searched the library, the study, and the bedchambers, and she still needed to continue her search in the ladies' solar. At least she had an idea of where to start.

As she entered the great hall, everyone was seated for the meal. Her husband rose in a gentlemanly fashion and pulled out her chair.

"Ella." His voice was low and deep.

She lifted her brow. "Alexander." She sat down next to Rosalia, who held Lachlann on her lap. The boy smiled when Rosalia kissed his rosy cheeks. "How do ye fare? I see ye live," Sybella said.

Rosalia giggled. "I am well. And ye?"

"The same."

Rosalia nodded to Ciaran. "I donna think we got ourselves into too much trouble last eve, did we?"

Ciaran's hand froze midair as he was about to take a drink from his tankard. "I think MacDonell and I agree 'tis the last time we leave your *seanmhair* to watch over the two of ye."

Aunt Iseabail's eyes widened. "Whatever do ye mean?"

"Ciaran…" Rosalia warned.

He leaned forward, resting his arm on the table. "It seems our women entertained themselves last eve by getting knee deep in their cups and then practicing swordplay in the ladies' solar…with their daggers."

Aunt Iseabail gasped and held her hand over her heart. "Truly? I must admit I am a wee bit surprised at the two of ye. Why would ye want to scrape up your daggers? I would've grabbed the swords from Alex's study. After drinking three cups of ale, I was somewhat astonished I made it to my own chamber last eve in one piece."

Alex rubbed his brow. "Ye too, Aunt Iseabail? For the love of God, ye women must stop encouraging one another."

"Ye are far too serious, Nephew. 'Tis a good thing to have a lighthearted attitude every once in a while. It cleanses the soul. Ye might find it would even do ye some good."

Ciaran grunted. "Aye, MacDonell. We should get in our cups more often and then practice swordplay… in the ladies' solar."

Rosalia elbowed Ciaran in the ribs. "Cease."

Sybella finished her meal and tried to keep her mind still, a hard task when Alex was so close. Although she'd thoroughly enjoyed last eve, she couldn't afford to be distracted by romantic notions. And God help her, the man's nearness made her senses spin.

Finally, Alex stood and then bent and nuzzled her ear. "I will see ye later, Wife."

As she watched him walk away with MacGregor by his side, memories from last eve started to flood her. She mentally chided herself. She needed to quit dreaming and make her escape.

Shifting in the chair toward Rosalia, Sybella spoke as casually as she could manage. "'Tis a lovely day. Alex thought mayhap we should walk with Aunt Iseabail to the loch. The fresh air might do her some good."

Rosalia nodded. "'Tis a wonderful idea. What say ye, *Seanmhair*? Do ye want to take Lachlann and we'll walk to the loch?"

"I donna mean to keep putting ye off, but I will have to join ye later," said Sybella. "I promised Anabel something and I havenae yet started."

"Verra well." Rosalia rose with Lachlann in her arms. "Let me change him first, *Seanmhair,* and then I will meet ye in the bailey."

To say that Sybella felt guilty did not reflect the agony she felt with herself. She despised what she had become, resorting to spinning tales. And it bothered her to speak of Anabel that way. No matter, once she found the stone, her father would have to leave her and Alex alone. Her sire wouldn't have any other choice in the matter. She would make certain.

Sybella reached the solar and closed the door behind her. Glancing around the room, she saw a book sitting on the table next to her dagger. After fingering through the pages the second time, she knew there was nothing odd. She tapped the book in her hand and noticed two pictures that hung on the wall.

One portrait depicted a woman with long reddish hair, her flowing emerald gown blowing in the gentle wind. The picture to Sybella's right looked like the same woman in a sapphire gown, bending down to pick up a yellow flower.

Sybella lifted the first picture from the wall. She brushed her fingertips over the stone and felt for any movement or indentation. Nothing. She replaced the painting and then removed the second picture with the same result. She had never felt so frustrated in her life. Where the hell was the stone? At this rate, she would never uncover it.

She looked at the shelf that held the cups, under, over—not a damn thing. She moved the chairs, lifted the table, and even checked the floor. She refused to believe that this was a hopeless cause and forced herself to settle down. Who knew? Perhaps Aunt Iseabail held the stone in her chamber.

After putting things back in their rightful places, Sybella closed the door and made her way to Aunt Iseabail's chamber. Once she was inside, she straightened her spine and got down to the task at hand. She pulled out everything from Aunt Iseabail's trunk, searching through her clothes, jewelry box, anything and everything.

After realizing her hunt was another unsuccessful jaunt, Sybella stood and stretched her back. All of Aunt Iseabail's dresses were scattered across the bed; the woman's jewelry box had been dismantled; and the room was in complete disarray. Sybella had done it now. With her luck or lack thereof, Rosalia and Aunt Iseabail would return from their walk and catch her in the act.

She hastily replaced Aunt Iseabail's belongings and

made her way to the only other place she could think of that could hold the stone.

The unsavory pit of hell.

✌

A lady's laugh wafted through the air, and Alex watched as Rosalia, Lachlann, and Aunt Iseabail returned from their walk. With the sun shining brightly and no clouds in sight, no wonder the women laughed. A gentle breeze blew through the bailey and MacGregor lifted his son in the air.

Alex waited a moment, finishing his conversation with John. When Sybella did not appear, Alex walked over to his cousin. "*Tha i breagha an-diugh.*" *It's lovely weather today.* "I assume ye enjoyed your walk. Where is my wife?"

"She didnae come with us. She had something to do for Anabel. We did have a good time with Lachlann, though," said Rosalia.

Aunt Iseabail rubbed her hand over Lachlann's tiny back. "He is such a good lad." Turning her head toward Rosalia, Aunt Iseabail looked puzzled. "What was it, my dear, that I was supposed to tell Alexander?"

"I donna know. Ye only told me to remind ye to tell Alex something. I think it was about Sybella."

Aunt Iseabail tapped her finger to her lip. "And ye say Sybella is with Anabel?"

Alex rubbed his hand over Aunt Iseabail's shoulder. "Nay, I think she is making something for Anabel."

His aunt giggled. "I would love to see that, especially since your wife doesnae even know how to stitch."

"Pray excuse me while I drag her away from whatever she's doing. 'Tis too wonderful of a day nae to be out in the sun."

Alex knocked on Sybella's bedchamber door. When no one answered, he walked to the ladies' solar—and found it empty. He had the same result with the parapet, the kitchens, and the garden.

He walked back out into the bailey and ran into John. "Have ye seen my wife?"

John chuckled. "Have ye lost her?"

"Search the grounds. She isnae inside."

"Aye."

Something gnawed at Alex's gut. Sybella knew not to leave the castle without telling anyone. It was too dangerous after the MacLeod's attempt on her life. But if his wife was not in the castle, where the hell was she?

∽

Sybella found her way into the dungeon much easier than the first time. Since hell currently held no occupants, no guard slept at the entrance. Once again, she descended the stairs and was greeted with a chill. It was cold and damp, and she paused only long enough to light the torch.

"Welcome back to the pit of hell, Sybella," she said aloud. "Find the bloody stone or this is where ye will reside for the rest of your days." She held up the light, pausing. "I can do this. I can do this," she repeated for confidence.

The same unidentifiable muck lay upon the ground, and the chamber smelled of something rotten, decayed.

She didn't want to think about any more of that. She held up the torchlight to the heavy stone walls and iron bars that lined the narrow center walkway. She inched her way to the first door and held up the candle between the bars. As before, she waited a moment until the flickering light stilled.

She opened the door and walked in. There was no time to worry about what was there. Examining the walls, she ran her hand across the cool, slimy stone. She took one section at a time slowly, carefully. She did not want to come back here in the event she had overlooked something.

Sybella made her way to the second door, trying to ignore the shackles that lined the wall. The smell and overwhelming sense of dread would surely be her undoing, but she imposed an iron control on herself to continue. Following the same ritual she did in the first cell, quickly and as thoroughly as possible, she finished and made her way to the last door.

Praise the saints. Was that dried blood? When she became light-headed, she had no choice but to place her hand on the grimy wall for support. She paused for a moment when saliva pooled in her mouth. She wanted to take a deep breath but willed herself not to move, afraid she'd toss her contents.

She fought hard against the tears she refused to let fall, and for an instant, she almost gave up. But then she waved aside any further hesitation and entered the last cell where the MacKenzie man had been held and, God help her, died.

Damn.

"Dè nì mi?" What will I do?

When she didn't uncover the stone, Sybella extinguished the torch at the foot of the stairs. She climbed the steps, and as soon as sunlight bathed her face, she lifted her cheeks into the light and took a deep, penetrating breath. She felt relief to be out of the dungeon, but panic welled inside her because she still hadn't found the stone.

She looked up and spotted the men who walked the wall. In her best interest, she decided to move. She'd searched the library, study, solar, bedchambers, and dungeon. Surely Alex wouldn't hide the stone in the kitchens. The servants were in there all the time. She was running out of places to look.

Sybella walked into the great hall and was halted by the sound of an angry voice.

"Where have ye been?"

She turned to see Alex standing with his hands on his hips. "Alex, I…was searching for ye."

He closed the distance between them. "I have been looking for ye everywhere. Where were ye?"

"I was in the garden for a while."

"The garden? I thought ye were making something for Anabel."

She wrung her hands nervously. "Anabel, aye. I was stitching something for her and then decided to take a walk."

Alex froze.

Sybella became increasingly uneasy under his scrutiny and muttered, "I missed ye, Husband." She tried to depict an ease that she didn't necessarily feel.

She lowered her gaze to the floor and studied the MacDonell crest, every line, every curve. She suddenly found the clan crest utterly fascinating. The black raven was perched on a rock, engraved with sleek curves. The words "*Cragan an Fhithich*" encircled the bird in a protective embrace. *The Rock of the Raven.*

And that's when she saw it.

The eyes of the raven looked…different. One stone was whole and of a black pearl color, and the other was brown with a hole in the middle, exactly as Colin and her father had described it. God's teeth! She'd found the bloody stone.

When Alex spotted his wife in the great hall, he was relieved but somewhat confused. How could he have missed her when he searched the gardens, and why wouldn't she seek out Rosalia and Aunt Iseabail to take a walk? The lass behaved as if she would rather be by herself than enjoying the company of his clan.

Perhaps Sybella had grown tired of his kin the same as he had grown tired of hers. And worse yet, she presently couldn't meet his eyes. He didn't mean for his tone to sound so accusatory, but he was troubled when he couldn't find her, especially after the attempts on her life.

He raised her chin with his finger. "I was worried about ye, Ella. I searched the castle, and when I couldnae find ye…"

She became instantly wide awake and threw herself into his arms. "Oh, Alex." She pulled down his head and kissed him with passion. He wasn't sure if it was the words he spoke, but her mood was suddenly buoyant.

Wrapping his arms around her midriff, he lowered his hands, pulling her bottom close. She needed to feel what she did to him. When he remembered he was in the middle of the great hall, he pulled back and gave her a roguish grin. "'Tis too early to seek our bed."

"Aye, but that doesnae mean I cannae steal a kiss from my husband." She broke into a wide, open smile.

He leaned in close. "Ye can kiss me whenever ye'd like. Your body tastes like sweetened honey." He paused for added impact. "And so does your kiss."

She colored fiercely.

"My laird, my apologies for the interruption, but might I have a word?"

Alex gave Sybella a wry smile. "Pray excuse me but a moment." He looked at John, who stood with a blank expression on his face. John nodded Alex out into bailey.

"I see ye've found your wife," said John. "Where was she?"

"I must have missed her. She took a walk in the garden."

John's eyes narrowed. "Is that what she told ye, or did ye see her?"

"What are ye talking about?" Alex crossed his arms over his chest. When John didn't answer him, Alex repeated the question.

"Your wife wasnae in the garden."

Alex's eyes widened and he shook his head, puzzled. "What do ye mean she wasnae in the garden?"

"I stood upon the wall and I saw her with my own eyes."

There was a heavy moment of silence.

John was never one to make a play with words. For some reason, his friend's behavior unnerved Alex. "Well, out with it. If she wasnae in the garden, where was she?"

"The dungeon."

Seventeen

SYBELLA CLOSED THE DOOR TO HER BEDCHAMBER AND threw up her hands. She couldn't believe it. All of that hunting for the stone, and the darned thing was under her feet the entire time. How many times had she walked over the MacDonell crest? Of course Alex's father would want to openly display his victory.

Men and their trophies.

All of this uproar—over a rock. A small part in the back of Sybella's mind had hoped she wouldn't find the stone and that her father was simply wrong. But now that she'd uncovered her family's sacred seeing stone, she knew the truth of the matter. And to think, the rock had been under her father's nose the entire time. God's teeth! MacKenzie men had even slept upon the floor. Had her sire discovered the stone during her wedding…She shuddered at the thought. There would've been a massacre.

She walked over to the desk and sat down. Now that she had found the stone, she needed to make certain that Alex and his clan would be safe. Everything was now in her favor, but she still found it necessary to proceed with caution. She penned a missive to Colin, short and to the point. Once her brother read her words, he would tell her father. And she only prayed her sire would cease this madness, call off his hounds, and stop Alex from traveling to Lewis and killing an innocent MacLeod.

There was a knock on Sybella's door and she opened it to find the messenger. She handed the man the missive. "Take this to Kintail and deliver it only to my brother, Colin. Show it to nay one else. Do ye understand?"

"Aye, m'lady."

She watched the messenger depart and then closed the door. She lay down on the bed and sighed. In a few days this would all be over and perhaps she could start to act like the wife Alex deserved. She made a mental promise to herself that there would be no more lies between them. Knowing she had ultimately betrayed his trust, bouts of guilt continued to plague her more often than not. This whole turn of events needed to be over. Soon.

❦

"Are ye sure?" Alex asked John for the hundredth time.

"Aye."

Alex ran his hand through his hair. "What the hell would she be doing in the dungeon?" He paused. "And why would she lie to me?"

"I donna know." John kept his face consciously guarded and Alex knew it.

Alex was laird, supposed to be in charge, supposed to know everything that occurred under his own roof.

And if he was a good laird, he should even be able to predict things before they'd happen. The mere fact that he did not know what was going on with his own wife angered him.

He walked to Sybella's bedchamber and didn't even bother to knock. He simply entered through the adjoining door. She lay upon the bed, her golden locks spread out around her.

"Ella."

She sat up abruptly. "Alex."

"When ye told me that ye took a walk in the garden, did ye?" He folded his arms over his chest. "I will have the truth."

Her eyes widened. "Of course I did. Why do ye ask?"

"Some of my men saw ye…leaving the dungeon."

Her thin fingers tensed in her lap. She looked away hastily and then moved restlessly.

"Ye will answer me, and I am nae leaving until ye do."

She looked up at him and spoke tentatively as if testing an idea. "Aye, I was in the dungeon, but I also went to the garden."

"Why? 'Tis nay place for a woman. Ye have nay reason to be down there."

Sybella patted the bed beside her. "Please sit, Alex."

He sat down beside her and waited for her explanation while she chewed her lip and gathered her thoughts.

"I wanted to see it." As he was about to open his mouth, Sybella continued. "I wanted to see where ye kept the man."

He paused. "I told ye. He is dead."

"I understand that, but I had to see it for myself."

"Och, lass." He reached up and tucked her hair behind her ear. "Ye have naught to fear. Although I take my leave to Lewis, ye have my word as your husband that ye are safe, Ella. MacGregor will be here with ye. He has Rosalia and Lachlann. He will nae let any harm befall ye and Aunt Iseabail. And now ye saw for yourself that the man is dead and gone."

She lowered her gaze. "I must ask this of ye." For a moment, she was silent. "Are ye certain it was the MacLeod? What if the MacLeod wasnae the man responsible?"

Alex sighed. "Ella, the archer wore the MacLeod tartan. If nae a MacLeod, why would the man wear the clan colors?" He pulled her close. "Donna fear. When I return from Lewis, this will all be over. Until then, I donna want ye thinking upon such things."

She pulled back and brought her hand to his cheek. There was a spark of some unidentifiable emotion in her eyes. She looked as though she wanted to say something, but when he nodded for her to continue, she simply brushed her lips to his.

He pulled back and gave her a gentle smile. "I wish there was something I could say to ease your worry."

She took a deep breath, closed her eyes, and simply embraced him.

❧

Sybella wanted to tell Alex everything—how she was stupid enough to let her conniving father and brother convince her to search for the stone, how her marriage was all a bittersweet scheme to plot revenge, and how much she truly loved him. But until she got rid of that damned rock, she had to hold back. Nothing was for certain, and she couldn't afford to take the chance.

As she sat next to Alex and Rosalia for the eve meal, she forced her eyes not to look at the MacDonell crest on the floor. For if she did, she was afraid her actions would betray her purpose.

"What are ye making for Anabel?" asked Rosalia.

"I am stitching a scarf. And I must admit, I am nae verra good at it."

Rosalia giggled. "Aye, I know the feeling all too well."

Ciaran leaned forward. "My wife isnae allowed to stitch my tunics. Howbeit she borrows them often." When his eyes darkened and he kissed Rosalia, Sybella turned her head.

"How was your walk to the loch, Aunt Iseabail?" asked Sybella.

"It was verra lovely even though Lachlann slept most of the time."

"And he would've stayed that way, but ye kept poking at him, *Seanmhair*."

Aunt Iseabail waved her finger at Rosalia. "A grandson needs to spend time with his grandmother. Ye see him all the time. He can sleep on your watch."

Ciaran bent his head forward. "Aye, well, when he doesnae sleep this eve, we will be sure to take him to your chamber so ye can spend more time with him."

"I think ye make up these tales of my Lachlann. He is always a good lad."

Rosalia laughed as Alex leaned over Sybella, tapping Rosalia on the shoulder. "How did she fare?"

Rosalia shrugged. Lowering her voice, she said, "She was having a good day and kept up with the conversation. She even recalled that she wanted to tell ye something when we returned. Of course, she forgot specifically what she wanted to say, but at least she remembered that."

"Good. I think it helps when she walks and her mind is occupied with something. Thank ye, Cousin."

Sybella tapped Alex's thigh. "It seems Aunt Iseabail is having a good day."

He smiled. "Having Rosalia and Lachlann here helps to keep my aunt's mind busy. I think if Aunt Iseabail sits idle, her condition tends to worsen. And the fact that the woman gives Lachlann her attention directs her thoughts away from us."

She raised her brow. "What do ye mean?"

"The fact that ye arenae with child."

Sybella lowered her lashes, her husband's comment leaving her with an inexplicable feeling of emptiness. She wasn't sure exactly why, but she was somewhat saddened. Although under the current circumstances, bringing a bairn into this world was probably not the best of ideas. She felt trapped in her own lie.

She turned her head and studied Ciaran and Rosalia. Their love for each other was quite obvious. Seeing the two of them with Lachlann only further confirmed what she already knew. Instinctively, Sybella's hand went to her stomach. When the time was right, she could only imagine how Alex would react when they were blessed with such a precious gift.

After finishing their meal, Aunt Iseabail wanted to take a walk in the garden, and Sybella couldn't turn down another request. As Ciaran stood and pulled Lachlann from Rosalia's arms, Sybella watched the loving family walk out of the great hall while she waited for Alex and Aunt Iseabail.

She found herself standing on the clan crest. She looked down and discreetly ran her foot over the seeing stone. It did not come as a surprise when the rock did not budge. Nothing could ever be easy. She would have to get a chisel to get the damn thing out.

❧

Alex pulled out Aunt Iseabail's chair and helped her to her feet. He looked up as Sybella waited, gracing him with a smile. At least his wife wasn't turning down another opportunity to be with his family.

Aunt Iseabail took his arm, stepping down from the dais, and Alex almost stumbled when his aunt froze midstep. His arms supported her, but the woman merely stared at Sybella, who stood brushing her foot back and forth against the stone floor.

"Aunt Iseabail?"

After a long pause, his aunt finally turned to him. Her eyes displayed a liveliness that he hadn't seen there for quite some time. "I must speak with ye alone with much haste, Nephew." And with that, she turned on her heel and ambled toward his study.

"Ella, I will meet ye in the garden."

Sybella's eyes were gentle, understanding. "Are ye sure?"

"Aye."

Alex followed Aunt Iseabail into his study. She walked over to the chair and then, as if she had a second thought not to sit, started to pace. Her behavior started to unnerve him.

She gestured toward the door. "Close it."

"What is this about? What is wrong?" He shut the door and walked over to her, taking her arm. "Please sit, Aunt."

She wiggled her way out of his hold. "Alexander, please stop forcing me to sit. Will ye listen? I must tell ye something."

He sat down on the edge of the desk. "What is it?"

"The stone. Ye asked me about a stone."

He became instantly wide awake. "Aye, I did. Do ye remember?"

"Seeing Sybella made me..." Aunt Iseabail shook her head. "Dòmhnall could ne'er understand how the MacKenzie got away with things. The man always seemed to know to steal from our clan when it hurt the most—before the winter or before the harvest. My brother thought mayhap it was purely dumb luck, but several years ago, Dòmhnall heard tales from...I think it was a MacLeod that the MacKenzie had a seer in his clan. Ye know our family struggled to survive, sometimes barely able to make ends meet. Howbeit the MacKenzies were always blessed with good fortune. Do ye nae find that odd, Nephew? Dòmhnall believed it was the result of the seer."

Alex's eyes widened. "A seer? Ye donna need a seer to know when 'tis best to raid and plunder from a clan. I have ne'er known Father to embrace such tales. Tell me more about this stone."

She waved her hand at him. "Silence, Alexander."

He folded his arms over his chest while Aunt Iseabail continued to speak.

"I think one of the MacKenzie maids ran away and married a MacLeod, but I cannae remember all of it. At any rate, this seer could only foretell when he held a particular stone."

"Aunt Iseabail, I'm sure 'tis only a story to tell the wee bairns at night. Surely ye donna believe this. Granted, we live in the Highlands and I have certainly seen things that I cannae explain. But to have me believe there is a stone which this seer uses to foretell the future is—"

"God's teeth, lad, but ye are impatient," she bit out. "Ye remind me much of your father. Dòmhnall told me years ago when we burnt down the MacKenzie's church that he found the stone. This relic was of such importance to the MacKenzie clan that my brother trusted nay one. I was the only person he told and we spoke of it once."

"All right. Where is this stone and what does it look like?"

She made a circle with her hands. "'Tis of a brownish color, about this big, and has a hole in the center."

"Did Father give it to ye? Where is it?"

"Placed into the eye of the Rock of the Raven." When Alex raised his brow, she quickly added, "Under your feet in the great hall, Nephew." She finally sat down in the chair. "When I saw your wife running her foot over the eye of the raven, I remembered that was what Dòmhnall meant in his letter to ye. And the way your bonny wife studied the raven, it seems she has discovered her clan's stone."

For the first time in his life, Alex could say that he was rendered speechless. Aunt Iseabail was right about one thing: his father had never mentioned the fact that he held this seeing stone of the MacKenzies. And leave it to his sire to place the damn rock in the middle of the great hall, no less. Alex shook his head at his father's arrogance. Then again, his father had more than likely never expected Alex to wed a MacKenzie.

He suddenly had another disturbing thought. If the tale Aunt Iseabail spoke was true, the stone was something the MacKenzie would not easily forget. What better way for a MacKenzie to recover the stone than by offering the hand of his daughter to Alex.

He quickly shook off the thought as ice spread through his veins. He tried to think clearly, not permitting his emotions to rule. He refused to race to conclusions until he spoke with Sybella.

"Thank ye, Aunt. I would ask that ye donna mention this to anyone, especially Rosalia or Sybella."

Her eyes widened. "I may be old, but I am nae a daft fool, Nephew." She rose. "I know Dòmhnall risked discovery by taking the stone. I leave it to ye to make certain it stays where it belongs."

He nodded. "I will take care of it. Can ye see yourself to the garden?"

"Alexander…"

He waved her off. "Of course ye can."

Alex sat down behind his father's desk and poured himself a drink. He could not stop himself from pondering and wanted to put all of the pieces together. Did Sybella know? The question continued to hammer at him. Perhaps she didn't. He could not simply ignore how gentle and loving his wife was. She was everything the MacKenzie clan was not. And he was proud to call her wife.

A thought froze in his mind.

Even thinking about the idea killed him. But what if Sybella did know of the stone? The harder Alex tried to ignore the truth, the more it persisted. He downed the rest of his drink, realizing these wild ideas were driving him mad. He'd told Sybella repeatedly that he wanted nothing but honesty between them.

He decided to simply ask her.

Alex walked to the great hall and stopped at the clan crest. He never would've noticed that the stone was different in the eye of the raven if Aunt Iseabail hadn't told him. Now he could see it as clear as day. He bent down and tugged at the rock, making sure it was still secure in its place.

"Alex."

He stood as John walked toward him, a troubled expression upon his brow.

"What is it?"

John lowered his voice. "Mayhap we should go to your study."

Alex nodded and once again found himself walking to his study. When John closed the door behind him, Alex grunted.

"Am I going to need another drink? I've already had my fill with Aunt Iseabail." When John merely nodded, Alex sat down behind his father's desk and poured them both some ale. He handed John a cup. "I am almost afraid to ask."

"Alex, I am your friend. We are as brothers, but ye also made me the captain of your guard. I have a duty, responsibility."

Alex spoke hesitantly. "Aye…"

"There is nay easy way to say this, but I must." John took a drink from his tankard and then met Alex's gaze. "Did ye speak with your wife about the dungeon?"

Alex shifted in his chair, studying John for a moment. "Aye. She told me she was there."

"She told ye?" asked John, surprised.

Alex didn't really want to share Sybella's fears with John, but his friend was troubled over something. "She wanted to see where we held the MacLeod. She is fearful of me taking my leave to Lewis and thinks I leave her unprotected with MacGregor."

"The MacLeod man is dead."

"I tried to tell her the same, but ye know how lasses worry over naught. What is this about?"

"When I saw your wife from the wall, her behavior was odd, almost as if she didnae want to be spotted."

"I'm sure she didnae. I would have throttled her myself had I seen her. 'Tis nay place for a woman."

"I had one of my men follow her."

"What? For what purpose?"

"I donna know, Alex. Something isnae quite right. And being that ye spend many an eve tupping the lass, mayhap ye are blinded by her actions."

"What are ye saying? I think with my coc—"

John dropped a missive on the desk before Alex. "Read it."

"What is this?" asked Alex, picking up the letter.

"Read it," repeated John.

Alex read the words and his heart stopped.

Colin,

I found what you and Father seek. Please stop this madness before it is too late.

Ella

Eighteen

SYBELLA WALKED ALONG THE GARDEN PATH, CONTEM-
plating how she was going to free the stone from the
great hall floor. She would need to find some kind of
tool to loosen it. Perhaps she'd check the stables when
everyone was asleep. She had another disturbing
thought. Once she removed her clan's stone, there
would be a hole in the floor. She needed to find
another rock to replace the one she would take.

She sat down on a bench and watched Rosalia and
Ciaran play with Lachlann. Ciaran held his son up
in the air and Lachlan smiled from ear to ear. When
Rosalia reached out and touched her husband's arm in
a gentle gesture, his eyes held a tremendous amount
of love for the woman standing by his side.

As Sybella watched the family together, she didn't
notice her own lips curving into a smile. From what
Alexander said about his cousin, Rosalia had suffered
hardship and discomfort before meeting Ciaran. But
no one could tell from looking at the woman. Rosalia
was proud, strong. And Alex's cousin had certainly
found her inner peace and her one true love. To

be honest, Sybella was blissfully happy for Rosalia. And if Sybella was truthful with herself, perhaps she was even a bit jealous of the woman who stood before her. One thing was clearly evident: Rosalia was a survivor.

Every time Rosalia's eyes met Ciaran's, it was difficult not to notice the heartfelt love, understanding, and compassion that were exchanged between them. Sybella hoped that perhaps one day Alex would feel the same about her—well, as soon as she could clean up this mess her clan had created.

With that revelation, Sybella stood from the bench. "Pray excuse me. I think I will take a quick walk to the loch."

Rosalia turned. "Do ye want us to come along with ye?"

"Nay, ye stay with your bonny lad. I will return soon."

Sybella walked casually to the loch, her eyes searching the path along the way. There were no stones or rocks that would serve her purpose. She thought perhaps there might be more of a selection next to the water—at least, that was her hope.

Reaching the loch, she took a moment to merely stand there and admire the view. The sun was starting to set below the horizon, and the leaves rustled in the wind. She took a deep breath and let the fresh air stimulate her senses. When another round of painful memories started to invade her thoughts, she began to walk.

Tiny pebbles rolled onto the sandy shore. When she almost stumbled, she looked down and spotted a rock that would suit her purpose. She picked up the stone and wiped the gritty sand off the surface.

On safer ground now, Sybella paused to reflect a moment. She was astonished at the sense of completeness she felt at Glengarry. She truly loved everything about this place. From her home to the loch to her new kin, she could easily live out the rest of her days here. And as long as the man she loved was forever by her side…She smiled at the thought.

❧

Alex couldn't deny the evidence any longer. His wife was a traitor. A MacKenzie through and through. Curses fell from his mouth, and he knew that when he was crossed, his temper could be almost uncontrollable.

"What will ye do?" asked John.

Alex ran his hand through his hair, his movements agitated. "Before or after I kill her?"

John's eyes widened. "Alex…"

Alex looked up at the ceiling. "God's teeth, I can hear ye now, Father. I should've known the lass was naught but trouble from the start. Why in the hell would I even think about wedding a MacKenzie. Why?"

"Do ye really want me to answer that?"

Alex glowered at John, and the man had the nerve to raise his hands in mock surrender. "May I offer ye a suggestion?"

Alex closed his eyes and squeezed the bridge of his nose. "What?"

"Ye arenae going to speak with her now, are ye?"

"Speaking, nay. Throttling or running my sword through her, mayhap. Howbeit I donna trust her to speak the truth, and besides, she hasnae yet taken the stone. If I question her, she would simply deny it." Alex paused, his thoughts racing. "I want ye to keep to the shadows and watch her *every* move. I entrust ye to do this, nae one of the men. After she takes the stone, I want to see her hand it over to the MacKenzie. We will deal with the two of them at the same time."

"I am truly sorry, Alex. I thought the lass—"

"The lass doesnae matter."

John nodded and simply walked out.

Alex sat down and pounded his fist on the desk. "*An diobhail toirt leis thu!*" The devil take you!

The MacKenzie clearly had played him for a fool. The arse hadn't hesitated when Alex demanded two hundred fifty cattle as Sybella's dowry. No wonder! The woman was planted under his roof to deliver the seeing stone to the MacKenzie seer. How utterly convenient.

He shook his head in awe at the lengths of the MacKenzie's machinations. He could imagine the man sitting behind the desk in his study, a smug expression upon his face. The bastard had deceived a MacDonell—or so he thought. But maybe it wasn't too late. The MacKenzie still didn't have the stone. Perhaps there was time…

Alex couldn't calm his thoughts. What the hell was he going to do about the MacLeod? The man had tried to kill Alex's wife. The MacLeod would just have to wait his turn. Besides, Alex couldn't think about that now. He needed to solve one problem at a time.

Sybella's missive to her brother continued to haunt him. What did she mean when she wrote, "Please stop this madness before it's too late"? Was marriage to Alex so unbearable? She was clearly going to leave him after she delivered the damn stone to her father.

Alex's heart hardened, and he refused to think of Sybella and her innocent touches. He banished the thoughts of their stolen moments. The woman was nothing more than a MacKenzie wench who had played him for a fool. And to think he cared for the lass, thought of her as one of his own.

He walked briskly to the parapet before he attempted to do something he would surely regret. He wasn't sure how long he remained there, nor did he care. The silence was a blessing. Only when his head bobbed and jolted him awake did he finally seek his bed. But no sooner did he close his eyes than the adjoining door opened and closed.

Alex watched his wife as she approached his bed. At least he'd had enough sense left to keep the bedside candle lit. He closed his eyes and feigned sleep, not giving Sybella the chance to place a dagger straight through his heart. For a moment, she merely stood there and watched him, no doubt planning his untimely demise. When she reached out to touch him, he whipped out his hand and firmly grabbed her arm.

Sybella gasped.

"What are ye doing?" he asked, his voice hardening ruthlessly.

"Praise the saints, ye frightened me. I wanted to make sure ye and Aunt Iseabail were all right." When he didn't respond and his eyes darkened, she gently pulled to free herself from his grasp. "Alex…"

He released her arm and his eyes roamed to her

nightrail. He could see her creamy breasts through the thin material. "Seek your bed, Sybella."

Instead of heeding his command, the lass placed her hands on her hips. "What is the matter with ye, *Alexander*?"

Alex punched the lumps out of his pillow while she stood there gawking at him. The lass clearly didn't know how much danger she was in. When she finally walked away, he rolled over onto his side. And there she stood, lifting the blankets and crawling into bed with him.

His eyes widened. "What are ye doing?"

"I am sleeping next to my husband."

"I am in nay mood for bed sport, lass," he said dryly.

She turned to face him, placing her hands in a prayer-like position under her cheek. "Tell me what happened. I know ye are distraught over Aunt Iseabail. Did her memory fail again?"

How was he to tell her that it was the complete opposite and that Aunt Iseabail remembered the stone Sybella had been sent to recover? As the sultry tempt-ress lay there with her innocent looks, pretending to be concerned about his aunt, she had no idea how much he wanted to reach over and throttle her. The lass had some bollocks.

She lifted her hand and gently rubbed his cheek. "I see ye are troubled. Share your burden with me. I am your wife."

He closed his eyes and clenched his jaw.

A kiss as tender and light as a summer breeze brushed his lips. His eyes flew open as his wife nestled her body against his. She raised her hand to his cheek and pulled him closer, forcing him to deepen the kiss. What the hell was she doing?

He placed his hand on her shoulder and gently pushed her away. She hesitated and then her hand encircled his cock. She began to stroke him, and he unwillingly lost the last thread of self-restraint he had managed to hold on to. If this was the game the lass wanted to play, he would treat her like the MacKenzie wench she was. He would make this one encounter she would never forget.

He tossed her onto her back and lifted her legs to straddle him. Lowering his head, he gave her a brutal, punishing kiss, forcing her lips open with his thrusting tongue. He placed his hand behind her neck and wrung her hair in his fingers, tightening his grip. God, he would make her pay.

Releasing her hair, he skimmed her body over her nightrail and brazenly reached down and inserted his finger between her legs. Damn. The lass was so ready for him. She was so wet. Hot.

Roughly, he tugged her nightrail down past her shoulders until the fabric ripped beneath his hands. He lifted himself up, tearing at the material and exposing her breasts. He fondled one globe, its pink nipple marble hard.

His tongue caressed her sensitive nipples, which had swollen to their fullest, and his hand seared a path down her abdomen and onto her thigh. His tongue swirled its way down her ribs to her stomach while his hands roamed for pleasure points. Her tormented groan was a heady invitation. She lay panting, her chest heaving.

He stood on his knees and ripped her nightrail from

her body as she lay naked beneath his gaze. He wanted
to intimidate her. Make her ache like he was inside.
He consciously watched her expression as he spread
her legs open wide. She was fully exposed, and when
he saw reality set in her eyes, he buried his face into
her womanly heat.

He licked and sucked, torturing her with his
every move.

She reached down to touch him, but he wouldn't
have it. He pushed her hands away. Her musky scent
drove him wild. He sucked on her sensitive bud, and
when she writhed beneath him, he inserted his tongue
as she called out in bittersweet agony.

※

Dear God. She was so hot and dripped with sweat.
The way that Alex touched her drove her wild. She
wasn't sure what was wrong with him this eve, but
right now, she didn't really care. The man's touch was
purely divine.

The pleasure was pure and explosive. And her
release came upon her hard by her husband's expert
touch. When he pulled himself to his knees, she
reached down and encircled his manhood, but he
pushed her hand away. She wrapped her legs around
his thighs and he merely stared at her.

Without warning, he flipped her onto her stomach
and lifted her bottom in the air. She gasped as he
entered her from behind. His hands held her hips in
place with thrust after blessed thrust. At first, she was
shocked, but then she quickly rose to meet him in a
moment of uncontrolled passion.

He continued to take her and she was drawn to a height of passion she had never known before. She couldn't believe the magnitude of her own desire. She moved her hips in response, and Alex called out as he sought his release. When he leaned over her and his fingers gently squeezed her nipple, she abandoned herself to a whirl of sensations.

Alex flopped down on the bed and Sybella pulled up the blankets, snuggling into his chest. He did not embrace her as he always had and his arm lay draped across his forehead, his eyes closed. When he didn't speak, she lightly ran her fingers over his chest. Perhaps he was more troubled by Aunt Iseabail than he cared to admit. No matter, she was sure he would speak to her when he was ready.

Sybella swore she had just closed her eyes when she woke up to an empty bed. She stood, spotting her torn nightrail on the floor while memories flooded her from last eve. She couldn't help but sigh. She shook her head and rubbed her brow, remembering her husband's keen eyes and inscrutable expression. She wondered what had happened since his visit with Aunt Iseabail. At any rate, Alex was probably busy preparing for his travel to Lewis. She briefly wondered if her father would appear this morn and stop her husband from taking the MacLeod's head.

She walked to her chamber, washed, and quickly dressed. As soon as she opened the door, she saw Rosalia standing there with Lachlann in her arms.

"Sybella, I hate to be a burden, but could ye please watch Lachlann for a bit? Ciaran and Alexander practice their swordplay in the bailey, and Aunt Iseabail wants to take a walk to visit my uncle's grave. We left ye a tray in the great hall to break your fast."

Not realizing she had overslept, Sybella extended her arms. "It would be my pleasure." She took Lachlann and smiled. "We shall have a grand time."

"Thank ye. I shouldnae be that long and he has already been fed."

"Donna worry. We will get along just fine."

Sybella carried Lachlann to the great hall and sat down to break her fast. His little hands pounded on the table and then he started to chew on his fists. She played with him in between bites and was amazed that the boy never failed to put a smile on her face.

She kissed him on the top of the head. "Ye are such a bonny lad." He looked up at her with his azure eyes and smiled—with his fist still in his mouth.

When she finished her meal, she called his name and he looked up at her. "Why donna we watch the men practice their swordplay? Would ye like that?" She took his cooed response as a yes.

They walked out into the bailey and were greeted with the sounds of banging swords. Alex and Ciaran were surrounded by a group of men, and Sybella made her way over to a bench. She sat down with Lachlann, and when he spotted his father, his tiny arms flailed and his body shook up and down. It was almost as if the little man tried to greet his father.

Ciaran stopped and nodded to Lachlann. "Ye are still too young to pick up a sword, but let your father show ye how 'tis done."

Alex deflected Ciaran's blow and turned to face her. When their eyes met, Sybella smiled, but his expression darkened. He raised his broadsword over his head, striking Ciaran's with a loud scrape.

Sybella became instantly wide awake and flew to her feet.

❧

MacGregor grunted when Alex sliced his arm. "Watch it, MacDonell, lest ye forget this is swordplay." The man briefly stopped to check his scratch, but Alex continued to strike at him again and again.

"I didnae forget. I am in need of a bit of sport." When MacGregor came down hard on Alex's sword, pain shot up Alex's arm and he almost lost his grip.

MacGregor's eyes flashed a gentle but firm warning. "I donna mind sparring with ye, but if ye continue to swing at me like ye're in the heat of battle, I am going to fight back. And I ne'er lose."

Alex deflected another blow. "I was counting on it." He was trying to clear his mind the only way he knew how. It was only a matter of time before Sybella took the stone, and he needed to be prepared. He was determined that this would be the last battle with the MacKenzie. And Alex had no intention of losing.

MacGregor looked over Alex's shoulder. He dropped his sword and shoved Alex into the wall. "Your wife took her leave with my son. What the hell is wrong with ye?" he asked between clenched teeth.

Alex nodded for his men to depart and MacGregor released his grip.

"I prepare to raise arms against the MacKenzie."

MacGregor raised his brow. "Is there something ye want to tell me, or are ye just daft?"

Alex grimaced. "To be truthful, I donna even know where to begin."

"Howbeit instead of trying to provoke me into killing ye, we have a wee bit of ale and ye can tell me all about it."

Alex wiped the sweat from his brow. "Aye, let's speak in my study."

The men rested their swords against the wall and made their way to Alex's study. MacGregor closed the door and sat down in the chair while Alex poured them each a tankard of ale. Alex took a healthy mouthful and swallowed. He placed the tankard on the desk and looked MacGregor in the eye.

"My wife is a traitor."

MacGregor kept a blank expression upon his face. "And ye think this why?"

Once Alex opened his mouth, words flew out like a raging river. He told MacGregor the entire story and then some. After a while, he wasn't even sure of all he'd said. When he finished, MacGregor finally spoke.

"Ye need to think this through and donna let your anger guide ye. Aye, the lass sent a missive, but ye donna know the meaning of her words. Ye think ye do."

"Hell, MacGregor. What else could she possibly mean?"

Ciaran shook his head. "I donna know, but I have seen the way she looks at ye."

Alex sat back, momentarily rebuffed. "What has that got to do with anything?"

"All I know is that the lass looks at ye the same way Rosalia looks at me. And I know my wife loves me."

There was a trace of laughter in Alex's voice. "*Love?*

She doesnae love me. She betrayed my trust. She is a MacKenzie. She knows of the stone. She—"

"Hasnae taken it."

"Yet."

"I will give ye my advice, but ye will do as ye will. Donna speak with Sybella about this until ye know for certain. Mayhap she does know of the stone, but mayhap she also loves ye and isnae a traitor."

Alex clenched his jaw.

"I know this isnae easy for ye to hear, but ye see the lass with your Aunt Iseabail and Lachlann. How could someone with so much compassion do such a thing? All I can say is this—give your wife a chance. If she takes the stone, 'tis another matter entirely."

"I have John watching her every move."

"And ye are laird. Ye do what is necessary to protect your people." MacGregor poured himself another tankard of ale.

"I'll be damned if I let my clan fall to the MacKenzie."

"I would expect naught less."

Alex sat back. "Do ye think me a fool for marrying her?"

"I think ye did what was necessary to better your clan. 'Tis what we all do."

"But ye wed my cousin and she had naught."

"Now that is where ye are wrong, MacDonell. Rosalia had everything I could possibly want."

Nineteen

Sybella waited all day and nothing happened. No messenger. No Colin. No word of her father calling off this ridiculous quest to Lewis. She could no longer postpone the inevitable. She needed to remove the stone and place it back in its rightful place. If her clan wouldn't stop this madness, she would.

Nightfall had arrived some time ago, and she was somewhat surprised that Alex had not come for her. She opened the adjoining door and saw a mound on the bed. When she heard a low rumble, she knew he slept.

The time was now or never.

She wore her dark cloak and kept to the shadows. The men more than likely had sought their beds since they wanted to take their leave before first light. And since it was a warm eve, she thought perhaps they slept out in the fresh air as they had done for the last several days. At least, that was her hope.

Lachlann had provided her with the perfect cover this afternoon. She had managed to sneak to the stable and show him the animals while conveniently finding a couple of tools, which she'd hid underneath her skirts until she could remove them.

With the main torches extinguished, Sybella was able to move stealthily to the great hall. For a moment, she stood still, listening for the sound of any movement. Because it was late in the eve, her chances of discovery were lessened. At least she silently prayed that was true.

There were only two torches lit in the great hall, and neither one was close enough to suit her purpose. She lifted a torch from the wall and walked across the floor. Her footsteps were the only sound heard next to her nervous beating heart. Lowering the light, she illuminated the MacDonell crest.

She spun her head around as shadows danced across the wall. Her nerves were on edge. Did she hear something, or was it her imagination? A cold knot formed in her stomach. There was no time to falter. Sweat dripped down her brow and she wiped it with her cloak. And once again she was drawn to the clan crest.

The black raven's eyes mocked her. The stone was her future, perched on a rock with the words "*Cragan an Fhithich.*" *The Rock of the Raven.* And God help her, she needed to blind the raven in order for her clan to have sight. Relinquishing the stone was the only way.

Sybella placed the torch on the stone floor and knelt next to the crest. She fumbled under her cloak for the tools she had taken from the stable. Positioning the chisel next to the eye of the raven, she pounded the small hammer on top of it. When a loud bang shot through the hall, she froze.

Praise the saints. She'd never thought about the noise. Panic welled in her throat. At this rate, she would be here all eve and would surely be discovered. There was no time. She lowered the chisel again. After the third attempt, the stone was free. She quickly replaced the eye of the raven with the rock she had found at the loch.

To her dismay, that rock was too small. Of course, nothing could ever go the way she wanted. And worse yet, pieces of broken stone lay upon the ground. She couldn't fret about that now. She positioned the eye, securing it in place and brushing the loose particles around the rock as best as she could. She stood, stepping on the eye of the raven and packing it down in place. That would have to do. She grabbed the torch and replaced it on the wall.

The time of reckoning could not be postponed forever. Her decision came down to two choices: deliver the seeing stone to her father to protect Alexander or simply take the rock out of the equation. After everything her father had done, Sybella realized she had already made up her mind. The stone would never be enough. Her father wouldn't stop until Alex was dead.

She walked along the darkened wall of the garden. Fortunately, Aunt Iseabail had wandered out the garden gate so many times that Sybella knew where to find it. The sun would be rising in a few short hours and she needed to move. For a moment, she stood silently, watching and listening to the wall above. When she didn't hear or see anything, she made her way through the gate.

Hastening her steps, she walked with long purposeful strides to the loch. The light of the moon made the path visible enough to guide her. When Sybella reached the edge of the trickling water, she stopped. She held the rock in her hand and traced the smooth surface with her finger. What secrets did this mere rock hold? If this was a means of predicting the future, the seeing stone would be a dangerous weapon for her father to possess. Her sire was ruthless, trying to kill Alexander and placing blame on the MacLeod for an attempt against her life.

She raised her eyes and studied the loch, confident in her decision and knowing that whatever she did next would change her life forever. There was no turning back. Before she had an opportunity to change her mind, she turned to the side and stretched back her arm the way Colin had shown her. With all of her strength and might, Sybella threw her clan's sacred seeing stone into the cold depths of the loch.

"Ye throw as a lad, Lady MacDonell."

Sybella whipped her head around and her jaw dropped.

The captain of Alex's guard stepped from the shadows of the night.

"What?" she asked, her voice cracking.

He gestured to the loch. "I said ye throw as a lad. I donna know many lasses that can toss a rock the same as ye."

"Aye...I practiced many times with my brother."

John placed his hand on the hilt of his sword. "And how will your *brother* feel about this?"

With an innocent tone, she asked, "About what?"

"There is nay need to be coy with me, m'lady. I know ye took the stone."

Sybella began to shake as fearful images built in her mind. Would the man draw his sword and simply strike her down where she stood? She tried to keep her fragile control and her stomach was clenched tight. When she didn't speak, he closed the distance between them.

"Come now, Lady MacDonell. I watched ye take the MacKenzies' seeing stone from the great hall floor. I saw ye sneak out the garden gate, and I followed ye here to where ye tossed the stone into the loch."

The silence lengthened between them, making her uncomfortable.

"Please, I beg ye, 'tisnae as ye think."

He chuckled in response. "Then enlighten me."

She bit her lip, and her eyes darted back and forth. This man was Alex's friend and also the captain of his guard. What was she supposed to tell him? She must have hesitated too long for his tastes because he grabbed her by the arm and started to drag her toward the castle.

"Then mayhap I will simply take ye to my laird and ye can tell him what ye were doing out here so early in the morn. But I donna think he will be as understanding as me."

She pulled her arm away from him. "Please! Please wait!"

He stopped and stood to his full height. "I am listening, but I will nae ask ye again. Do ye understand?"

Sybella shook her head. "Aye. I knew about the stone."

"I gathered that much, lass," said John dryly.

"My father made this alliance so I could steal back our stone."

His eyes darkened dangerously, but he stood and listened. "Go on."

"My father told me that our clan had a seer, but I honestly didnae believe him. I've ne'er heard of such a thing, but he insisted Alex's father stole the stone from our clan."

"And ye thought to betray your husband and steal back the stone to give to the MacKenzie."

"Nay!" When her voice rose and he raised his brow, Sybella lowered her voice. "It wasnae like that."

He waited for her to continue.

She wrung her hands in front of her. "Well, it was like that, but I didnae want to do it. Things changed. I ne'er searched for the stone until my father insisted I retrieve what was taken and return it to my clan."

"But ye didnae. Why?"

An unwelcome tension stretched even tighter between them.

"I would ne'er harm Alexander. I was trying to keep him safe."

He took a small step closer. "Ye didnae answer my question."

She closed her eyes. "I love my husband. And I would rather see the stone destroyed than in the hands of my father." She paused. "He isnae the man I thought he was."

"Now that is the smartest thing ye've said yet. I could have told ye that, lass." John shook his head. "I cannae keep this from my laird. Ye must tell him the truth or I will. And he will know before we take our leave to Lewis this morn. Do ye understand?"

She paused. "Ye cannae let Alexander travel to Lewis."

"The MacLeod tried to kill ye—twice."

"Nay, he didnae."

"Lady MacDonell, I'd like to think I'm a verra patient man, but ye have a way of making me become verra impatient."

"John," she said, calling him by his Christian name in the hope that he wouldn't see her as the enemy. She reached out, and the muscles of his forearm hardened beneath her hand. "Ye must believe me. I am loyal to my husband, but if I tell ye…I cannae have harm befall my clan. Nay matter what they have done, they are still my family."

"And so is your husband." He sighed. "I am nae the laird, m'lady. I only follow his orders. I can make ye nay such promises. Now tell me why ye think the MacLeod isnae responsible."

There was a heavy moment of silence.

"Because the man ye held in the dungeon was my father's man."

∽

Alex walked into the great hall to break his fast. He finally managed to get some sleep since he knew John watched over his beloved wife. When memories of Sybella started to flood him, he merely reminded himself that she was a deceitful MacKenzie wench. Nothing more.

He was immediately drawn to the clan crest on the

floor. He wondered how long it would take for the lass to be tempted to remove the eye of the raven. A small part of him silently hoped that she wouldn't and perhaps their tender moments were truly that.

He looked down and noticed the rock was loose. Well, it could've been the fact that it wasn't the damn seeing stone. He lifted his eyes to find his wife standing in the entry to the great hall. Her widened eyes couldn't mask her guilty expression if she tried. Instead of following John's advice to wait, Alex felt his temper quickly rearing its ugly head.

Thundering toward his wife, Alex grabbed her roughly by the arm. His fingers dug into her soft flesh. "I will speak with ye now." She practically had to run to keep up with him as he pulled her along behind him.

"Alex, please. Ye are hurting me."

"Your arm is the least of your worries." He lessened his grip, and once he closed the study door, he thrust her away from him. "Ye betrayed me."

"Please calm down. I didnae."

"Donna tell me to calm down. Where is the stone?" he demanded.

"Alex, please."

"Where is the stone?" he repeated.

"I donna have it. I—"

"Donna play games with me."

"I speak the truth. I—"

He threw back his head and roared with laughter. "Ye speak the truth? Since when does a MacKenzie ever speak the truth?"

"I know ye're angry, but let me explain."

"Where is the stone? Ye will give it to me. *Now*."

"I donna have it. I threw it in the loch." She took an abrupt step toward him and lifted her hand to his cheek. "Please listen to me. Ye must believe me. I lov—"

He pushed her hand away and his eyes narrowed. "Ye took the stone only to throw it away in the loch? Careful, your lies are becoming tangled, *Wife*. I was a fool to marry ye, but at least I was wise enough to have my men follow ye. Whether ye tell me or nae, I *will* find that damn rock. And ye *MacKenzies* shall ne'er have it."

She looked hurt and tears welled in her eyes.

"Your game is over, lass. I know everything. The only reason your father arranged this marriage was for ye to steal back the stone."

"Alex, ye have to believe me. I—"

"Do ye honestly think I care?" He heard his bitterness spill over into his voice.

She hesitated. "How long have ye known? Last eve when ye laid with me…Did ye…Did ye think I could…"

He smirked.

"Alex, after what we shared…"

"I gave the MacKenzie wench a good tupping was all."

He felt the sting of the slap, and Sybella's eyes burned with fire. "My father is many things, but he was right about something. Ye are a wicked man, Alexander MacDonell. Lest ye forget, your clan stole my clan's seeing stone. Your clan burnt our church to the ground…while a piper encircled it playing a bloody melody!"

Alex wasn't about to tell her the piper had been his idea. He needed to get back to the task at hand. "And ye betrayed me."

"And that is truly all ye see," she said as her voice faded. Sybella placed her hand over her heart and looked him in the eye. Her gaze was clouded with tears. "With all of my heart and all that is mine, I truly loved ye, Alexander MacDonell. Mayhap one day ye will nae be blinded by your hatred and will open your eyes to see what was before ye."

"All I see before me is a damn MacKenzie who feigned herself off as my wife in an attempt to betray me and my clan. Ye are naught more than a MacKenzie whore."

And with that, she smothered a sob and fled.

⤳❦⤳

Sybella needed time to erase the pain. Ice spread through her veins and she felt an acute sense of loss. Alex's words had hurt her beyond recognition, and her misery was so prominent that it was actual physical pain. Her anguish controlled her. Trapped in her own lie, she was defeated.

She ran to the stables. When she grabbed her saddle and carried it to her horse's stall, the stable hand approached her.

"M'lady, please let me do that for ye."

"Nay, I will saddle him. Thank ye." She didn't dare look the man in the eye. She wasn't exactly sure what she was doing, but she suddenly found Glengarry extremely suffocating. She needed air, needed to breathe, and needed to be as far away from Alexander as possible.

Sybella pulled her mount over to the riding block. With nothing but the clothes on her back, she galloped out the gate and did not look back. Someone called to her in the distance, but she knew the voice was not her husband's. No matter, she was dead to him.

She rode hard, fast, and her horse thundered beneath her feet. Tears blinded her and she had to trust her mount to see. Alex's words replayed in her mind and a stab of guilt lay buried in her chest. She pulled on the reins for her horse to stop and covered her face with her trembling hands, giving vent to the agony of her loss. Her breasts rose and fell under her labored breathing. She took deep breaths until she was strong enough to hold her head up.

She kicked her mount to continue to the only place where she knew she'd be accepted.

Kintail.

❧

John called out to the daft lass, but she rode through the gates of Glengarry like the hounds of hell nipped at her heels. He turned and yelled at one of his men.

"Go after her! Bring her back!"

One of the guards charged out of the gate after Lady MacDonell, and John shook his head. As they had agreed, the lass went to speak with Alex to tell him about the stone and Lewis. And from the looks of things, John had a fairly good idea of what had happened.

He found Alex in the first place he looked, sitting behind his father's desk with a tankard of ale. John closed the door behind him.

"Already ye are in your cups?"

"She took the stone."

John sat down. "I know. Ye had me follow her, remember?"

"Where is it?"

John paused and his eyes narrowed. "Your wife didnae tell ye?"

Alex sat back and rubbed his hand through his hair. "Of course she didnae. She told me she threw it into the loch."

"She did." Alex was silent for a moment and John sat forward. "What exactly did she tell ye?"

Alex shrugged. "I did most of the talking. After a while, I could nay longer listen to her lies."

"And did your wife tell ye that she loves ye?"

Alex smirked. "I donna know what she said. If she did say that, it was spoken conveniently after I caught her in another one of her lies."

"I want ye to listen to me verra carefully, Alex. I love ye as a brother, but sometimes ye are naught more than a daft fool."

Twenty

SYBELLA RODE INTO THE BAILEY OF HER FAMILY HOME. For some reason, the formidable, gray stone castle was not as welcoming as she remembered it being. With not a single tear left within her to cry, she handed her mount to the stable hand and simply walked into the great hall.

Everyone was seated in time for sup, and they all looked up and spotted her at the same time. She merely stood frozen in the entrance, dirty and defeated, as Colin raced toward her.

"Ella, what are ye doing here? What has happened?"

"I've come home, Brother."

He placed his hand on her shoulder. "Where is the MacDonell?"

"He doesnae come. 'Tis too late, Colin. He knows everything." Her voice was barely above a whisper.

Colin wrapped his arm around her shoulders. "Come in, Ella. I cannae believe ye traveled all this way by yourself."

She dropped her lashes quickly to hide the hurt. "I've taken one of my husband's prized mounts.

Please have one of the men see the horse returned to Glengarry at once."

"Donna worry about that now."

Her father approached her. "My dearest daughter, we didnae expect ye. What are ye doing here?"

She glanced to the end of the table to see that Mary's expression was one of concern. Sybella lowered her gaze and looked back at her father. "I have come home." Knowing her anguish peaked to shatter the last shreds of her control, no other words came to mind.

Mary rose and hugged Sybella. "I have missed ye. Why donna I have a bath drawn for ye, and we will get ye something to eat and drink." Mary rubbed her hand gently up and down Sybella's back.

"Where is the MacDonell? Surely ye didnae come alone. I have arranged for his passage to Lewis," said her father.

All Sybella could do was give her sire a blank stare. This was entirely his fault. Because of his machinations, she lost the love of her life. And she found the only place she was welcomed was in her own personal hell, and of course under her father's roof, which was basically one and the same.

Colin shook his head. "Nae now, Father. We must take care of Ella."

Mary guided Sybella to her chamber and neither one of them spoke. Mary opened the door and Sybella sat down in a trancelike state on her old bed. The men carried in the tub and the steaming buckets of water, and Sybella didn't even notice they had departed until Mary helped her undress.

Sybella's mind was numb as she lowered herself into the tub. Even the warm water didn't help to soothe her nerves. For once, Mary must have sensed Sybella's unease because she left her to her own devices—although, the woman showed her concern and returned with a nightrail and a tray of food.

Mary sat down on the bed and smiled with compassion. "What has happened, Sybella?"

Her voice broke miserably. "I betrayed my husband."

Instead of chastising Sybella like Mary always did, Sybella's cousin-by-marriage merely sat and listened. In truth, Sybella needed a friend, or at least one person who did not judge her. She'd forgotten what that felt like.

"Do ye know our clan has a seer?" asked Sybella, her voice sounding distant.

Mary's mouth dropped open. "A *seer*? Nay. Who?"

Sybella shrugged. "I donna know."

"What does this have to do…How did ye betray the MacDonell?"

Sybella rubbed her hands over her face. "Several years ago when Alexander's father burnt our church, he stole our seer's sacred stone. This seer apparently could foretell the future with this stone, and the last he foretold was Father's success on Lewis."

Mary stared wordlessly.

"Father and Colin knew Alexander's father held the stone, and when the MacDonell died, Father arranged for me to wed Alexander. But what Alexander thought to be an alliance formed between MacKenzies and MacDonells was naught more than another MacKenzie scheme to steal back the stone."

Sybella rubbed the wet cloth up and down her arm.

"Father's man shot an arrow aimed for my head so that Alexander would keep me within the walls of Glengarry to search for the stone. When I took too long to find it, Father's man tried to kill my husband. The man was captured and wore the MacLeod tartan to make it look like the MacLeod was responsible. At any rate, Alexander was to travel to Lewis to kill the MacLeod because of Father. Now my husband knows all and I betrayed him."

"Sybella, I cannae believe what ye speak is true. How could your father do this? How could your father expect *ye* to do this? The MacDonell is your husband."

"Alexander nay longer cares what becomes of me. I am only another deceitful MacKenzie in his eyes."

Mary knelt beside the tub and touched Sybella's shoulder. "I donna know what to say."

"There is naught left to say. I am home where I belong. I deserve my fate." Sybella rose from the tub and grabbed the drying cloth. She donned her nightrail and took a sip of mulled wine from the tray that Mary had brought.

Sybella raised her eyes to find Mary watching her.

"Praise the saints. Ye love him."

"It doesnae matter. I mean naught to him."

Mary wrapped her arms around Sybella. "All this time and ye finally found love. *Tha mi duilich.*" *I am sorry.*

Sybella's head was bowed into Mary's shoulder, her body bent over in despair. Again, she was assaulted by her sick yearning for the husband who no longer wanted her and who could never love her.

She was nothing.
Nothing but a MacKenzie.

≈

"If what ye say is true, why wouldn't she tell me?" Alex continued to pace in his study.

John smirked. "Hell, did ye even give the lass a chance? Ye barely let her speak and were verra quick to judge."

"I need to go after her."

"I sent one of my men and he should be back by now. Let's go to the bailey and see if he returned with your wife."

Alex and John were walking out into the bailey as the rider dismounted from his horse. The rest of Alex's men stood around, preparing to travel to Lewis.

The guard approached them, shaking his head. "Lady MacDonell had too much of a start. Her horse was too fast. I lost her."

"Damn. Which direction was she headed?" asked Alex with concern.

"Toward Kintail."

Alex ran his hand through his hair. "God's teeth. This is naught short of a disaster. Mount up. We ride to Kintail."

"I shall be here when ye return. Donna worry about Sybella."

Alex turned around to see MacGregor standing with Rosalia. "I donna have time to explain, but I donna travel to Lewis. We take our leave to Kintail to bring back my wife."

Rosalia's eyes widened. "Kintail? When did Sybella leave for Kintail?"

Alex felt guilty enough. He didn't need his cousin placing a dagger through his cold heart.

"Do ye want me to come with ye?" asked MacGregor.

"Nay, if ye could stay here and keep an eye on Aunt—"

"Nay worries." MacGregor slapped him on the shoulder. "Bring back the stone in one piece."

"I could care less about the stone. I will bring back my *wife*."

MacGregor's only response was an approving smile. "I told ye she loved ye."

"What are ye two talking about?" asked Rosalia.

MacGregor draped his arm across his wife's shoulders and led her away.

Since the men were already prepared to travel to Lewis, they didn't need long to be ready to ride. Alex probably didn't need to take as many men as he was, but he would rather have too many by his side than not enough, especially because he didn't know what he would face when he met up with the MacKenzie.

The bastard was ruthless, using Sybella to do his bidding. Not only did the man have someone try to kill Alex, but the fool had someone take a shot at Sybella—his own daughter. What if the archer would've hit her?

The men mounted up and thundered out the gate. With a score of his best men, Alex pushed his mount faster. Fire fueled his veins and his eyes were dark, dazzling with fury. And to think he was supposed to travel to Lewis to take the MacLeod's head. He only knew one thing for certain.

He would come back to Glengarry with his wife

by his side and return with a head that was not the MacLeod.

✎

Sybella's bedchamber door opened and she sighed. "Mary, I donna really want to talk to ye right now."

"Well then, mayhap ye will speak with me."

She jolted upright. "Father." He closed the door and Sybella rose from the bed, wrapping a blanket around her.

He walked over to the sitting area and sat down in a chair. "Please, join me."

Sybella reluctantly sat down and faced her father, his arm resting casually on the table.

"Where is my stone, Daughter?" A sudden chill hung on the edge of his words.

She shot him a cold look. "Where is your bloody stone? Ye donna ask if I'm all right. Your archer took aim at me in the forest, and then your man tried to kill my husband. Ye blame the attempt on the MacLeod and then try to have my husband do your bidding. 'I need ye to gain your husband's trust and be a dutiful wife. That is all I ask of ye.' How dare ye! Ye used me to get your precious stone and still planned on harming Alexander. I am your only daughter. Why, Father? I demand to know why."

Her sire had the nerve to chuckle in response. "Ye know naught of politics, Daughter. The MacDonell was naught but a thorn in my arse for years. If ye want the truth, I'll give it to ye. The *truth* is that I was going to marry ye off to the MacLeod in order to stay in His Majesty's favor. The *truth* is that Colin had a better idea to wed ye to the MacDonell so that ye could bring back our stone. The *truth* is that ye are merely a woman and what ye think doesnae matter in the ways of politics. Now I ask ye again, Sybella. Where is my stone?"

Her voice was cold and lashing, and she mocked his tone. "The *truth* is, Father, that your precious stone is gone—forever out of your grasp."

"I donna have time for your foolish behavior. Ye were always a willful child. Howbeit ye are a clever MacKenzie. Even if the MacDonell discovered what ye were about, ye would've still taken the stone and preserved what is ours. Now where is it?"

"I donna have it."

He grabbed her forcefully by the arms. "The last Ennis predicted was Lewis. I need to give him that stone, Sybella."

"*Ennis?* Anabel's father is your seer?"

A muscle ticked in his jaw. "I will nae ask ye again."

"Then I will only need to respond once. 'Tis sleeping in the cold depths of the loch where it waits for your cold, black heart."

His eyes darkened. "Enter!" Two of her father's guards opened her bedchamber door. "Take her." Each man grabbed Sybella by the arm and started to lead her out the door. Her father's voice was soulless. "I know ye have the stone. Until ye come to your senses and give it to me, ye can sit—"

She whipped her head around. Shock and anger lit up her eyes as she faced him. "In the dungeon? Ye would place me in the dungeon for a rock?"

"That stone is our clan's future. Ye, my dear, are

nae. What kind of father would I be to place ye in the dungeon? Throw her in the pit."

She paled.

In the middle of the night, she walked through the darkened halls in her bare feet dressed in nothing more than a nightrail and a blanket. She shivered, but it wasn't from the cold. The pit was where her father threw the most unsavory of men...until they died. Their faint screams could sometimes be heard from the kitchens. Perhaps her father only had the men escort her to frighten her. Of course, that was it because her sire would never treat her this way. He couldn't. She was his daughter. The daughter of the MacKenzie laird. A lady.

Sybella quickly pushed back the thought when they descended the cold, damp stairs. The smell overwhelmed her senses, reeking of bodily excrement and making her gag. The guard reached down and lifted the gate from the floor while the other lowered a ladder. They forced her to climb down.

She took one step and tears welled in her eyes. "Please donna do this. I beg ye."

"We donna question our laird's command. Please climb down, m'lady."

With no choice but to descend into the devil's dungeon, she reached the bottom and the men lifted the ladder. The gate locked over her head and she was embraced by darkness. Muck of unknown origin squeezed between her toes and when she tried to step, she slid and fell into something thick and wet.

She screamed.

The hole was dark and foreboding, and she felt a

wretchedness she'd never known before. A raw and primitive grief overwhelmed her. She pulled herself to her feet, and when she slid again on the slimy floor, she sat down.

Sybella felt something move on her lap. She reached down and grabbed a ball of wiry fur, whipping it away from her body. Dear God, her father left her alone with the rats. She gulped hard, hot tears slipping down her cheeks. Perhaps Mary or Colin would hear her.

"Please help me! Please help me! I'm here! I'm here!" she screamed. "Mary! Colin! Help me! Let me out!" When she heard no response, she bellowed, "*Mo mhallachd ort!*" *My curse on you!*

When cursing her father didn't work, Sybella's tears choked her. Her throat was raw from her screams of terror, her teeth chattered, and her body trembled. A sensation of intense sickness and desolation swept over her.

She jumped.

"Where is the stone, Sybella?" Her father's voice echoed from above. "Tell me where 'tis and I'll lower the ladder."

"*Cha leig thu leas.*" *Don't bother.*

"Ella, stop this madness and tell me."

"I told ye. The stone is at the bottom of the loch."

"Why must ye be difficult? Ye are so much like your mother."

"Thank ye."

"I give ye fair warning. Ye arenae coming out of there until ye give me the stone."

"Ye will ne'er destroy Alexander! Ye are naught but a *mhic an dhiadhail!*" *Son of the devil.*

His voice hardened. "Then ye can sit in the bowels of hell."

Sybella shouted in a mix of anger and fear. She was furious at her vulnerability to him. Alex and John were right. Her father was a horrible man. As she sat in her darkened prison, she knew her only hope was if Mary or Colin would hear her. She would scream until she had no more voice left to give.

⸻

Colin was sitting down to break his fast when Mary walked into the great hall. She took her seat and was quiet, withdrawn. She seemed worried. Angus leaned over and whispered something in her ear.

"*Madainn mhath*," Colin said to her. *Good morning.* "Have ye checked on Ella this morn?"

Mary's eyes clung to his, analyzing his reaction. "Is it true then? Did ye do all of that to your own sister?"

"*Wife*," Angus warned.

For the first time in his life, Colin saw Mary blatantly ignore her husband. "I asked ye a question."

"Ye donna understand," said Colin.

"And what part do I nae understand?"

"Mary," said Angus in a firm tone.

"Donna 'Mary' me, Angus." She turned and her eyes narrowed at Colin. "Ye placed Sybella in a situation she couldnae possibly win. Ye asked her to choose her clan over the man she loves. Nay woman could be expected to make such a choice, a sacrifice."

His eyes widened. "She loves him?"

"Is that so hard for ye to believe?"

There was a heavy moment of silence.

"Have ye checked on Ella this morn?" he repeated. "Have *ye*?"

"That is enough, Wife."

She pushed away her trencher and stood. "It seems I've lost my appetite. Pray excuse me."

Colin watched Mary storm out of the great hall with Angus nipping at her heels. In truth, Colin shared Mary's opinion. He was disappointed in the man he'd become. Beyond trying to protect Sybella from the MacLeod, he realized he should've been protecting her against her own clan. He wondered when he'd lost sight of the difference between right and wrong.

He wasn't sure how long he sat at the table alone, but when his father didn't come to break his fast, Colin was somewhat surprised. No matter, now that his sister was home, he would try to make amends.

Colin ambled through the halls and found himself in front of Sybella's door. He knocked, and when she didn't answer, he opened the door.

"Ye will nae find her in there."

He turned around to find his father standing in the hall. "Where is she?"

"Recovering my stone."

Twenty-One

THE AMBER RAYS OF THE SUN WERE STARTING TO SET as Alex and his men rode into the bailey of Kintail. They were greeted by a wall of armed MacKenzie men with unsheathed swords. Alex glanced around as archers stood upon the parapet, waiting for their laird's command. Blood fueled him and Alex didn't care if King James's own men were in attendance. He would fight the bloody lot of them. He had a purpose, a mission, and no one would stand between him and his wife.

He couldn't believe Sybella had made the journey alone, without an escort, with only her hurt to guide her. Hell, he could be so blind. His wife had portrayed nothing but kindness, and he hadn't even given her a chance to explain her actions. He'd assumed the worst. Remembering the look in her eyes when he said those hurtful words made him feel like a complete idiot. He needed to make things right. And he would start now.

The MacKenzie walked into the bailey, confident, arrogant. "Laird MacDonell, what brings ye to Kintail?" he asked with an air of indifference.

Alex dismounted, his hand on the hilt of his sword. He didn't need to look to know that John flanked his every move. His men encircled him, protecting him from the archers. As he had planned, five guards proceeded on foot, ready to take out any archers that dared release their arrows.

"I've come for my wife."

"Ye mean my *daughter*? For what purpose?" The MacKenzie's eyes grew openly amused and his lips curved into a cynical smile.

"Ye attempted to kill me and blamed the MacLeod. Be thankful I donna run ye through right where ye stand. Return Sybella or I will take your head."

A devilish look came into the MacKenzie's eyes, and he threw back his head and roared with laughter. "Ye dare give me commands? I am Laird Kenneth MacKenzie. I donna take orders or listen to demands made by a mere MacDonell sow. Know your place, lad."

The MacKenzie men cheered as Alex's guards stood firm, not listening to the bastard's taunts. Alex's father and Donald had taught them well. They were not foolish enough to give the arse anything to use against them. When Alex hesitated to respond, the MacKenzie continued his rant.

"My daughter returned home because ye arenae man enough to get her with child. I believe she compared your cock to that of a mere bairn."

Alex simply raised his brow and smirked. "I find talking with ye is *mar a bhith a' bruidhinn ri each 'na chadal.*" *Like talking to a horse in its sleep.* "I will nae ask again. Give me my wife."

The MacKenzie started to pace. "Ye think ye can

merely ride into Kintail and give me demands? *Tha thu gòrach.*" *You are foolish.* "Let's make a trade, shall we? I want the stone. Give me the stone and I will give ye Sybella."

❧

Colin paced and ran his hand through his hair. "Where the hell is she? I have been searching for her all day. She didnae break her fast, and she didnae come for the noon meal. How could she take her leave when her horse is still in the stable?" he asked for the hundredth time.

Mary's expression was troubled. "I donna know. I have checked everywhere. She arrived with only the clothes upon her back, and I took them last eve to be washed. I know she was distraught, but surely she wouldnae wander off in only her nightrail. And her boots are still by the bed. Are ye sure your father said she took her leave to recover the stone? How could she ride back to Glengarry without a horse?"

"She didnae ride back to Glengarry. The stone is nay longer there. I donna like this. Something isnae right. Angus, ye check the parapet and we will search again."

Colin and Mary checked the bedchambers, opening all of the doors and peeking in. They went to the ladies' solar and his father's study, and no one was within. They searched the library, running out of places to look. As a result of their limited options, they happened to walk into the great hall at the same time as Angus.

"She isnae on the parapet."

When a loud commotion broke out in the bailey, Colin gave a brief nod. "I donna have time for this, Angus. See what that's about and check the stables again while ye're out there. Mary, come with me."

They walked to the gardens in the back of the castle and called Sybella's name. All of the signs indicated that his sister still remained at Kintail, but she was nowhere to be found. A thought froze in his brain and he shuddered. There was one place he had neglected to look.

The dungeon.

Mary shook her head and approached him. "She isnae here."

"There is a place I didnae search. I donna want ye coming with me. 'Tis nay place for a woman."

Mary reached out and touched his arm. "Please tell me your father wouldnae place Sybella in the dungeon. Surely he wouldnae do such a thing. Please tell me he wouldnae, Colin."

She paled when he closed his eyes.

"I am coming with ye." She ran to keep up with him, but he didn't bother to slow his pace.

"Mary…"

"Naught ye can say will stop me. Let's find Sybella. Enough time has passed. I am sick with worry."

That made two of them. Colin had no time to argue. He descended the stairs to the dungeon, pausing only long enough to light the torch. He didn't notice the chill in the air or the rat that gnawed on something in the corner. He was too concerned about his sister.

"Ella!" Mary called from the bottom step.

"Ye wait here." He walked over and held up the light to the first, second, and third doors. Only empty shackles lined the walls, and the dungeon had no occupants. Colin shook his head, his misgivings increasing by the moment. "She isnae here."

"Where could she possibly be?"

"I donna know. I have nay choice. 'Tis time to have speech with my father. I am mad with worry." He put out the torch as Mary lifted her skirts and ran hastily up the steps. He was somewhat surprised that his cousin's wife, who regularly preached about propriety, had remained by his side in the dungeon. This was the first time he had seen her throw caution to the wind. It was apparent that Mary was as worried about Sybella as he was. They proceeded to the great hall as Colin mentally prepared himself to confront his father.

"Lady Mary…"

Colin turned to see the cook standing with her young daughter by her side. The girl's arms were wrapped around her mother's waist. When the woman spotted him, she flinched and took a step back before his obviously frantic expression.

She lowered her voice as Mary approached. "My apologies, m'lady, but 'tis difficult to work on the meal for the morrow with all of that screaming. And pardon me for saying so, m'lady, but having my daughter hear that over and over isnae good for young ears. That *'thalla gu taigh na galla.'" Go to hell.*

Mary looked at Colin, and he raced to the one place that had haunted him as a child.

৵৵

Sybella could no longer scream. Her voice had deserted her, the same as her husband. Darkness enveloped her and the muck swathed her. And when the smell no longer bothered her, that's when she knew no one was coming for her.

She closed her eyes and wanted to succumb to blackness. She prayed the gods would take her now. She was no longer frightened and no longer angry, and her throat ached with defeat. Her mind was languid, without hope. Her head was bowed, her body slumped in despair.

The pain in her heart was a sick and fiery gnawing, but it could've been one of the rats that crawled on top of her. The last traces of resistance had banished and she had given up all hope. She was lost.

She wanted to die.

Her only regret was that Alexander would never know how much she loved him. When she finally spoke the truth, he hadn't believed her. There were too many lies. She'd betrayed him. Her own husband. And for what? For a clan who didn't give a damn about her and threw her away like a piece of garbage.

Being in the pit was a fate far worse than death. She sat in hell with no means of escape, wondering if her father would bury her or let her mind and body decay down here with the rats. If Sybella had a knife, she would put an end to this brutal torture.

She placed her head back on the slimy wall as something with legs crawled in her hair. And taking one last breath, she realized she didn't care.

❧

Some part in the back of Colin's mind couldn't fathom the cook's words. His sister had been thrown into the pit. He was breathless with rage. His heart hammered against his chest and his breathing was labored.

He threw open the gate from the floor and lowered the ladder. "Ella…" He wasn't sure what frightened him more: that Sybella didn't charge up the ladder or that she didn't respond.

"Sybella," called Mary.

Colin didn't hesitate. He climbed down the ladder and couldn't see a damn thing. "Ella…Dear God, Ella, please answer me. Come to me, Sister, and escape this madness." He lowered his hand and then realized she probably couldn't even see it.

"Did ye find her?" asked Mary from above.

"Nay. I cannae see and she doesnae respond. Ella, are ye here?"

He stepped off the ladder and almost slid in place. He reached out in front of him, but it was so dark. He shuffled his feet and almost stumbled over what he thought felt like a leg. How he prayed it was Sybella's. He knelt down and found an arm. "'Tis all right, Ella. I am going to get ye out of here."

He gently lifted her to her feet and she was limp in his arms. "Mary, I have her. Steady the ladder." He bent down and hefted Sybella over his shoulder and then turned, fumbling for the ladder. "Hold on, Sister. 'Tis all right." Colin climbed out from the depths of hell, and when he reached the top, Mary gasped.

"Oh, Sybella."

He lowered his sister to the ground and propped

her up against the wall. Mary brushed away her own tears and knelt down beside Sybella. Looking up at him, Mary smothered a sob.

"How could he do this? How?"

Colin studied Sybella, who sat with a glazed expression upon her face. She still wore her nightrail, which was caked with muck. She was filthy. Her hair was matted, and every spot of her ivory skin was covered with something unthinkable. When a centipede slithered its way from under her hair, Colin reached over and grabbed it. He threw it to the ground and crushed it under his boot.

Mary's eyes widened and she told the cook to have a maid draw a bath for Sybella.

Anger lit Colin's eyes and he replied sharply, "Are ye able to care for her?"

Mary nodded.

He took off as though his arse was afire. He was furious and his thoughts raced dangerously. His father had gone too far. His own daughter. Colin's sister! He remembered Sybella long ago as an innocent lass and how she used to spy on him. And then he pictured her now. His breath came raggedly in impotent anger. God help the person who stood in his way. Several thoughts came to mind, but only one rose above all others. It was time that Colin made his own choices—for better or worse. He was no longer his father's pawn. And neither was Sybella.

He spotted his father as soon as he entered the bailey. Barely giving himself enough time to recognize over the score of MacDonell men that had arrived, Colin drew his sword. When he heard his father's

words, there was no turning back. It was about time
he stood as a man and protected his family.

"I want the stone. Give me the stone and I will
give ye Sybella," said his father. His father turned and
his eyes widened. He looked down to find a sword in
the middle of his gut being pulled out by his only son.

"*Ceusda-chrann ort. An diobhail toirt leis thu.*" *The
agony of the cross upon you. The devil take you.*

His father fell to the ground with a thump.

Colin bent over, catching his breath. He was so furious that blood pounded in his brain. He could barely
think, anger consuming him. His sire definitely had
an easier fate bestowed upon him than the one Colin
would've given him had he had ample time. Colin
lifted his eyes to find the MacDonell watching him.

"I am nae like my father, and if ye give Sybella
a chance, ye will find she isnae like him either. She
loves ye."

"Where is my wife?"

⤝⤞

Sybella sat in the tub as Mary and the maids bathed
her—twice. "Ye should have left me."

Mary rinsed Sybella's hair. "I donna want to hear
ye say that again."

"Do ye think that Colin will be all right after…"

"Aye. I donna think Colin had much of a choice.
Your father…lost his way. I want ye to think about
yourself now. Colin did what was necessary and he
will be a fine laird."

"I love him, Mary." Sybella closed her eyes as tears
fell down her cheeks. "For as much as I jested with ye

about Angus, I now see. I was such a fool for throwing it all away."

Mary gestured for the maids to depart and she handed Sybella a drying cloth. Looking over Sybella's shoulder, Mary smiled. "Mayhap 'tisnae too late."

Sybella pulled her nightrail over her head. "Ye didnae hear his words, Mary. Ye didnae see the look in his eyes. He hates me." She closed her eyes, placing her hand across her brow. "What have I done?"

"Mayhap ye made your husband realize what a dolt he can be."

Her eyes shot up in surprise.

Alexander smiled with compassion and opened his arms. Mary quickly departed as Sybella ran into her husband's embrace. "Alexander, I am so sorry! I love ye with all my heart. I donna want to lose ye. My heart truly breaks." Tears streamed down her cheeks.

He looked down at her, wiping away her tears with his thumb. "Ella, I was such a fool. Can ye ever forgive me? I didnae mean the words that flew carelessly from my lips. And ye were right. I was too blinded to see what was before my verra eyes. *Tha gaol agam ort.*" *I love you.* "I want ye to come home where ye belong, by my side."

She placed her head against his broad chest and held him tight. "Then ye must believe me that I donna have the stone. I—"

He pulled back and touched his finger to her lips. "Shhh…I know. Donna worry about it. 'Tis over." He tucked a loose tendril of hair behind her ear. "Colin told me what your father did to ye. Please tell me ye are well." He ran his hands up and down her arms.

"It was terrible, Alex, but I was more frightened at the thought of losing ye."

He paused and pulled her close. "That will nae happen, lass. From this day forward, I promise ye that. Please promise me there will be nay more lies between us."

"Aye."

"Then if we are being truthful, there has been something I have been meaning to tell ye."

She pulled back and her expression was puzzled. "What?"

"I loved ye from the first time I saw ye at the waterfall, Lady Sybella MacKenzie of Kintail. Ye plagued my thoughts for years and I always wondered what became of ye. Ye are the bonny lass that filled my dreams." He smiled and gave her a roguish grin. "And your lips taste of sweetened honey. In fact, I will tell ye a secret. I'd really like to taste them now."

He lowered his head and she licked her lips.

"Alex, ye are so verra wicked."

Epilogue

SYBELLA SAT AT THE TABLE ON THE DAIS IN THE GREAT hall surrounded by MacDonells and MacKenzies, and her smile broadened in approval. Men and women laughed as if they had not a care in the world. For the first time since she could remember, she was blissfully happy, fully alive. She no longer felt the burdensome chains of betrayal.

It was good to be home.

She couldn't believe a sennight had already passed since the death of her father. And this jovial mood was exactly what the clans needed. The dreaded nightmare was over and it was finally time to heal old wounds. A little voice pulled her from her woolgathering.

"Come on, Lachlann, ye can do it," said Anabel. She held out her arms as Lachlann took unsteady steps into her embrace. "Ye did it!"

Rosalia smiled. "He has taken a fancy to ye, Anabel."

Anabel stood tall, proud. "I think I get along better with the wee lads than with my brothers."

Colin rubbed the top of her head. "Your brothers may jest with ye now and again, Anabel, but they will always look after ye and love ye." He turned to Sybella and they shared a smile.

A warm hand came down on Sybella's shoulder and she reached up to grab it.

"Aunt Iseabail is in the garden with William. Should I be worried?" asked Alex, sitting down beside Sybella.

"Nay, I have a feeling William would ne'er let anything happen to her."

"I suppose ye're right." Laughter filled the hall and Alex took a drink from his tankard. "My men are glad to be home from Lewis."

"'Tis quite obvious. And ye really think things with the MacLeod will settle down now?"

"Now that Colin is laird and we have withdrawn our men, we shall see. With His Majesty's men arriving on the isle, there isnae much the MacLeod could do now anyway."

"I suppose."

"Come now, Ella. I told ye that I donna want ye worrying about such things."

"How can I be worried when I have such a strong and handsome protector?"

Alex lifted his brow, and as he was about to speak, Ennis approached the dais. "Thank ye for inviting us to the celebration. Anabel loves seeing ye, my lady."

"I wish I could see her more often. Ye know how much I simply adore her. At times, I wished we lived closer to Kintail."

"That doesnae mean we cannae come to pay ye a visit." A mischievous look came into Ennis's eyes and he lowered his voice. "Besides, I donna think ye will have the time, Lady Sybella. Ye will soon have your own bairn to raise."

Sybella's mouth dropped and Alex sat forward. "What? What did ye say?"

"Aye, Laird MacDonell, your wife is with child."

She stammered in confusion. "Are ye for certain? I thought ye couldnae see without the stone."

A sheepish smile crossed Ennis's face. "That's what I told your father, lass. I was aware of what he did to the MacLeod's women and children, and knowing that, I could nay longer aid him in his endeavors. I ne'er wanted blood on my hands. I only tried to help our clan." Alex was about to speak when Ennis looked him in the eye. "Aye, ye have your heir. He is a healthy lad."

Sybella didn't even realize Ennis had walked away when Alex pulled her to her feet. He lifted his hand to her cheek and held her close. "Ye have made me the happiest man alive, and nae only because ye carry my son. *"Tha gaol agam ort,* Ella." *I love you.* His eyes were tender, compassionate.

She placed his hand to her stomach and laced her fingers with his. "Alex, I love ye with all my heart. And I'll need ye now more than ever." She laughed in sheer joy. When he raised his brow, puzzled, she rolled her eyes and added, "Ye heard Ennis. A lad. Just what I need. Another bad boy of the Highlands."

Here's a sneak peek at

My Highland Spy

by Victoria Roberts

Highlands, Scotland, 1609

"SHE'S HERE."

"Damn."

"Aye, well 'tis too late to turn her away now, Ruairi. What did ye expect? How long did ye think ye'd be able to hold King James at bay? Ye havenae shown your face in Edinburgh and didnae send Torquil…"

Laird Ruairi Sutherland thundered his way to the great hall and didn't bother to let the captain of his guard finish his response. Why would he? Fagan clearly knew how Ruairi felt about His Majesty and the man's ridiculous commands. As if he would send his only son to the Lowlands to learn the King's English. King James had no respect for Scotland or its people. And Ruairi would be damned if he'd give in so easily without a fight.

He entered the great hall and walked toward the English lass. Her brown hair was pulled back into a tight, unflattering bun. Her face was austere, her manner haughty. The woman held herself as if she graced him with her presence. He didn't like her at all.

"A bheil Gàidhlig agad?" Do you speak Gaelic?

The woman merely stood there, mute.

He looked at Fagan and smirked. Turning back toward the woman, Ruairi's eyes darkened. *"Thalla dachaigh." Go home.*

"Just place the trunk right there. Thank you."

Ruairi's eyes widened in surprise as another woman entered the great hall. Her smooth ivory skin glowed and the corners of her mouth turned slightly upward. She had a wealth of red hair, loose tendrils that softened her face, and her lips were full and rounded over even teeth. She seemed elegant and graceful. And for the first time since he could remember, he had no words to express the sight before his eyes. The woman was simply...beautiful. Who was this lass?

She lifted her skirts and walked over to him, greeting him with a warm smile. "I see you've met my driver's wife, Mary. You must be Laird Sutherland. It is a pleasure to make your acquaintance. I am Mistress Denny."

Carried away by his own response, Ruairi failed to notice the woman waited for him to answer. In fact, he had one hell of a time trying to suppress his admiration. When her cheeks reddened under the heat of his gaze, he cleared his throat and nodded at Fagan.

"'Tis a pleasure to meet ye. I am Fagan, the captain of Laird Sutherland's guard." The lass looked puzzled, and then Fagan added, "My laird doesnae speak English."

Her eyes widened and her jaw dropped. "I see... And what of Lady Sutherland?"

Fagan paused. "Lady Sutherland has passed away."

Ruairi eventually came to his senses when the pounding of his heart finally quieted. Although the woman was here to educate his son, Ruairi didn't need to learn the ways of the English. He was a grown man. He had survived twenty-nine years on earth without the help of those bloody English bastards. And besides, the lass was now in the Highlands, his beloved lands, which were a far cry from the English border. As far as he was concerned, she could keep her ways to herself. He was bound and determined not to make this easy for her—as if he would roll over like a good dog because his liege demanded obedience. As soon as King James gave the Highland lairds the respect they deserved, perhaps he would feel differently. But for now, Ruairi certainly wasn't going to tell the lass that he understood every word she spoke, and he sure as hell wasn't going to mention the fact that his wife had died—nearly two years ago.

❧

With all her might, Ravenna held back a groan. She'd traveled all the way from London to the bloody Highlands only to find out the laird didn't speak a word of English. How would she be able to figure out if the man conspired against the Crown if she didn't understand a word of Gaelic? Praise the saints. The man couldn't even communicate with her. This was nothing short of a disaster. She was stuck in the Highlands with a widowed laird and his son. She didn't like this at all.

Trying to compose herself, she gave Laird

Sutherland a sympathetic smile for the loss of his wife. She stretched her neck to look up at him because the top of her head only reached the middle of the massive man's chest. His green eyes continued to study her intently. His brown hair had traces of red and was fairly straight. Somehow she knew that she would never forget a single detail of his face. When their eyes locked, her breath hitched in her lungs and her heart turned over in response. Her gaze roamed to his powerful set of shoulders and he stood there like he didn't give a damn about her or what she thought of him.

She heard herself swallow and she cleared her throat. "You have my sincere condolences on the loss of your wife."

When he raised his brow, Fagan spoke, and she presumed the man translated her words. The laird must have understood because he nodded in response and then left without as much as a backward glance.

"Your trunk will be carried up to your chambers," said Fagan. "Ye must be weary from your journey. I will escort ye to your room and leave ye to rest." He was about to walk away when Ravenna spoke.

"Might I at least meet Torquil?"

His eyebrows shot up in surprise. "Ye arenae weary?"

"Captain, I've come all of this way. I'd like to meet the boy."

The man was just as big and imposing as Laird Sutherland. His dark hair hung well below his shoulders, but he had a kind, almost tender, smile. "Fagan, if ye will."

Ravenna nodded in response.

"I am nae sure where the lad is at the moment, but I will be sure to introduce ye when he returns."

"Very well. I suppose I will unpack my trunk."

❧

Ruairi took his seat at the table and felt the lass's eyes upon him, judging him. The woman probably thought he was some kind of barbarian, as all those pampered English bastards thought of his kind. He wasn't thrilled to have her here, but the sooner Torquil took to his lessons, the faster the lass would be back in her own country and not underfoot.

When the conversation drew quiet, a very small part of him felt a little guilty for deceiving her. He should probably work with her to help Torquil so that she could be on her way home. After all, she was only a woman and basically doing as she was told. And Ruairi liked the lasses—not necessarily English lasses— but lasses nonetheless. And this particular woman was not so sore to the eyes.

He gave her a brief nod. *"Ciamar a tha sibh?"*

"He asks how ye are," said Fagan.

She sat forward and took a drink from her tankard. "Tell me. How do I answer him that I am fine?"

While Fagan instructed Mistress Denny, Ruairi sat and listened, somewhat surprised the lass had wanted to answer him in his native tongue. After several botched attempts, she turned and gazed at Ruairi with an intense look upon her face.

"Tha gu math." I am fine.

Torquil clapped and his eyes lit up upon his governess' efforts to speak Gaelic. Ruairi hadn't seen that look on his son's face in quite some time. The boy was only six when his mother had died, and Ruairi knew his son missed her.

"She would like a tour of your home. Will she teach Torquil in the library?" asked Fagan in Gaelic.

"Aye. I will take her after we sup."

Fagan's eyes grew openly amused. "Must I come along to translate?"

"I think I can manage," he said, annoyed.

Fagan smiled at the lass. "My laird will escort ye and show ye his home after we sup."

Ruairi didn't like the way her face lit up when Fagan spoke to her. The woman clearly didn't know that the captain of his guard was only doing what he was told to do. He wondered if she'd still smile at Fagan that way if she knew the man only followed Ruairi's command.

"That would be delightf—"

"Ravenna, I want to come too," said Torquil in Gaelic.

Ruairi's brow rose when he heard Mistress Denny's Christian name spoken from his son's lips. "Torquil…"

Her gaze became puzzled at the sight of Ruairi's displeasure, and the lass placed her hand over her heart. She leaned forward in the chair. "Fagan, is the laird upset because Torquil called me Ravenna?"

"Aye."

"Please tell Laird Sutherland that I asked Torquil to call me by my given name because it was much easier on his tongue. It was difficult for the boy to say 'Mistress Denny.' And if it suits the two of you, you may both call me Ravenna as well."

Fagan turned up his smile a notch. "Ravenna…A verra bonny name for a verra bonny lass. The name suits ye."

Ruairi scowled. What the hell did Fagan think he was doing? Was he actually trying to woo the lass? God's teeth! The chit was English, a sworn enemy. Ruairi was aware that he probably shouldn't have been so aloof toward her. After all, she would report back to His Majesty. When he gave his captain another dark look, Fagan only lifted a brow and then had the audacity to smirk. The man would pay for that one later.

For the remainder of the meal, Ruairi sat and listened while the woman laughed at all of Fagan's jesting, sent smiles…at Fagan, and asked questions about Ruairi's home…to Fagan. Clearly, Ruairi couldn't answer, his only option to sit mute. Perhaps this wasn't one of his most brilliant ideas. Mistress Denny must think him daft. He took another drink from his tankard and tried to think of all the ways to kill the captain of his guard.

Her gentle laugh wafted through the air. She was a bonny lass with her slim waist and long red tresses. In truth, her nearness was overwhelming, but the feelings she stirred within him had nothing to do with reason. After all, it had been quite a long time since he had shared his bed with a woman. When visions suddenly appeared of the sultry temptress lying beneath him, a cynical inner voice cut through Ruairi thoughts. He hated when his cock ruled his mind. He brought his tankard to his lips and took another big gulp, quickly realizing he needed something much stronger than what was in his cup.

Ravenna was by no means blind to Laird Sutherland's attraction. Her instinctive response to him was powerful, but she mentally took a step back. What was she thinking? What had she become? And what kind of man made her mind race with purely wicked thoughts? He had just lost his wife. He was in mourning. Besides, since he didn't speak English, she was forced to obtain her information for the Crown elsewhere.

She deliberately switched her attention to Fagan. If anyone should know what was afoot, it should be him. He was the captain of Sutherland's guard, after all. She didn't like the thought of using her feminine wiles against him, especially since she favored the looks of the handsome laird who sat beside her in a rugged, dangerous kind of way.

When Laird Sutherland abruptly stood, Ravenna presumed the meal was over. She thanked Fagan for his hospitality and followed the laird. His kilt rode low on his lean hips and the muscles under his tunic quickened her pulse. He appeared to fill out the material quite nicely.

She continued to follow him around, not minding the view at all, as he led her from the library to the kitchens and then to the ladies' solar without speaking a word. He gestured with his hand and they walked out into the fresh air and into the gardens.

The last of the summer blooms lined the path. Yellow and red flowers led to a stone wall that was about waist high where the laird stopped and waited for her. She walked up beside him and looked over the wall. The white waves of the ocean crashed below on jagged rocks that stuck out from the shore. She inhaled the fresh saltwater air and closed her eyes, letting the breeze comb through her loose tendrils.

When she opened her eyes, he was watching her. He shifted his weight and stood to his full height. He stood so close that a piece of his long hair whipped her cheek. She could easily drown in the depths of his emerald eyes. She suddenly found it difficult to breathe and caught the smell of his spicy scent as it wafted through the air.

For a brief moment, Ravenna forgot who she was and what she was sent there to do. Something intense flared through her entrancement, which made her tingle in the pit of her stomach. No man had ever looked at her that way.

What was the matter with her?

The man had enough burdens. He was mourning for the loss of his wife and now had to raise his son alone. And here she was acting like some virginal chit who floundered over the man's good looks.

Ravenna cleared her throat. "It's quite unfortunate that you do not speak English." When she saw a slight hesitation in his hawk-like eyes, she added, "Praise the saints. I don't know what's wrong with me. You stand there, so handsome, sporting your kilt. Frankly, I don't remember any of my other assignments being quite so...desirable."

The smoldering flame she saw in his eyes startled her.

"Ye are my son's governess, but I would take ye verra willingly to my bed."

Ravenna paled.

COMING SEPTEMBER 2014

Acknowledgments

A very special "thank you" goes out to the following people:

To my agent, Jill Marsal, for your endless encouragement.

To my editor, Leah Hultenschmidt, for supporting my dreams.

To my dad, who tells everyone he is the cover model for my books and that Sourcebooks photoshops his head. You're doing a great job, Dad, and the ladies think so, too!

To my family, who can spot a tartan and a Scottish festival a mile away.

To Sharron Gunn, my resident Gaelic expert, *mòran taing* for your always willing attitude and assistance.

To Mary Grace, who continues to be my rock and who I'm proud to call my friend. I could never do this without you. You are truly the reason my dream is alive. I'm so glad you're with me on this journey.

To my readers: You know who you are! For the ones who travel two hours to see me at a book signing, who constantly promote my books via word of mouth and social media, who believe in me and give me endless encouragement, and for your pictures, letters, and smiles, I thank you from the bottom of my heart.

About the Author

Victoria Roberts writes sexy, Scottish historical romances about kilted heroes and warriors from the past. An avid lover of all things Scotland, she simply writes what she loves to read. Prior to ever picking up a romance novel, she penned her first young adult novella (never published) at sixteen years old. Who knew her leather-studded motorcycle hero would trade in his ride and emerge as a kilt-donning Highlander wielding a broadsword?

Victoria lives in western Pennsylvania with her husband of twenty years and their two beautiful children—not to mention one spoiled dog. When she is not plotting her next Scottish romp, she enjoys reading, nature, and antiques. For more information about Victoria, visit her website at www.victoriarobertsauthor.com.

Temptation in a Kilt

by Victoria Roberts

❧

She's on her way to safety

It's a sign of Lady Rosalia Armstrong's desperation that she's seeking refuge in a place as rugged and challenging as the Scottish Highlands. She doesn't care about hardship and discomfort, if only she can become master of her own life. Laird Ciaran MacGregor, however, is completely beyond her control…

He redefines dangerous…

Ciaran MacGregor knows it's perilous to get embroiled with a fiery Lowland lass, especially one as headstrong as Rosalia. Having made a rash promise to escort her all the way to Glengarry, now he's stuck with her, even though she challenges his legendary prowess at every opportunity. When temptation reaches its peak, he'll be ready to show her who he really is… on and off the battlefield.

❧

"Wonderful adventure with sensual and compelling romance." —Amanda Forester, acclaimed author of *True Highland Spirit*

For more Victoria Roberts, visit:

www.sourcebooks.com

X Marks the Scot

by Victoria Roberts

———— ❧ ————

He's fierce, he's proud, he's everything she was warned against.

Declan MacGregor hadn't a care in the world beyond finding a soft bed and willing woman... until he had to escort Lady Liadain Campbell to the English court. The woman needles him at every turn, but he can't just abandon her to that vipers' nest without protection.

Liadain wasn't thrilled to be left in the care of her clan's archrival. It was as if the man never had a lady tell him no before! And yet as whispers of treason swirl through the court and the threat of danger grows ever sharper, her bitter enemy soon becomes the only one she can trust...

———— ❧ ————

Praise for *Temptation in a Kilt*

"Well written, full of intrigue, and a sensual, believable romance, this book captivates the reader immediately." —RT Book Reviews

"Filled with everything I love most about Highland romance..." —Melissa Mayhue, award-winning author of *Warrior's Redemption*

For more Victoria Roberts, visit:

www.sourcebooks.com

Sins of the Highlander

by Connie Mason and Mia Marlowe

———— ∽⊱⊰∾ ————

ABDUCTION

Never had Elspeth Stewart imagined her wedding would be interrupted by a dark-haired stranger charging in on a black stallion, scooping her into his arms, and carrying her off across the wild Scottish highlands. Pressed against his hard chest and nestled between his strong thighs, she ought to have feared for her life. But her captor silenced all protests with a soul-searing kiss, giving Elspeth a glimpse of the pain behind his passion—a pain only she could ease.

OBSESSION

"Mad Rob" MacLaren thought stealing his rival's bride-to-be was the perfect revenge. But Rob never reckoned that this beautiful, innocent lass would awaken the part of him he thought dead and buried with his wife. Against all reason, he longed to introduce the luscious Elspeth to the pleasures of the flesh, to make her his, and only his, forever.

———— ∽⊱⊰∾ ————

"Ms. Mason always provides a hot romance." —RT Book Reviews

For more Connie Mason and Mia Marlowe, visit:

www.sourcebooks.com

Lord of Fire and Ice

by Connie Mason and Mia Marlowe

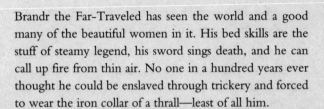

Brandr the Far-Traveled has seen the world and a good many of the beautiful women in it. His bed skills are the stuff of steamy legend, his sword sings death, and he can call up fire from thin air. No one in a hundred years ever thought he could be enslaved through trickery and forced to wear the iron collar of a thrall—least of all him.

Katla the Black isn't just called so for her dark, silky hair. His new mistress has a temper as fierce as a warrior's and a heart as icy as the frozen North. But inch by delicious inch, Brandr means to make her melt…

"The love story is steamy and well crafted." —Publishers Weekly

"Compelling with a rich narrative, strong characters, and non-stop action." —RT Book Reviews, 4 stars

"Intriguing and absorbing…There are several surprising twists and lots of passion." —Long and Short Reviews

For more Connie Mason and Mia Marlowe, visit:

www.sourcebooks.com

To Conquer a Highlander

by Mary Wine

❧

Her father will surely kill them both when he finds out what they've done...

When Torin McLeren discovers his neighbor's plot against his king, he takes their daughter as his prisoner, thereby stopping her father's plot from going forward. But that leaves him with a woman under his roof whom he can't ignore, and not just because she's his enemy's daughter...

Shannon McBoyd decides to use her captor to experience passion for the first time, and then to destroy him. But her plan goes awry because once she has lured Torin into her bed, she no longer wants to hurt the one man who seems to value and understand her...

❧

"Not to be missed." —Lora Leigh,
New York Times #1 bestselling author

"Deeply romantic, scintillating, and absolutely delicious." —Sylvia Day, national bestselling author of *The Stranger I Married*

For more Mary Wine, visit:

www.sourcebooks.com

Highland Hellcat

by Mary Wine

He wants a wife he can control...

Connor Lindsey is a Highland laird, but his clan's loyalty is hard won and he takes nothing for granted. He'll do whatever it takes to find a virtuous wife, even if he has to kidnap her...

She has a spirit that can't be tamed...

Brina Chattan has always defied convention. She sees no reason to be docile now that she's been captured by a powerful laird and taken to his storm-tossed castle in the Highlands, far from her home.

When a rival laird's interference nearly tears them apart, Connor discovers that a woman with a wild streak suits him much better than he'd ever imagined...

"Among the intrigue of clan power, there is a wonderful love story." —*Night Owl Romance*, Reviewer Top Pick

For more Mary Wine, visit:

www.sourcebooks.com

Highland Heat

by Mary Wine

---- ❧ ----

As brave as she is impulsive, Deirdre Chattan's tendency to
follow her heart and not her head has finally tarnished her
reputation beyond repair. But when powerful Highland
Laird Quinton Cameron finds her, he doesn't care about
her past—it's her future he's about to change…

From the moment Quinton sets eyes on Deirdre, rational
thought vanishes. For in her eyes he sees a fiery spirit that
matches his own, and he'll be damned if he'll let such a wild
Scottish rose wither under the weight of a nun's habit…

With nothing to lose, Deirdre and Quinton band together
to protect king and country. But what they can accomplish
alone is nothing compared to what they can build with
their passion for each other…

---- ❧ ----

*"Dramatic and vivid…Scorching love scenes threaten to
set the sheets aflame."* —*Publishers Weekly* starred review

"A lively and exciting adventure." —*Booklist*

For more Mary Wine, visit:

www.sourcebooks.com